The Ancient Blood

The Ancient Blood

A Novel by Steven Wilson

To Priscilla, for everything.

Chapter 1

I will tell you a story.

Chapter 2

A white man called Jessup dug into a bucket of grease and rubbed it into the hub of a wagon wheel. He had come to this spot with his wife and child with other wagons, which had gone on, leaving him alone. To the *Tsis Tsis' tas*, The People the white man called the Cheyenne, it was the time when the Moon When the Green Grass was up; but the land where this white man was, was dry, with short brown grass for as far as any man could see. He had come from the East where the white man lived. Many white men did this, but they did not understand how to get along on this land. They could not always find water, carried too much in their wagons, and would leave their belongings all along the journey. They were foolish. They brought chairs, beds, and large crates with white men clothes, and even a big box that made music. This was too much for their horses; and sometimes the horses died, and a man could see their bones bleached white by the sun. Sometimes, it was the white man's bones.

Jessup had not taken care with his wagon; and the captain of the train had told him that they would not wait on him, that he must see to his wagon and then catch up with them. This captain was named Jack and he was always talking in a loud way, as if he was sure the sound of his voice would keep him safe. There were seven wagons and a pack mule train, which were hired by a man looking for big bones. It is said these bones belonged to large animals well before The People came to this land, but no one knows for sure. The man who hired the wagons and some others dug in the ground and became very excited when they found bones.

So, this white man Jessup smeared grease on the hub and then went to the other side and did that as well. His back was sore from bending over, as he looked at the sky in the distance. Gray clouds were rolling across the horizon to the east, trying to eat up the sun. The wind had raced ahead of the clouds and stroked the short grass as if warning there was a storm coming. There was even some lightning. The air got cold, which happened sometime during the Moon When the Green Grass came up. Sometimes it would also rain or snow.

Jessup felt the hands of the cold wind touch him, and he pulled his coat close to him like a man does when the air is like that. No one can control the wind when it becomes angry. His girl child was a little way away from the wagon, and his wife was trying to calm the horses. She was afraid because they were all alone, and she had not wanted to leave her home where the white man lived. She was sad about leaving her family.

Jessup's child called out to him and said, "Papa? Papa, look I have found a dog." She was a small girl with light hair and wore a dress with red polka dots that blew around her legs in the wind.

He walked toward her and found her petting a brown dog with white spots. The dog wagged its tail because it was happy to find someone on the wide prairie.

"Do not get close to that dog," Jessup warned her. He thought someone had let it run off from another wagon train, because it was very thin, and its ribs pushed through its sides. Still, the dog wagged its tail and appeared to be friendly.

"Can I keep it, Papa?" the girl said while petting the dog.

The dog ran around her little legs and kept close to her, all the time watching Jessup as if it were uncertain about what the man would do. It looked at him with his dark eyes.

"We cannot keep a dog," Jessup said. He bent down and rubbed the grease from his hand on the grass and watched the dark clouds. He thought if they left now, they could catch up with the wagon train when it stopped to camp for the night. Suddenly a gust of wind came rushing by, kicking up some dust with it, almost snatching Jessup's hat from his head, but he was quick enough to hold on to it and pulled it down tighter. White men always wore wide-brimmed hats because the sun burned their skin and turned it red.

"Please, Papa?" the girl implored as she held the dog closer to her.

He did not answer but walked back to his wife who kept her head down so that the dust flying around in the air because of the wind would not sting her eyes.

Jessup was angry about the wagon, and he thought Captain Jack was a fool; and he was angry at his wife because she cried for her family far away where the white men lived. Now, he was angry with his daughter because she had found a dog that needed to be fed and watered when there was not enough food and water for the family itself. He thought maybe he should have gone on his own and left his wife and daughter behind so he would not have to care for them.

He was about to take the cup and dip it into the water keg on the side of the wagon when he heard his daughter scream. He looked around frantically but could not see her. He told his wife, "Stay with the horses!" afraid that the wind would make them nervous, and they might run off. He ran back to where his daughter was with the dog. He thought the dog had bitten her, and that made him angry.

What he saw instead was a sight that stunned him. His daughter was lying on the ground and her insides were thrown about the grass and the thirsty dirt ground below drank up her bright red blood. Meanwhile, her head lay a little further away from her body. He froze at that moment, his mind unable to comprehend the scene before him. The burst of cold wind struck him with an even greater force this time, taking his thoughts away with it. He seemed to have lost his voice. He could not shout, let alone let out a whisper.

He heard his wife cry out behind him. It was high-pitched, unlike a human sound, more akin to the cry of an animal that has been wounded and is afraid. Jessup ran back to her.

Two of the horses lay on the ground, dead, with their guts spilled over the other two horses, wet and shining in the remaining light. The two horses reared in fright, crying out and trying to break free from the harness; they fought each other, jerking the wagon forward.

He called out to his wife but did not see her. He wondered if the wagon had run her over, or the horses had kicked her. Maybe she had been killed. He could not think of what to do. His daughter was dead, he did not know where his wife was, and the two horses were stumbling over the bodies of the other two dead ones.

The air had stopped moving as if it were afraid, and it stank of things that had been dead for a very long time, like the bodies of buffalo killed by white men and scattered over the ground.

Then he saw what had killed the two horses, and what had probably killed his daughter. It was very tall, nearly as tall as his wagon. His wife was hanging from its mouth, with her arms and legs jerking back and forth as if she was dancing; but it was because the creature that had her in its mouth was chewing on her body. Her long yellow hair hanging down was streaked with blood that fell on the ground in streams.

A great fear came into his heart so quickly that his body would not listen to his mind telling him to run away. His legs were rooted into the ground so that they would not move, like the tree of a cottonwood grove alongside a river. Then the creature that had his wife in its mouth looked at him with very dark eyes, grinning at him, like a madman grins at the moon.

Chapter 3

Walking Man was tall for a Cheyenne warrior, and he was known to be thoughtful. Some Cheyenne, who called themselves *Tsis Tsis' Tas,* which meant The People, did not give as much thought to things as this Kit Fox warrior. A few said the Walking Man thought too much.

He walked with grace and purpose. Often, he would listen in the Council until the others had spoken, and then he would speak. When he did so, he would comment respectfully on what each of the men had said. Some men said Walking Man would take another man's idea and talk about it around until it was thought the idea came from him. Others said that he would take the best of what others said and offer it to the council. He was not a chief, but that did not matter. He was well-thought-of, and sometimes that was better than being a chief.

He watched the other members of the war party as they examined the ground, looking for signs of the white soldiers. Old Turtle had found the track first and let out a shout, and Many Horses came and found another sign; but buffalo had traveled across the earth, and their hooves cut up the ground which made it hard for anyone to find anything.

There were about twenty warriors in the party, which was a good size if they came across any white soldiers. Most of them were Kit Fox Soldiers, although a few were from Dog Warrior Society; and three, One Eye, Fool Dog, and Red Horse, were from the Shield Warriors Society. There was one Contrary called Little Raven, who always had a good story to tell when asked or even if he was not asked. He liked to laugh and make others laugh.

Walking Man's Kit Fox thought themselves better than any other society and did not have to paint their bodies like some of the other societies, wear a feathered headdress, or carry an eagle-bone whistle or a rattle made of buffalo hoof like the Dog Men. They did wear their hair braided with leather strips painted red and crow feathers in their hair. They wore buckskin or dark woolen-cloth leggings and carried a heavy blanket because it was the Moon When the Green Grass Came Up, and sometimes the weather was harsh.

But each warrior of a society thought themselves better than others. That was the nature of a warrior society.

There was one more in the party. A woman. She was called Comes-a-Pony, and she rode with her younger brother, Left Hand. She was not from the Kit Fox nor Dog Warrior. Some women went to war with their husbands and some after their husbands had been killed. Comes-a-Pony was neither. She was thin for a Cheyenne woman, almost as tall as Walking Man which was unusual. She rode a red pony with three white stockings and a dash of white on its forehead. She called him Wind because he was fast. Her face was narrow, unlike most *Tsis Tsis' Tas* women, and her eyes dark and searching. She could ask questions and give answers to them by looking at a man. One old chief said Comes-a-Pony said more with her eyes than any man with words. Some said even if any warrior society asked her to join, she would not. Her loyalty was to her brother, as his was to her. This was well known among the Cheyenne.

She did not dress as a woman. She wore a doe-skin shirt with a long tail that hung to her knees. It was gaily decorated in glass beads of many colors such as red, yellow, green, and blue, and porcupine quills, with shells from the river sewn in two rows down the front. Instead of a skirt, she wore a pair of white soldier's trousers that had been cut down to fit her. She kept her hair in two long braids that hung down to her shoulders and no one could recall her hair unbound by red ribbons. Once a brave hoping to interest her in his intentions, brought her blue ribbons and a felt hat that he had bought from a white man. She told him, "I will give the ribbons to my brother and the hat to my pony." He went away humiliated and told others. Since then, no other brave approached her.

The warriors gathered, waiting for the trail to be struck. They were grouped by society which was common.

Black Antelope spoke to Wolf Chief. They were both Dog Warrior Society. "This is a waste of time," Black Antelope said. Wolf Chief nodded. He always agreed with Black Antelope. They had known each other since they were boys.

"Walking Man wants to be a member of the Council of Forty-four," Black Antelope said, although Wolf Chief had not spoken of the Council of Forty-four. He did not care for Walking Man. They had words some time before, but no one knew what was said.

"He is too young for the Council," Wolf Chief said, but he was not satisfied. He decided he should say more. "He is not wise or a great chief. He thinks too much of himself. I have heard others say this."

This was true. Wolf Chief married an Arapaho called Buffalo Moon, and she was the one who had said it. She would tell others what a wonderful husband

Wolf Chief was and that their tipi was always filled with deer or buffalo meat. She said this whenever the women went out to gather roots or pomme blanches, until after a while, the other women started making excuses not to go. They were tired of her constant bragging. They did not think as much of her husband as she did. She blamed Walking Man for this.

"He is not wise," Black Antelope agreed.

"Walking Man was the cause of all that trouble with Broken Dish," Wolf Chief continued. He liked to say things that he thought Black Antelope wanted to hear. This was just after Broken Dish was asked to give up the Sacred Medicine Hat Bundle. His wife Standing Woman was so angry that her husband would no longer be the Keeper of the *Issiwun* that she did away with it. That caused much ill will. This was especially bad because the *Skiddi* Pawnee had taken the Four Sacred Bows, given to The People by Sweet Medicine, during a big fight on the South Loop River. This was the time before many white men came across the land. It was said that Sweet Medicine had warned The People that bearded men with long sticks that held fire would come. He was talking about the white man. Wolf Chief reminded Black Antelope about this many times.

"I do not believe Walking Man is as thoughtful as people say," Black Antelope continued. "Let us go speak to him." Wolf Chief nodded and they galloped up to Walking Man, riding close to his pony to make it shy away from them. This gave them some power.

Comes-a-Pony saw the pair approach Walking Man and she said to her brother, "Those two want something."

Left Hand saw them as well and said, "They will try to make Walking Man lose his temper."

Comes-a-Pony stoked the neck of her pony. "He will not give them satisfaction. I think there is no emotion in Walking Man." It was said among the Cheyenne that Comes-a-Pony found Walking Man attractive, but that something had happened. It would make no difference if she did, some people thought. It was also said that his indifference caused her to be ashamed of her feelings. She seldom spoke to the Cheyenne warrior afterwards; and when she did, her words were cloaked in ice.

"I think we are wasting our time," Black Antelope said to Walking Man. "Maybe we ought to have everyone looking for a sign." That was how it was. If Walking Man said the rain was coming, Black Antelope said the sky would be fair all day. "Let us ride in that direction to find the soldiers." He pointed toward the Big Horn Mountains.

Walking Man did not look at him. He knew Old Turtle, Many Horses, and Left Hand, and maybe Bull

Bear were the best trackers, so he let them look for a sign. He did not have to be the one who found it.

Wolf Chief said, "We should go find the white soldiers." When they were boys tending to the pony herd, it was said that Wolf Chief was tied so closely to Black Antelope that where one went, the other had to follow.

"Do you speak for the Dog Society?" Walking Man asked. He was a reasonable man. His voice did not change, no matter what he said. He always spoke evenly, giving each word much thought. Some said it was a gift. Others said he was born without feelings. Comes-a-Pony would have agreed.

The words angered Black Antelope, so he waited before he replied. This was uncommon for him because when he spoke, his words were sometimes filled with bitterness. Some *Tsis Tsis' Tas* said that he was so driven by ambition that he was never satisfied. It was a hunger, one older warrior allowed, that must be constantly fed. "I think we are wasting time. I think we should send some men north so they can cut the white soldiers off. Wolf Chief thinks there are just a few soldiers."

"Well," Walking Man said. "The Dog Society should do what they think best. I will wait for the trackers to find a sign. Then we will know how many white soldiers there are and where they are going."

Black Antelope was humiliated but not because of what Walking Man said. It was how calmly he spoke the words. He jerked his pony around and rode back to the other members of his society. Wolf Chief followed him.

While Walking Man waited for the trackers, he saw Little Raven sitting on his gray pony with the spotted rump. He thought it strange that Little Raven was looking over his shoulder to the east. He did not move. It looked like he saw something that held his attention. His pony pulled a little grass from the ground to eat, but Little Raven did not move. One Eye and Eagle Head raced by on their ponies, trying to outrun one another, and still, he did not move. Little Raven appeared to be made of stone. Walking Man swung his pony around, which he called Moon, even though the pony was brown, not white like the actual one. He walked Moon up to Little Raven, carefully, in case Little Raven was asking *Maheo* for guidance. He would wait until Little Raven was finished speaking to the Great Spirit.

Little Raven spoke first, without looking at his friend. "Do you feel the cold wind?" He spoke as if the words had come to him across the prairie, like a man who marvels at a bank of distant storm clouds.

"I feel the wind because the wind is never still."

"This is a different wind. I think it has lost its way."

Walking Man was surprised at Little Raven's manner. He was very serious with his words, as if he was speaking with a great weight on his chest. This was not like Little Raven. The Contrary was always in good spirits. But now, Walking Man thought, he was troubled by something.

One Eye rode up to them. "Black Antelope is talking to the Dog Society warriors. He is telling them that they should go off and leave us. I think the Shield Warriors want to go with them."

Bull Bear shouted and raced his pony around in a circle. Many Horses followed and then galloped up to Walking Man. He grinned in excitement.

"We have found the trail. Bull Bear found it first, but then I did. It is not very strong, but it is enough."

"How many soldiers?" Walking Man asked.

"I say ten, but Bull Bear says eight. I say ten."

One Eye said, "The Dog Society want to ride off. Black Antelope is talking them into it."

Many Horses looked towards Walking Man. "What will you do?"

"We will follow the trail. When we find the white soldiers, we will fight them. We will take their horses and guns and all the cartridges they have. When we get home, we will show The People all that we have gotten.

When Black Antelope and the others get home, all they will have is empty pemmican bags and tired ponies."

Many Horses shouted in glee and rode off to tell the other Kit Fox Soldiers. Walking Man stayed with Little Raven, who had been silent during the exchange with Many Horses.

"What troubles you, friend?" Walking Man asked Little Raven.

Little Raven turned to Walking Man, his eyes wet and glistening in the light. "I think there is something out there that frightens the wind."

"Can you tell what it is?"

Little Raven did not answer the question which puzzled Walking Man, so he asked, "Have you seen something?"

"Do you remember Likes-to-Dance?"

That was a strange question for Little Raven to ask. Everyone knew the story of Likes-to-Dance. He was a good man who took to walking away from camp, sometimes two or three days at a time. When he came back, he would not talk; and after a while, it was decided that his mind had something wrong with it. This sometimes happens in old age when *mahta'sooma* leaves the body but Likes-to-Dance was a young man. His father did not know what to say and his mother wept for her son. One day he did not come back, so

Walking Man and some others went to look for him. They found some wolves fighting over the body; and after the braves chased them off, they saw that there was a big cut on Likes-to-Dance's neck. The knife was still in his hand.

"I remember him," Walking Man said.

Little Raven spoke, his eyes set on the horizon. "I wonder if I have become like him. I wonder if there is something wrong with my mind."

The words shocked Walking Man, but he did not let on that they had. "No," he said. "I think you are just tired. We have come a long way." He thought the news would cheer Little Raven, so he said, "They have found the white soldier's trail."

It did not seem to matter to Little Raven. A man could talk to his pony and get more of a response than Walking Man got from Little Raven. The Contrary was like a man who could not see or hear and, therefore, ignored all around him. He saw only what lay on the edge of his mind. "I think," he replied, "there is something out there."

Chapter 4

Lieutenant Homer Sweet had Caesars Commentaries balanced on the pommel of his saddle, reading as he led the patrol on a slow march under a blazing sun that beat on the backs of the riders. What few clouds were in the sky were featureless and fleeting. The air was hot and kicked up racing dust sprites that chased each other across the knee-high grass and scrub bushes. Clouds above had been so weakened by the wind that they followed one another in a white mist. There was nothing inviting about the land. It was broken by rolling hills, and gullies cut into the earth from spring run-offs. The ground was hard, baked by the sun until it refused to give way: a prairie. God had taken some pity on the land and peppered it with green grass, junegrass, western wheatgrass, and fringed sagewort, which did their best to add variety to the monotonous landscape. Sometimes it was green and sometimes brown, but it never changed completely until one left the prairie and went into the mountains or found sandstone formations in the foothills, gleaming under the sun. Sagebrush huddled in clumps, blue against the brown grass. The wind pushed them across the prairie, where they died; skeletons seeking absolution. There were a few stunted juniper trees; and down in a gulley, a man might find cottonwoods to build a fire with, if he was lucky. Silver sagebrush grew on the edge of the ravines but none down in the ravines. Buffalo shared the land with grouse, ground squirrels, tiny sage mice, elk, wolves, and other animals. Little rain fell, and the few streams flowed largely with brackish water. A man could even find bands of snow in June, caught along the lee sides of the shrubs. The land was neither one thing nor the other which made crossing it difficult. God had become bored making the prairie, so He raised up the land, peppered it with rolling hills, and carved Rocky Mountains out of stone.

The wind? The wind never ceased moving. Sometimes in violent bursts and other times in a constant, unyielding surge. It snatched up saddle blankets when men tried to saddle their horses and whipped dust into their faces until they became angry, or worse, ventured to the edge of madness. Mostly, it was content to roam over the land at a steady pace.

It was true that a man could see for miles; but, after a while, what he saw never wavered, so it didn't make any difference.

Sergeant Taliaferro, behind Sweet, watched as the lieutenant pulled his watch from a coat pocket, snapped open the cover, and read the time. The sergeant was thin, and his trousers always sat low on his hips. He looked to be the sort of man that never ate enough, with his coat hanging limply on his frame. But he was used to men following his orders and knew all the tricks of an old soldier's trade. And if he had to use his fists to convince a recruit what had to be done, well, he would do it. In garrison, he wore faded blue blouse and sky-blue trousers; but his brass buttons were gleamed, and his boots were shined. His hands and face were deeply tanned; and when he removed his hat, his forehead was stark white where it had been deprived of sunlight. He knew the army. He knew soldiers. And he knew which officers would listen to him and those who wouldn't. The first benefited from his knowledge. The second were simply tolerated.

Now what the hell does he care what time it is? Taliaferro wondered. Time don't mean a goddamned thing out here unless you had to be someplace or do something. Right now, all they had to do was ride.

Following side by side in pairs were Smallwood, Wagner and Jones, and Collier and Mendelson. Ashcroft was about a quarter mile back as rear guard, struggling to keep his horse from bolting. She was a new mount for the soldier, and the two despised each other. Stewart was about the same distance in front as the Point. Nobody wore a uniform. Uniforms were too hard to replace. They looked more like a band of street ruffians than soldiers. Their patched trousers were strengthened by canvas inserts, their blouses were sweat-stained, and their hats were a combination of the shapeless army-issued and civilian ones. If the lieutenant had given it any thought, he knew Caesar would have been appalled by the slovenly appearance of these soldiers.

Sweet, who wore a red flannel shirt with patches on the elbows, shifted a bit in his saddle, pushed his glasses back up on his nose, dog-eared the page, and closed the book. His face was sunburned, and wispy red hair did its best but failed to cover his upper lip. Grow a mustache, he was told, it'll keep your lips from sunburn. He envied the men with thick mustaches. His was a boy's attempt to look like a man. He held his hand up to stop the patrol. "Halt. Prepare to dismount," he ordered. "Dismount."

The men swung out of their saddles as Taliaferro whistled for Stewart and Ashcroft to rejoin the patrol. Sweet untied a checkered handkerchief from around his neck, used it to clean his glasses, wipe the sweatband of the straw hat he wore, and then tied it back in place. He led his horse out of the column, looking back over the prairie.

Taliaferro joined him, taking a quick pull from his canteen. "Don't worry a bit about Porter," the sergeant said. "He's half Indian. Ain't nothing going to happen to him. He'll be along shortly."

Sweet nodded, rubbing his mounts muzzle. His ass hurt, and his legs were stiff. He'd ridden more on a few weeks of campaigning than he had his six months since leaving the Point.

Mendelson turned his horse, keeping it between him and Taliaferro. "What do you think about the general?" he asked Collier, glancing at the slight lieutenant.

Collier looked at him and then toward Sweet. "He's all right, I guess. For an officer."

"See him reading a book? Ain't that some way to lead a command?"

Collier shrugged. "He's an educated man."

"I'd rather have an old soldier leading the command," Mendelson said.

Collier took a handful of grain out of the feed bag and held it under Mike's muzzle. The horse sniffed at it and began eating. "You keep talking about commands like this is the column. We ain't but half a dozen. All we have to do is ride on until we find Gibbons. Besides, Taliaferro will keep him on the straight and narrow."

Jones, a small man with a broad face and thick mustache moved in close to them. "Tell me the truth, Mendelson? Does anything make you happy?" He was English and spoke precisely. He had the look of a soldier but not the manner.

The question irritated Mendelson. "I ain't talking to you, Lord Walter. Just think of it. A boy general and a nigger for a scout."

"You know I don't like that word, Mendelson," Jones said.

"Yeah, there's a lot I don't like, but nobody pays attention to what I want." His eyes darted around to make certain no one was watching. He patted his saddlebag in anticipation.

Wagner, small even for a cavalryman, tightened the coat straps around his greatcoat perched on the pommel. He was an old hand, quiet, competent. He seldom spoke unless someone asked him a question, and then his answers were brief, without elaboration. He walked around his mount, Judy, checking to make sure that his blanket was tightly strapped on the cantle, and the straps coiled and slid into the buckle, so they did not hang loose. He pulled on the cinch strap to see if it was snug enough to hold the saddle in place, but not so tight that it bound the horse. Like the others, he carried his canteen high under his left arm, with his haversack strung under his right. He could have secured both to his saddle, but horses sometimes run off; and a man afoot in this land was bad, but a man without food and water might as well just lay down on the hard earth and die. He patted Judy on the rump, satisfied with his investigation, and slid the carbine sling holding his weapon so that it hung at his waist. The broad leather strap ending in a snap clip attached to the weapon crossed from his left shoulder and across his chest. The weapon hung loosely on his right. He carried a Springfield, while some of the men had Sharps. His Colt Army Issue single-action revolver was in its holster on the cartridge belt, butt forward, on his left hip.

"Don't you take nothing for granted?" Collier said, watching the ritual. He was a short, stocky man with course features and blue eyes.

"No," Wagner replied. His speech was burdened with a thick Bavarian accent. "If I find something wrong, I mend it right away. If I keep everything where it belongs, then the sergeant, he has no cause to fault me."

Mandelson decided to pitch in. He always had an opinion. "He don't trust anybody. Not even himself."

"How long you been in, Phil?" Collier asked Wagner.

"A while. I think maybe," he calculated silently, "twelve years."

"A while!" Mendelson snorted. "You won't catch me in this army for no twelve years."

Collier scoffed, "The army wouldn't have you for twelve days if soldiers didn't keep running off to hunt for gold." His interest returned to Wagner. "You was in the war, weren't you? What regiment?"

Wagner settled the picket rope and pin on the saddle, so it was secure. "I fights with the Eleventh Ohio."

"You ought to know this country, then."

"I never got this far," Wagner admitted. "I tell you one thing I learn out here." He reached into the top pocket of his jacket and pulled out a pistol cartridge, showing it to Collier. "I keep this fellow handy in case things go wrong. No Cheyenne ain't gonna catch me alive. You fellows ought to do the same."

"What? Kill yourself?" Collier said.

"It's better than being skinned alive," Wagner said. "They get ahold of you and you gonna wish you listened to me."

"They ain't human," Mendelson said. "I say, kill every one of them. Men, women, and child."

"You can't be serious?" Jones said. "Do you really mean you would kill children?"

"Nits make lice, Lord Walter. Kill them off and there won't be no Indian problem. I seen what happens when they get ahold of you. Tony Stiller got hisself captured not five miles from Fetterman. They chopped off his nuts, cut him up something terrible, and shot him full of arrows."

Smallwood called out, "Here comes Porter."

Sweet watched as the scout, a black man wearing a tan hat in a Montana peak, closed the distance at a gallop, reining up just short of Sweet and dropping to the ground. The scout was a solemn-looking man until he smiled, which he did readily. His skin was the color of coffee with just a spot of cream. Taliaferro threw him a canteen. He pulled out the cork stopper, took a drink, and tossed it back to the sergeant. He jerked his head to lead the lieutenant away from the men. When he was satisfied with the distance, Porter made his report. "I seen a dust cloud about ten, fifteen miles back."

Sweet said, "Do you know who it is?"

"I know who it ain't," Porter answered, reaching for his water bag. He poured a handful of water into his hand and rubbed it on his face, his skin glistening. "It ain't Crow because those boys are sticking close to Crook. It ain't Shoshone because they're headed in the wrong direction." He took a swig, cupped his hand again, and held it under his horse's snout. He tipped the bag, filled his hand, and watched while the animal consumed the water, licking the scout's hand. "Drink up, Randy, but don't eat my hand." He hung the bag on his saddle horn. "That leaves Sioux, Cheyenne, or some boys from Gibbons. I wouldn't bet on Gibbons, though."

"But there's no way to tell for certain?"

"Nope. If you're up to it, I figure we drop back a bit, find a hill, and see what we can see."

Sweet thought over the idea. He realized he was still holding the book. He hid it behind his back. "Should I send the men on ahead?"

"I would," Porter said, hooking the stirrup over the saddle horn so he could tighten the saddle's cinch. He finished and patted his horse's shoulder. "We can catch up to them easy enough."

"All right," Sweet said. "Sergeant Taliaferro? If you please?"

Mendelson twisted his face at Collier. "If you please."

Porter waited as Sweet carefully explained the situation to the sergeant, glancing at the scout to see if there was anything else to be said. There was.

"If I were you, Lieutenant, I'd have your boys go until they find a gulley and wait for us there."

"Yes," Sweet said. "Of course. Take them on a while, Sergeant."

"We won't be but a bit," Porter said to Taliaferro as he swung onto the saddle. "We'll catch up with you by and by."

Sweet slipped the book into his saddlebag and was mounted before he realized he didn't know where his binoculars were. He dug through his saddlebags while Porter waited. The lieutenant held them up in triumph. Porter kicked his horse into a gallop, followed by Sweet.

They raced across the ground, Sweet's excitement, and dread mounting at the same pace. What if they were spotted by the Indians? What if there were too many of them? A hundred thoughts flew through his mind. They became fragments, splinters, darting about with the urgency of a frightened man.

At the depot before he set out for West Point, he heard the colonel's voice. "Do your duty, boy, don't fail me," delivered with just a hint of disappointment.

"Yes sir," he had replied.

The air was still and hot, the railroad platform crowded. He felt sweat running down his forehead. His father, the colonel, was stiff with irritation. He had things to do, he reminded his son. Important things. He always had things to do. His mother was sobbing, patting his arm nervously. He did not want to be a soldier.

"But then what, boy?" the colonel said. A clerk in some shop? Pull yourself together for God's sake." The colonel was a man dissatisfied with most things — unsmiling, brusque, and intolerant. He did not *talk* to his wife and son; he issued orders.

Sweet locked his legs around the mount; his butt danced up and down in the saddle, and his arms flapped like the wings of a bird struggling to take off. He forced his horse to slow so that Porter rode just ahead. So that Porter did not see how poorly he rode.

"You will be a cavalryman, boy. Full of dash and elan. When you get some years in, you can move up to staff. That's what I did. Did well enough for me. Field and staff. That's how it should be."

But horses frightened him. It seemed that everything unknown frightened him. Lieutenant Sweet was a man uncertain about most things. He wasn't like his father. He didn't have his father's self-confidence. His father had a way of looking at him with mild disappointment. The colonel's eyes would narrow, and he would look away as if trying to conceal his concerns about the boy who was his son.

"For God's Sake, act like a soldier."

Now, he was the officer-in-command about to encounter the enemy. He knew he had to act like a soldier.

He wondered if he was doing everything right. Maybe he shouldn't have ordered the men to go on? No, Taliaferro knows what to do. He'd find a ravine, let the men graze their mounts, and wait on his return.

"You're to take these dispatches to Gibbons," the major had ordered. The column had stopped for the day and was making camp.

No, no, I can't do that, he thought but the packet was in his hands before he had a chance to speak. "You're to note sources of water and the general condition of the ground."

"Dash and elan," the colonel had said over dinner one night. "That's what the cavalry is."

"I'm sending this man, Porter, with you. He is highly competent," said the major.

"Mr. Porter?" Sweet said. "Do you know how many there are? I mean Indians."

"Oh," Porter thought it over. "I suppose twenty, twenty-five or so. I didn't get close enough to tell for certain. Judging from the size of the dust cloud, I'd say that's a good number."

Sweet was amazed. "You can tell how many there are from a dust cloud?" He felt terribly inadequate. He cataloged it as another failure.

"If I get close enough, I can tell what they had for supper," Porter said, and then smiled at the officer. "Anyway, we'll see."

The young man wondered if he would ever be as knowledgeable as Porter or the other officers in the column. He stood mute as they gathered around the campfire drinking coffee and telling stories. Laughing. Nothing troubled them. Their faces were suntanned and crisscrossed with wrinkles, and their eyes sparkled with comradeship. They were old soldiers with flowing mustaches and uniforms cobbled together over years of campaigning. They stood easily, confident, taking everything in stride. He was ashamed to stand next to them.

Porter pointed to the right. "Let's head for that rise."

Sweet felt his stomach drop. "What if they see us? I mean…"

"Now don't get worried, Lieutenant. We've got some distance on them so that's a plus. They might not find our trail but that ain't likely. Cheyenne can track a moonbeam at noon. They might decide they don't want to fool with us, but I'd be surprised if they did."

"Can't we outrun them?"

Porter brushed his hand along his jaw in thought. "Well, there's outrunning, and then there's outrunning.

Our best bet is to keep a good pace, but not so fast that we kill horseflesh. You boys are mounted on grain-fed horses, and you carry just enough feed to get them from one point to another. Indians graze their mounts if there's anything to graze. Indian ponies ain't picky eaters. Their ponies don't carry nearly the weight army mounts have to tote. If we don't lose our heads and go charging off, everything will work out."

"Thank you, Mr. Porter," Sweet said, although he wasn't certain why he was thanking the scout.

Chapter 5

Porter and Sweet dismounted and started to climb a low ridge before Sweet realized he had forgotten his binoculars. He returned to his horse, dug them out of his saddlebag, and rejoined Porter, who had waited for him. Before they reached the top, the scout removed his hat. "Take off your skimmer, Lieutenant. Gives us away as white men."

Sweet took off his hat. "Are they that close?" he asked as they knelt, below the edge of the ridge.

"No," Porter said, "but they've got eyes like an eagle. Almost as good as mine."

They crawled the remainder of the way. At the top of the ridge, Sweet handed his binoculars to Porter. On it was a brass plaque inscribed Col. Honor Sweet to His Son.

Porter shook his head. "Don't need 'em." As he scanned the prairie, he said, "I don't think a man can make a machine better than God made a good set of eyes." He glanced at Sweet settling the binoculars against his glasses. "Cup your hands right at the looking part if you would. Cuts down on the light shining off the glass." He watched as Sweet searched the horizon. "Got'em yet?"

"I think I see movement out that way, but I can't tell what it is."

"Oh, it's them alright. Cheyenne, I'd guess. Maybe twenty, twenty-five, or so."

Sweet lowered his binoculars. "What are they doing?"

"Three things a Cheyenne does well. Track, fight, and consider. Four if you count riding. They're riding fools for sure."

"Consider?"

"They always talk things over. Everybody gets a say, and then they consider all that's said and make a decision. That's what those folks are doing now. Trying to find our trail and talking things over. Indians ain't like the army. They don't got a general to say go do this or that. If a particular brave is respected enough, they'll listen to him."

"I thought a chief…"

"No," Porter said, pulling a plug of tobacco from his coat pocket. He offered it to Sweet, who shook his head. The scout bit off a chunk and began to chew.

"No. There are fighting chiefs, and holy chiefs, and some that act kind of like governors. They've all got opinions that the others listen to, but they don't give orders. In a fight, it's every man for himself." He was silent for a moment, watching. "That tricky son-of-a-bitch."

"What?"

"Can't you see nothing with those things?"

"I don't…"

Porter chopped the air in the direction of the war party. "There's a bunch just broke off and started moving north. I bet you dollars to donuts that big fellow sent them that way to cut us off if we try to get back to the column."

"What big fellow?" Sweet asked.

"No offense, Lieutenant, but even with those things, you're blind as a bat. There's a big fellow sitting out there on a brown horse. We might as well get back to the patrol." They returned to their mounts. Porter squatted next to his horse, and Sweet, not knowing what else to do, did the same. "Here's what I figure," the scout said, pulling out tufts of grass as he spoke. "We can head northwest, kind of angling toward the Big Horns. We'll keep that other bunch on our right. That bunch with the big fellow will likely keep on our tails. If we run into them that just took off, we can head for the mountains and maybe lose them. We'll do the same if the following bunch catches up with us. It's a damned sight better fighting from behind a rock than out in the open. But, with any luck, we won't have to fight. I figure things will be all right if we keep a good distance between us and them."

"How many are in that party?"

"The ones on our trail? Ten or twelve, I guess. So that leaves about ten or so who took off. That ain't a bad number to tangle with, but I'd just sooner not get in a fight with anybody. Our chances of outsmarting them is better than outfighting them. That is, if they keep going north."

"But you said you thought they were sent out to keep us from returning to the column?"

"That's exactly what I said, but that don't mean that's what they're going to do. Another thing about Cheyenne. They're a crafty bunch. You think you got'em figured out, and they go and surprise you."

Sweet felt useless. "But we won't be able to make good time if we go into the mountains." He tried to keep his voice even so that Porter wouldn't notice his fear.

"That's true. But if we're slowed down in the mountains, then those rascals are slowed down as well. We might end up wearing out our mounts and walking to Gibbons' column, but, at least, we'll get there with our scalps intact. You ain't been out here long, have you?"

Sweet hesitated before answering. "No. Not too long, Mr. Porter."

"I see," the scout replied. "Well, the good news is I ain't been killed yet. You listen to me, and I'll do my darndest to get you back to your station in one piece."

Chapter 6

Wooden Leg and Bull Bear rode ahead, weaving back and forth over the ground to make certain they did not lose the trail. Three of the Shield Warriors Society had decided to remain with the Kit Fox, which pleased the others because the number in the party would have been seven without them. Seven is an unlucky number and even the Kit Fox would have thought it a bad omen. One of the Shield Warriors was a brave called Red Horse, who had the impatience of a young man. He was always riding about because he had a big black horse, and he liked to show how well he rode. It was said that he liked another man's wife.

Many Horses trailed beside Walking Man for some distance before he spoke what was on his mind. "What is wrong with Little Raven?"

"Something is troubling him," Walking Man said, but he could not say what; and even if he knew, he would not say it. That was how Walking Man was. He did not often say what he was thinking unless he had thought about it until there was no need to think more. That was how he got his name. When he was young, he was called Standing Up because he was tall for a boy. Later, when his habit was to walk alone in thought, his name was changed to suit his manner.

"He is not telling stories," Many Horses said. "He is not singing. He is always telling stories or singing, which made my heart light. Now he rides alone behind us."

Walking Man twisted to catch sight of Little Raven. He was walking, leading his gray horse with the spotted rump. His head was down. Far behind him Walking Man saw dark clouds stretched across the horizon. "Little Raven said the wind has lost its way."

"Oh?" Many Horses replied. "The wind is always losing its way. That is its manner. Sometimes Great Roaring Thunder beats it with his whip, and the wind races to get away."

"I think we will ride for a while and then make camp to rest our ponies." He was about to ask Many Horses if he thought the wind was cold.

"Maybe *Veeho* is playing tricks with his mind?" Many Horses offered because he had seen some men who avoided others when they had nothing to say. It could have been the mischief-maker spirit *Veeho*, but sometimes it was only the actions of a man. He was speaking of Likes-to-Dance.

A great shout came up. Walking Man saw Red Horse racing toward them, leading a buckskin pony by the reins. "See what I have found!" Red Horse was very excited and rode around the war party. He pulled up next to Stone Forehead and sprang from his pony, stroking the buckskin's muzzle. One of the Shield Warriors braves called out, "See what Red Horse has!"

"Where did you find a Crow pony?" Stone Forehead asked.

"Back there," Red Horse said. "It's mine now. The Crow made it a present to me because they do not care for their ponies." The warriors knew it was a Crow pony because it was painted like a Crow pony with red hoof marks to make it run faster, and there was a black hand, painted on its flank for everyone to see.

Stone Forehead said to Walking Man, "I wonder if there are more Crow ponies back there?"

Walking Man said nothing but rode up to Red Horse. The other Shield Warriors braves and some Kit Fox were admiring the Crow pony and commenting how lucky Red Horse was to find him. That was not what Walking Man thought.

"It is a fine pony," he said because Red Horse was filled with pride. If young men think they are being challenged, they become angry and want to fight. "Where did you find it?"

Red Horse was pleased that Walking Man said it was a fine pony. "Back there," he nodded toward the ground they had just come across.

"Did you see any Crow or sign of Crow?"

"No," Red Horse said, stroking the pony's ear, and smiling.

"No sign of white men?"

"No," Red Horse said again. "No sign of anyone. Just my new pony. I will find a good name for him."

"You should," Walking Man said and then said to the others, "Let us go on some more, and then we will camp for the night." He galloped up to Bull Bear, who led the warriors. To him he said, "Red Horse has found a Crow pony."

"I see that," Bull Bear said.

"The pony may have run off and come a good distance. But I do not think so."

"That is true."

Walking Man said, "I think it would be good if someone went back to look for a sign."

Bull Bear, who was older and shorter than Walking Man, and had a thick chest like a bull buffalo, said, "I will ride back a bit. If you find a Crow pony without Crow, maybe they are not far away. White soldiers, too. The Crow are dogs for the white man." With that, he spun his pony around and galloped toward where Red Horse's pony had been found.

Red Horse raced back and forth among the warriors showing off his new pony. He pulled up next to Left Hand and Comes-a-Pony and slowed to a walk alongside them. Comes-a-Pony rode with her Sharps rifle laid across the pommel of her rawhide saddle. It was a long gun and not as handy in a fight as a shorter carbine; but it had more range, and she was a good shot. She had tied a rope from the stock to its barrel so she could carry it over her shoulder.

He tried to catch Comes-a-Pony's attention. "See what I have found."

Comes-a-Pony did not look at him. "A pony."

"The Crow lost it and I found it," he said, disappointed that she did not look at either him or his new treasure. He tried again. "I have three ponies now. These two and the one I let my cousin ride."

"What do you think of that, Little Sister?' Left Hand said.

"I do not think of it at all," Comes-a-Pony answered. She still did not look at the Shield Warriors brave.

Red Horse was stung by her words. "When I get back, women will sing of my exploits. They will tell of my Crow pony." He kicked his pony into a gallop, and leading the Crow pony, rode off.

The war party rode on until the sun was just returning to the earth. They found a deep gulley and made camp so that no one would see a fire unless they were almost on top of them. They pulled their blankets from their ponies, took their water jugs and parfleche bags, built a small fire, and lay down. Walking Man watched as Little Raven made his camp a little way off. Soon there were clouds over the sky, and the moon and stars went away. The ponies, who had gone a good distance, settled into a sleep. Sometimes they would wake up and blow through their lips. All the warriors were asleep except Many Horses, who kept watch, and Walking Man. He squatted near the fire, putting a little dried grass or twigs on it, until he stood and walked to the top of the gulley.

The *Tsis Tsis' tas* do not count time like the white man. They will say, "It was seven winters ago," or "It was the Drying Grass Moon when Young Wolf fell from his pony and died." White men kept time like they kept everything else. They divided the hours and days and tried to hold them. *Tsis Tsis' tas* knew that time was as natural as the sun passing in the sky or how long it took one man to ride from one place to another.

Or how long Bull Bear had been gone.

Walking Man paced for some time, trying to see through the darkness as he looked for Bull Bear. He listened but heard no sounds. He walked across the prairie. He had gone a distance when he thought he saw the shimmer of a fire. He carried a Henry rifle with the barrel wrapped in leather because he knew a brave that had a Henry, and when the brave dropped it, the cartridges could not move through the tube underneath. So, he wrapped the barrel in leather and kept just six or seven cartridges in the tube.

Walking Man cocked the rifle slowly, watching the fire all the time, and moved towards it. He thought maybe Bull Bear had decided to camp here, but that made no sense because it was just a short distance from the others. Bull Bear would have ridden on until he met up with the braves.

Down in a gulley, not as deep as the one where the others slept, he saw an old man.

The old man was *Tsis Tsis' tas.*

His presence confused Walking Man because it was a very strange occurrence. He did not expect to see anyone on the prairie except Bull Bear. He lowered his rifle and watched the old man skin a prairie dog and hold the meat on a stick over the fire. The old man spied Walking Man and motioned for him to come down. Waking Man knelt at the top of the gulley and looked around. This was very strange.

"Come down, come down," the old man said, gesturing again. His voice was high and cracked with delight as he spoke. "Do not be afraid of me."

"I do not know you."

The old man laughed a little, turning the stick in the fire. "This is true. But I have some tobacco and a little prairie dog, and we must talk."

Walking Man stood slowly, and keeping the Henry across his chest, went down into the gulley. He stood a few feet away and studied the old man. He wore a white man's blue shirt, and a green-wool breechcloth, with a red blanket thrown over his shoulders. His bony knees stuck out from under the breech cloth. His long gray hair was pulled to the back of his head and tied with a leather thong. His shirt had porcupine needles and beads sewn into it on the breast and down both arms. He hummed a song that Walking Man did not know, while he cooked the prairie dog. He put the stick down and picked up a calumet pipe with a long, wooden handle, which had three grouse feathers tied to it. He pulled a white man's canvas pouch from the pocket of the shirt and put some tobacco in the pipe bowl. He held it out to Walking Man. "You might as well sit and smoke. You cannot stand there all night."

Walking Man sat down with the Henry across his lap, watching the old man as he picked up a stick from the fire and gestured for Walking Man to put the pipe in his mouth. Then the old man blew on the glowing tip of the stick, lit the pipe, and waited until the tobacco had caught fire.

Smoke came into Walking Man's mouth and lungs, and it was warm. After just a bit, Walking Man said, "I did not expect to find anyone out here." He was being polite. He did not ask any questions. Still, he was disturbed because of the situation. Such a thing had never happened to him before. He had never even heard of such a thing. He was suspicious of the old man because he did not understand who he was or what he was doing there. He would reason this thing out, he told himself. Then he realized the old man was alone, meaning, he had no pony. This was almost too strange to comprehend. A thought pushed itself into his brain so hard that he flinched. The old man could be a *maiyun,* but then he dismissed the idea because the *maiyun* came as plants or animals. *He could have been of the Maiheyuno,* Walking Man thought. The idea made his heart tighten, so he concentrated on smoking the pipe.

"I will tell you a story," the old man said. As he spoke the words, they traveled over the fire and disappeared with the smoke.

Chapter 7

"Many winters ago, nobody really knows how many," the old man said. "The *Tsis Tsis' tas* lived in lodges, far to the east. This was before they met the Red Talkers, who made them a gift of ponies. They were farmers and did not follow the buffalo as they do today. Before their enemies and friends pushed them out of the land. How is the tobacco?"

Walking Man nodded.

"Good." He held up the stick and examined the prairie dog and put the carcass close to the fire to continue cooking. "We did not know the *Suh' Tai* then. That would come later. The *Tsis Tsis' tas* were content with their lives. One day, during the Deer Rutting Moon, some hunters came back to their village and told a story. They said they were out in the forest and could find no game, and the silence was so great that even the leaves did not brush against each other in the wind. They said they had heard wolves howling, but not like any wolves they had heard before. The village did not believe the story, but a medicine man said maybe some warriors should go out to find the wolves. Seven warriors went out. They did not come back. It is said that this is why seven is an unlucky number for the *Tsis Tsis' tas.* The old chiefs sat down and made a plan. They would send out a big war party to kill all the wolves, and then the game would return. There was celebration and dancing, and a big party went out. Roundabout thirty braves. When they were gone, The People in the village heard an animal call out several times, like it was seeking its mate. Or maybe it was hurt and crying out in pain. It was said the sound turned the water to ice, and the sky gray, and the wind as cold as that of the Strong Cold. It was unnatural. The people in the village were afraid.

After a while, three warriors returned to the village. They were all that remained of the thirty who had gone out. They could not speak, and they shook as if some sickness had invaded their bodies. They lay down and the villagers covered them with blankets and kept them close to the fires in the center of a lodge. The medicine men were called, and they did all they could. No one in the village knew what to do. Finally, one of the three men died, and another ran off. One brave remained and told the story."

The old man examined the prairie dog and then continued his story.

"He said they went into the forest but could find no sign of wolves. He said, all the time they felt they were being watched. They spent more time in the forest hunting until, one by one, the braves disappeared. The other hunters were afraid and angered. The others heard howling and then the men's screams, but when they went to look for them, they found only bits of them. The bodies were torn apart. Entrails were flung into the tree limbs, patches of blood covered the ground, heads were crammed in the forks of trees. The man said that those who remained kept close together and watched the forest, but they were afraid. The howling became louder and came all the time. More of the warriors disappeared; and the others, those who lived, decided to return to the village. The brave said he had never known such fear. He said they ran as fast as they could until they could run no more; and they made a place in a creek, where a bunch of rocks had fallen during a flood. They hid behind the rocks. They would make their fight there. The man shook so much as he told the story that it was hard to understand him. He said whatever made the howling circled them all night, taunting them. He said they built a big fire so they could see the creature that was not a wolf should it come at them at night."

Walking Man realized he was biting down so hard on the pipe stem that his jaws ached. He took the pipe out of his mouth before it broke his teeth.

"Finally, early in the morning, before the sun was born, the thing that was not a wolf came for them. He said he and the two men stayed with the fire at their back. He said it stank of long-dead buffalo, and the wind turned cold around them. The thing was terrible, with eyes like the embers of a strong fire. During the fight, other braves were killed. The man did not say how, because the memory was too painful. The man began to cry for the friends he had lost and what he had seen. He spoke no more and died." The old man looked up at the sky. "I cannot see the stars or moon, but I know it is only a little while until the sun comes again. I must go soon, but I will finish the story. The people became afraid of what they had been told; then they did a bad thing. They set fire to the forest to kill the creature. They called it the White Devil because of what the brave told them. He said it was big, with gray skin that was almost white. It was covered by hair. One should never do such a thing, burning down the forest. I think it angered *Maheo*. Then they moved far away to a wide river and built a fort made of earth with stakes on top. They kept a big fire burning and watched for the thing that had killed the braves. It never came. They were safe from it. But sometime later, men came and pushed them off the land. Cree, and Ojibwe, and some Lakota. Then *Maheo* gave them ponies and taught them to ride. Maybe it was the Spaniards. Those were Red Talking white men who wore iron shirts. The *Tsis Tsis' tas* met the *Suh'Tai,* lived in tipis instead of lodges, and quit farming and followed the buffalo. That is everything I know."

Walking Man said nothing as the old man stirred the fire with a stick. He did not eat the prairie dog.

"Why do you tell me this?" Walking Man said.

"This thing that is not a wolf has come again," the old man answered. "This White Devil is hunting for men. For women and children. It comes with a great hunger. The hunger is more than for food. It eats fear. It washes its body in blood and chases men to see them run until they can run no more; and when the thing is satisfied, it rips them into pieces like a woman tears a piece of cloth. It will come for you, Walking Man. You and your braves. Then it will go to your village."

Walking Man stared at the old man. "How do you know my name?"

Chapter 8

Walking Man stood on the prairie, alone. The old man was gone. A cold wind stroked his arms and pulled at his legging. He held his Henry rifle and heard voices behind him. He turned to see the warriors pulling the blankets from their ponies and making camp. They were laughing. It was the same moment before he found the old man. He had not moved from the ravine.

Stone Forehead called to him. "Why don't you come down and eat something?"

Walking Man heard the mournful call of a bone flute and, in the darkness, saw Comes-a-Pony sitting next to a fire, playing. He wondered what she would say if he told her of his vision. For an instant, he thought he should tell her. She would understand and perhaps help him explain what he had seen and heard. He felt a twinge of loneliness. She stopped playing, and the flames danced over her face as she glanced at him. The moment was gone, and he knew he would not speak to her.

"He is waiting on Bull Bear," Fool Dog, one of the Shield Warriors said. He folded his blanket and lay down, digging through his parfleche bag.

"Bull Bear will find us," Stone Forehead said. "Maybe he will wait until the moon reappears."

Walking Man looked at the sky and then saw a streak of lightning cut into the darkness many miles away. Thunder followed. He smelled rain.

I will tell you a story.

Worry tugged at him as he watched the others settle in. What was the thing that had come some time ago? How could it live so long? He walked down into the ravine and stared at the small fire made from the scraps of a cottonwood tree that had lived in the ravine and then died, its white corpse shattered by strong winds.

He knew of only one White Devil. They came from the east and took everything. They ate up the land and killed the animals to make The People starve; and if that was not enough, they killed the *Tsis Tsis' Tas* or made them go live where the hunting was no good. That was the White Devil.

"We will stay a little while," he told the others. "Then we will go after the white soldiers." He saw Little Raven at his camp, away from the others and walked over to him. "Something has got hold of you,

Little Raven," he said. "You ought to tell me about it, and maybe I can help."

Little Raven ate a handful of berries and shook his head. "I cannot tell you because I do not know." He looked into the sky. "I wonder why the stars were taken away. I always feel better when I see the stars, my brothers." The wind picked up, moaning. "There is something wrong with everything. I feel it. The wind is unhappy, and the stars have hidden themselves away. Something bad is coming. Perhaps I will be killed by the white soldiers. Perhaps my soul knows this and is sad."

Lightning cracked the darkness again, and this time, the thunder followed closely behind.

"Rest," Walking Man said. "Then we will go after the white soldiers." He went back to Moon, pulled off the blanket, and wrapped it around his shoulders. He climbed to the top of the ravine, sat down, and laid the Henry across his lap. He talked to *Maheo*. "I do not understand. Did you bring me the old man to warn me? I cannot do anything without your help. Give me a sign that I will know what to do. Let no harm come to Bull Bear." The wind answered him by tugging at the blanket. It grew stronger, and this time, there was thunder but no lightning. He thought he heard a wolf howl, but it could have been the wind racing across the prairie. He tried to reason out what he had heard, because he valued reason and clear thinking and the notion that all things are revealed to him after careful thought. That was how Walking Man was. That was his strength. But tonight, had been like a clay pot thrown to the ground and shattered into a thousand pieces; and when he tried to put it back together, none of the pieces fit. He felt fear creeping into his soul. A cold rain began to fall. He thought there would be snow in the morning, and maybe the white soldiers would be easier to track. Maybe they would catch them quickly, kill them, and go home. You should leave the white soldiers and go home, a voice inside of him said. Yes, he agreed. But the warriors would not understand. He was taking victory away from them because an old man had come to him in a vision. They would want to kill the soldiers, capture their ponies, and take away guns and cartridges. They would ride home and be celebrated.

Come-a-Pony lay down on a buffalo robe Painted Feather, a girl whose mother had died and whose father had been killed by whites, had made for her. The girl had come to the tipi that Left Hand shared with his sister and said, "You have no one to cook for you or mend your clothes. I will do so." She spoke to Comes-a-Pony, not to her brother. Painted Feather was small and very thin, and someone said she had the wasting disease; but she but was always busy gathering buffalo dung, sweeping the earthen floor of the tipi, or cooking. She had made the fine doe-skin shirt that Comes-a-Pony wore and had given it to her as a surprise. When Comes-a-Pony had put it on, Painted Feather inspected it to make certain it fit her.

Comes-a-Pony played her bone flute, and Left Hand smoked a pipe. "You should go and speak with Walking Man, Little Sister."

She lowered the flute and said, "I have nothing to say."

"He is a good man. It will do no harm."

She played a few notes before she answered her brother. "Walking Man has no time for anyone besides Walking Man. Why should I waste my words on him?"

Left Hand rolled over on his blanket, put his hands under his head, and studied the sky. "You ought to have a husband. It is not so bad to have a husband."

"You have no wife. Why do you want me to have a husband?"

Left Hand considered the question before replying. "I will find a wife someday. It is not necessary for me to have a wife now. She would just get in the way. Now I can go anywhere I like, and no one would complain. A wife would just get in the way."

Comes-a-Pony started to play the flute, but then said, "I will find a husband when you find a wife." As she played, she saw Walking Man sitting alone, tapping a stick on the ground in thought. You think too much. Maybe one day you ought to do something without thinking. She continued playing.

After a while, Walking Man decided he had his answer. The thing that was not a wolf. The thing the old man spoke of was white men. They killed the buffalo to deny the *Tsis Tsis' tas*. They ate up the land. Their words were hollow, and their greed was never satisfied. Walking Man reasoned out what the old man was warning him about. Death was coming. Death was the white man.

He pulled a blanket close to his body in satisfaction. Now he knew. Now he understood the vision. The knowledge gave him calm. He listened as the hollow sound of the flute floated over the ground and into the darkness. He thought of Comes-a-Pony, but then sleep made his blanket warm and his body soft so that it relaxed into the ground.

But inside, a tiny voice called to him. Like a man speaking from far away whose words lost power as they traveled across the ground. There was sound but only a little was recognizable about the words.

A White Devil, the old man called it.

Chapter 9

The patrol had taken shelter from the wind in a gulley, but despite the protection, Sweet had ordered that no fire be made. Taliaferro suggested that maybe it would be best to build a small fire and roast a little coffee. "Begging your pardon," Taliaferro had said in a low voice so that no one else heard. "It would be good for the men to warm their bellies a little. They might not get the chance for a while."

Sweet chastised himself for not thinking of the men's wellbeing and then found he was angry at Taliaferro for pointing it out. "Yes," he said, trying to sound decisive. "Let the men make coffee and eat."

"Yes, sir," the sergeant said and went off to see to the men.

Two of the men searched for scraps of wood washed down into the gulley by the spring rains. They found enough to make two small fires. The rest of the men drew coffee beans from their haversacks, crushed them as well as they could between two rocks, and poured the remnants and water from their canteens into cups next to the fires. After a bit, steam rose from the cups. They ate a handful of red beans cooked earlier and some salt pork seasoned with vinegar, washing it all down with coffee. Then they lay down with their reins wrapped around their wrists without unsaddling or hobbling their horses.

"Post two men for guard detail," Sweet ordered Taliaferro, "and have them relieved in two hours." He was satisfied with his orders, more so when Porter nodded after he gave them, which Sweet took to be a sign he had done the right thing. He wondered if the men would sleep and envied those that did. His mind would not let him rest, so he sought out Porter and found some comfort in being close to the scout. He sat down.

Porter handed Sweet a piece of stick candy. "I don't have many vices, but I can't seem to get my fill of this. The sutler keeps a batch on hand because he knows I'll buy him out."

"What do we do next?" Sweet asked

Porter bit off a piece of candy and rolled it around in his mouth. The sun was a faint memory, and heavy clouds were moving in from the east. "I wish we had the moon tonight, but wishing don't make it so. I guess we'll wait a few hours and head out. I'll take the lead, and you and your boys can follow, one right after the other. Tell'em to latch on to the fellow in front of them and not let go. It'll be darker than the inside of a well digger's ass out there, and I don't want no one wandering off."

"Yes," Sweet replied. "Should we proceed at a walk, Mr. Porter? To save the horses, I mean?"

"If I was you, Lieutenant," Porter said, "after it gets light enough, we don't bump into each other, I'd get on a trot and stay there. It'll be rough on the horses and men, but I think it best to keep some distance between us and them Cheyenne."

Sweet told himself he should have thought of that. He should have ordered it before Porter had said anything. "What do you think the Indians are doing? Right now, I mean."

"Oh, I reckon they've settled for a while. They'll eat up the distance in daylight. Our job is to stay one step ahead. Fast enough to stay out of their hands but not so much that we wear out our mounts too soon and end up afoot."

Sweet shivered and took another bite of candy.

"I'd tell the boys to go easy on their water if I were you. Later, come daylight, I'll set off ahead to look for some."

Sweet didn't like the idea of Porter leaving the patrol, but he didn't say anything. He didn't want the scout to know he was afraid to be on his own. He felt like a boy. "It sure is cold, isn't it?"

"Yeah, weather out here is always hard to figure. You get snow in summer and heat in winter, and the wind never stops. Drive a man crazy if he'd let it." He slid the remainder of the stick candy into the pocket of his buckskin coat. Porter's horse tried to pull away. The scout jerked on the reins. "Settle down, Randy. You ain't going nowhere."

Jones, lying next to Smallwood, pushed an envelope at the trooper.

"What's this?" Smallwood asked.

"It's a letter," Jones said in a whisper. "I want you to mail it, if anything happens to me."

Smallwood sat up. "What the hell are you talking about?"

"Please?"

"Hang onto it and mail it yourself."

Jones brushed the dust off the envelope. "It's to my father. The Right Honourable Charles Balsam."

"Didn't think Jones was your real name. Anyway, quit talking like that. Porter'll get us out of this mess."

"You're my bunkee. You're supposed to help me out."

Smallwood shook his head and snatched the envelope from Jones, sliding it into his shirt. "You're going to get real surprised if I get killed instead of you."

"No. No, I know what's going to happen."

"Ain't you the cheery one? How do you know that?"

Jones shrugged. "Just a feeling, I guess. I've had it for a while."

"Where you from? I mean before?"

"Kent," Jones said. "In England."

"Ain't never been. Pretty far from here?"

Jones said, "A lifetime."

"Well," Smallwood said. "What was it?"

"What?"

"When a fella signs up, it's usually because of one of three things. The drink, cards, or a woman. Anyway, it's because there's trouble behind it. Which is it?"

Jones shook his head.

Smallwood shrugged, "Suit yourself."

Mendelson crawled over to the two men. "Ain't you asleep?"

"Does it look like it?" Smallwood said. He sniffed the air. "You'd better be careful Taliaferro, don't smell that who-shot-john on your breath."

"I ain't worried about him. It's the general up there. I'd like to get home with my topknot on." He held out his hand, palm up. "Hell, it's starting to rain."

Victoria, Ashcroft's horse, pawed at the ground. "Settle down, you bitch."

Collier laughed. "Ain't you two ever gonna get married.

Ashcroft tugged on the reins. "A hundred mounts at the depot, and I draw this one. She's as stubborn as a mule."

"Look at it this way, bunkee. You could have been one of those poor souls Crook put aboard jackasses."

Victoria snorted in protest. She was a big mare, black, sixteen hands high with a broad face. A few of the soldiers at the remount depot chuckled when Ashcroft drew Victoria. He soon found out why. She tried to bite him when he took her reins, she resisted his commands, she swung her head to brain him when he tried to saddle her, and she ate everything in sight, including the top boards on her stall.

"I think I'll get rid of her when nobody's looking," Ashcroft said.

Collier shook his head. "You just don't know how to handle women. You got to be gentle like, that's all I'm saying. Buy her a nice dress. Maybe some flowers."

"I'd shoot her if it weren't a waste of a good cartridge."

The rain increased, cold, big drops battering hats, covering saddles, carried by the wind so it felt like it was coming from straight ahead. The men went for their ponchos, taking off their hats and slipping them over their heads. It would help a little but do nothing to keep out the cold. The rain increased.

Sweet was on his feet, wishing he had bought a felt hat instead of the straw one, but the sutler who sold it to him insisted it was ideal for hot weather. What hot weather? The weather had been mild until they reached Fort Laramie, then it turned cool. Like a fall day, Sweet had thought, and he decided campaigning wasn't as difficult as everyone said.

Porter pulled his horse close to him. "We ought to go now, Lieutenant. If the rain keeps up, it'll cover our tracks. Besides, this ground is hard as granite and flash floods come down these gulleys pretty quick if there's a hard rain. This ain't no place to be if it comes a flood." He held out his hand, letting the fat drops bounce off it. "If this ain't hard, it'll do. Remember. You tell them boys to get right on my ass and stick there. It's bad enough in pure dark, but the rain'll make it a hundred times worse."

Sweet called out, "Sergeant Taliaferro? Mount the men. We're going to move out."

Jones swung into his saddle. Two years before, he had bought a brown corduroy coat from a trail hand down on his luck. He paid a laundress to repair the rips and tears and add a flannel lining. He wore it on every campaign. He kept his pipe in the right-hand pocket and his tobacco pouch and matches in the left-hand pocket. He'd lost one of the bone buttons and replaced it with one made of gutta-percha. The coat had its imperfections, but then so did men; and Jones had learned to accept them. The elbows were worn, and the cuffs frayed, and the tail edge was nearly gone from the time it had rubbed against the saddle. They had grown comfortable together, man and possession; and Jones attributed some luck to the coat. Soldiers were odd that way. Superstitious, wary of change.

But this patrol was different. They had come away from the column, and each mile farther away from the post had brought a sense of loss for Jones. He did not understand the feeling. He had been on campaigns before and looked forward to them because they broke the monotony of garrison life. This? This was different.

Jones looked about, as if searching for something. There was that and the feeling that he was being watched. He even thought about asking the lieutenant if he could use his binoculars, just to see if he could locate the unseen watcher. But that was impossible. Troopers did not approach officers asking for anything. Officers were on one plane, and troopers on another. Their worlds never intersected. Any communication, any contact was through company sergeants, like Taliaferro.

And Taliaferro would listen with patience like he always did and then screw up his face while he said, "Permission denied." That would be the end of it.

The patrol was mounted and moving at a trot, troopers with their heads down, trying to keep the hard rain from stinging their faces. Occasionally, Taliaferro would appear out of the gloom to make certain they were holding their intervals.

Collier shifted stiffly in his saddle. "Two saddle blankets," he said under his breath. "Two goddamned saddle blankets and it still hurts."

"What's the matter?" Smallwood asked.

"Rheumatize. Every time this animal moves, it's like a knife in my back."

"You're lucky. It could be piles. I get them every once in a while. Hurts like the fires of hell."

After about an hour, Sweet called a halt; and the men, except Collier, dismounted, walking, leading their horses. Collier hesitated, swung his right leg out, and stepped gingerly on the ground. A searing pain shot through his spine. "I don't know how much longer I can keep this up," he said as Smallwood led his horse past him.

"I got some liniment in my saddlebags," Smallwood said. "Try that when we stop. At the rate we're going, everybody's gonna need some."

When they had walked about a mile, Sweet stopped them again and ordered them back into the saddle.

The men prepared to mount their horses. Collier slid his left foot into the stirrup and willed himself to take the pain.

"Mount." When the men were in their saddles, Sweet called, "At the trot, march."

A flash of lightning illuminated the patrol, huddled figures on sodden horses, moving so tightly together that they could have been one, long animal. Many legs, many heads. Some of the men uncorked their canteens and held them out to collect water. It wouldn't be much, but it would help.

"Sergeant Taliaferro?" Sweet said. The sergeant rode up next to him. "How are the men?"

The question surprised Taliaferro. He didn't think Sweet was asking about the welfare of the men. The lieutenant wanted the sergeant's opinion about his leadership.

"Just fine, Lieutenant. Ain't nobody complained to me." What kind of an officer was the army sending out here, anyway?

"I know this pace is difficult," Sweet pressed. "It's hard on horses and men."

Yes, it is, Taliaferro thought, *but so is being butchered and scalped.*

Porter, ahead of the patrol, heard a wolf's pitiful wail in the distance, surprising him. Animals, even wolves, often sought protection from storms: a rocky overhang, a cluster of downed cottonwood trees. They did not come out unless they had to. Unless they wanted to. He heard it again, off to the right. It seemed to follow them, as if the wolf was tracking the patrol; but he shook the idea from his head. Wolves, animals, avoided men. Men were killers to be approached only in desperation, or if the animals were defending themselves or their young. This was different, and there was something unsettling about this wolf's call. It was mournful, haunting. A hollow sound. It was as if the creature was calling to the men.

Jones pulled his hat tightly over his head and rode with one hand clutching his collar. The cold rain stung his face. He heard the howl.

His head snapped up, and cold water trapped by the brim of his hat poured down the back of his neck.

He trembled due to the cold and even more because of the cry from the distant animal.

Porter, leading the men, drifted back so that he was alongside Lieutenant Sweet. "Looks like this rain is going to keep up which suits me just fine. Here's what I'm going to do. It's near light, so I'm going to strike out ahead, see if I can find us some water. You're going to spot a big old mountain. Tallest one in the range. Can't miss it. Head straight for it, and I'll find you along the way."

Sweet realized he would be alone. "What if the Indians catch up with us?"

"Well, there's always that possibility, but I don't think that'll happen. This rain is going to cover our tracks. They'll waste some time trying to find them again. That mountain is north of here, so you'll veer off the course we've been keeping all this time. Don't stop for nothing. Walk'em, trot'em, and lead'em, but don't stop. This is a long fight." He noticed the troubled look on Sweet's face. "Look here, Lieutenant. I've been out here for a while. We keep our senses about us, and we'll be alright. Those Cheyenne ain't going to do nothing, unless they think they've got an advantage. Don't give them one. And if they catch up to you, find good ground, keep'em at a distance, and slip away in the night. It's a cat and mouse thing. No need to tell you who the cat is."

"Yes," Sweet said, not certain he could do anything Porter suggested. Fear came back, almost making his body ache.

"Funny, ain't it?"

"What?" Sweet asked. "What's funny?"

"I ain't seen an animal in a while. Course, a party of any size usually scares them off, but a soul could expect to see at least something. Flying or on the ground. Maybe watching from some ways off. But I ain't seen nothing. Not hide nor hair."

Porter kicked his horse into a run.

Sweet watched the scout disappear into the rain. He heard a noise off to his right. He wasn't sure what it was. Plaintive, dissolute, a prolonged moan. He was afraid again and ashamed that he felt the way he did.

He was at war. He had come from the majesty of an army on the march, long columns of infantry, cavalry galloping into position. Wagon trains that stretched to the horizon. Young staff officers, filled with self-importance, galloping along the line, Crook in his canvas suit, guidons flying, and Sweet, the warrior. No, not yet. Now was the chance that he could go into battle. This was different. This was not The Death of General Wolfe. This was no painting with stilted figures, heroically posed. This was not of Benjamin West's making. No one would honor his death. He was not a noble soldier. He was a boy. And his passing? It would be of some note but nothing more than a casual mention in dispatches.

He felt like crying. He could, he rationalized. No one would see his tears in the rain. The men rode with their own thoughts, so his existence was of no importance. He took a deep breath and slumped in his saddle – a warrior afraid of war.

Chapter 10

The Cheyenne rode out just before dawn. The rain had stopped, the sun nothing but a smear in the sky, its warmth hidden by gray, motionless clouds. Mud splattered the ponies' legs up to their knees. Bull Bear had not yet returned, and the warriors spoke in hushed tones. Old Turtle and Left Hand rode back and forth on the left, like an old woman sewing stitches into trouser legs, looking for a sign. One Eye and Eagle Head made the same zigzagging pattern on the right. It still smelled of snow, but the air was not cold enough to make it so.

Stone Forehead rode up to Walking Man and spoke. "This is not a good time. First, it was hard to find the soldier's trail; and when we did, the rain came and washed it all away. Now no one has seen Bull Bear, and that is troubling. Someone should go back and look for him. Maybe he fell off his horse and hurt himself."

"He will come soon enough," Walking Man said. He did not believe his own words. He did not believe them because he could not get the image of the old man out of his mind.

"I think having Shield Warrior's braves with us has been bad luck."

"It was never so before," Walking Man said. His reason began to re-emerge, but it was not yet strong. The old man's presence made it so.

"Maybe we should go and look for Black Antelope. Maybe he has had better luck."

The idea angered Walking Man. "Do you think that the Dog Soldiers have better luck than the Kit Fox? Are we children to go running from one place to another?" Heat flowed through his body, and he turned his head away from Stone Forehead so the brave could not see his shame for his words.

Stone Forehead jerked his pony to one side and joined the others looking for a sign.

Walking Man sat on Moon and considered what he had said. Something was happening to him. He thought of the old man. He remembered Little Raven's words. He heard the wolf howling in his mind. The world was twisted.

Stone Forehead, Old Turtle, Left Hand, Eagle Head, Many Horses, and the three Shield Warrior's braves rode up to him. Wooden Leg continued looking for sign. It was Stone Forehead who spoke, "We think it is a good time for a council."

Comes-a-Pony followed them but said nothing.

"We have not found the white soldier's trail yet," Walking Man said.

"We will find it," Stone Forehead said, "and finding it, we will catch the white soldiers and kill them. But we think it is time for a council."

Walking Man nodded and dismounted, squatting near Moon. The others followed, except Comes-a-Pony. She hooked her right leg over the pommel of her saddle and rested the butt of her rifle on her thigh.

Eagle Head said to Comes-a-Pony, "We are having a council."

"Yes," she said.

"You can come and join us," Many Horses said. He was always hospitable.

"I can hear you from here," Comes-a-Pony said.

Old Turtle was the oldest braves, so he spoke first. "Some things have troubled me. Bull Bear has not returned, and that is not like him. Little Raven is no longer singing or telling stories. He stays by himself. First, the wind is warm and then it is cold, which by itself is no great thing, but with the others, it is of concern. I have heard brother wolf calling many times.

He calls from all directions. I think maybe we have done something to anger him. We should send after Bull Bear."

"The others went off and left us, but that is to be expected, I suppose. They were not Kit Fox warriors," Wooden Leg said. "The only good thing to happen is Red Horse finding that Crow pony." Red Horse had tied the reins of the Crow pony to his own pony's so that they ran side by side.

The others spoke when it was their turn, and Walking Man listened respectfully. They were all concerned about the way things had been. When it was Walking Man's turn to speak, he scrubbed the ground with his hand and began assembling pebbles in a small circle as he spoke. "I grew angry with Stone Forehead, and for that I am sorry. That is not the way to behave."

Stone Forehead nodded, accepting the apology.

"The others went off because that is what they decided. Black Antelope is a good warrior. Maybe they will find the white soldiers first. I have heard the wolf as well. I do not know why he follows us. Maybe he is keeping the bad spirits away. I have spoken to Little Raven. I have seen this sort of thing before, but not with Little Raven. A cloud comes over a man, and he is silent and stays away from others. After a while he gets better. I am concerned about Bull Bear. I think it would be a good idea for two braves to go back and look for him. We will go on after the white soldiers."

The others considered Walking Man's words. "There is more," he said. And he told them about his vision.

The warriors were silent as he spoke. He was careful to tell them the event as he remembered it. Finally, he finished and said, "I have given this some thought, and I think the old man was warning me about the white men's coming. He is the White Devil. You know how it is. First, a few came and then many. We signed papers and listened to them, but I know the white men cannot be trusted. They gobble up everything they see."

One Eye said, "The old man did not tell you, his name?"

"He did not. But he knew mine."

Eagle Head said, "Maybe it was the spirit of an old chief."

Red Horse spoke next. "I don't believe in visions. I have heard people speak of them, but I think it is something they made in their mind and did not understand it."

"No," Stone Forehead said. "Visions are a good way for a man to find his path." To Walking Man he said, "I think you are right. I hate the white men. They defile our women and make our braves sick with whiskey. They put their names on paper and say that is their word and we should trust them. None of them are honorable. They cannot be trusted." He asked Walking Man, "Maybe he knows about White Chief Crook and his army coming? He has many soldiers and a big wagon train."

"The others, too," Eagle Head. "They say Long Hair will join Crook."

"Yes. That is true as well," Walking Man said. As he spoke, Walking Man moved the little stones around.

Stone Forehead continued. "This vision gives me strength. It is a warning about the white men. They are the devils with red eyes. Let us go find the white soldiers and cut them up. We will scatter their bodies around until they cannot find their hands to make war or their tongues to lie. Then we will go back and join the others and rub out Crook and his men. That way, we will kill the White Devil."

Fool Dog agreed. "I think Stone Forehead is right. This vision warned us about the white men, but we already know about them. But this is more white soldiers than ever before. This will be a big fight."

One Eye joined in. "Maybe the vision was telling us that we will win this big fight and chase the white men from our land. This could be."

Old Turtle, who said very little even when there was good reason to talk, said, "What about Bull Bear? We must send someone to look for him."

Red Horse spoke up. "I will go. I will find him," he announced, looking at the others for recognition. He wanted their attention so that they knew he was a brave warrior. He did not fear anything. He would ride away and find Bull Bear, and the others would know how courageous he was. When they returned home, the others would sing of his bravery, and the women would look at him with desire. "I have two ponies; and if one gets tired, I will ride the other one. I will show that Crow pony how a *Tsis Tsis' tas* rides."

"Someone else should go with you, in case there is trouble," Stone Forehead said.

The words offended Red Horse, and he jumped to his feet, speaking with anger. "I will go alone. I do not need another to ride with me."

Walking Man stood and said kindly to the young brave. "Stone Forehead meant only that he did not want you to come to harm." He hesitated, and then spoke. "Go find Bull Bear but be careful. Maybe his pony is lame, and he cannot catch up with us." When Walking Man said this, he thought it might be true. But his mind whispered that there might be another reason that Bull Bear had not returned. He did not want to listen to his mind.

Red Horse shouted in triumph and swung onto his pony. His mount sprang forward with the Crow pony tied to it, and Red Horse said, "I will find Bull Bear." He swatted his pony's rump with a coup stick and rode off at a gallop.

"What do you think?" Walking Man asked Comes-a-Pony. She had not spoken during the council. She had let her pony graze contently, while the others said what they wanted.

She said, "Why did the vision come to you? Why not Eagle Head or Wooden Head?"

"I do not know," Walking Man replied.

"I think," she shifted her leg from the pommel, "maybe, it was *Veeho* playing a trick on you."

Many Horses spoke first, "That is not likely."

"Why?" Comes-a-Pony said sharply. "Because it was Walking Man and not Eagle Head or Wooden Leg who had the vision." Eagle Head started to speak when she said, "You asked me to speak. I have done so."

"Comes-a-Pony is right," Walking Man said. "The vision could have come to anyone else, but it came to me. Why, I do not know. Maybe one day I will find out. Do you think I am right?" he asked Comes-a-Pony.

"It was your vision," Comes-a-Pony said. "Not mine. Stone Forehead agrees with you. What do the others say?"

One by one, the Cheyenne said they thought Walking Man was right. The vision warned of the white man. The White Devil.

Walking Man took Moon's reins. "Let us catch up with the white soldiers and kill them. My vision has told us what we must do. "

The others mounted and rode off except Left Hand, who said, "Little Sister? Why do you doubt this? Because it came from Walking Man?"

The question angered Comes-a-Pony, but she could not be cross with her brother. "No, brother. If it were not *Veeho* playing a trick on us, then why would Walking Man have a vision about something we already know?"

"Maybe to warn us a big fight was coming."

"We do not need to be reminded," Comes-a-Pony said, "Ask the *Wutapai* band, or the Oglala, or Arapaho. Every time we trust the Whites, they steal from us or kill our people. Maybe there will be a big fight, and we will kill lots of white soldiers. Maybe it is something else." She rode off, leaving Left Hand alone. He watched her rejoin the others and thought over her words. Visions foresaw things that would or could happen, not what already has passed. If that were true, then there was something else the Cheyenne should fear. Something unknown. Something that was coming.

Chapter 11

Taliaferro walked back along the line, leading Mike. The black gelding followed behind him, head down, mane hanging limply, still soaked from the rain. The sergeant knew the horses were in bad shape. They hadn't had a good rest in some time. They would get worse as time and miles went on. They would seep life like a bucket with a tiny hole. They could walk, and the life would drip from them. But when they broke into a trot and kept that pace, the life would drain out of them faster; and after a while, the bucket would be empty.

A cavalryman knows his mount. Knows how much it will take, and when it has given up. They were dying because they had come a hundred hard miles from Fort D. H. Russell to Fort Laramie and another hundred miles from Laramie to Fort Fetterman. That's what a horse did: go until it couldn't go anymore.

And a cavalryman afoot was infantry. What the Cheyenne called 'walk-a-heaps.'

A cavalryman fed and watered his horse before he did anything else. He put fresh straw in its stall, and when he could, gave it a slice of apple, or more likely a carrot from the company garden. He would brush its coat, clean its hooves, and when needed, paint its sores with medicine. It was a bond, man, and horse. A soldier knew: you take care of your mount, and it'd take care of you. They were like benevolent ghosts in their white canvas stable fatigues while they tended to their horses, hovering around their mounts like spirits at a séance.

Now they were eight days out with the Indians chasing them with little grain for the horses and barely enough water to keep the men going. The wind was cold, coming from behind, the sky sullen and unfriendly. The water that had pooled in depressions reflected clouds still too heavy with rain to move.

"Mind your intervals," Taliaferro said. The rain had soaked saddles and saddle blankets, and the horses' withers would be rubbed raw from saddles that hadn't been removed in days. Cinches were biting into their bellies, and two of the mounts had thrown shoes. Their hooves would fester, and they would go lame. Every step through the mud was a struggle. When they led their mounts, men slid, cursing, holding onto their horses for support. Horses struggled to pull their hooves out of the muck and take a step. Too tired even to fight if one horse got too close to another. The animals tolerated each other because they were just too worn out to do anything else. Pretty soon, their muscles would lock up because they didn't have enough water. They got a little from the puddles that spotted the ground but not enough to help. Not nearly enough. When their muscles failed them, they'd drop into the mud and die.

The men knew this, but there was nothing they could do. They knew when a horse just loses its will to go on. Oh, they'd walk when led; but in a while, they would just stop walking.

Just like a soldier.

He filed in next to Smallwood. The old soldier's head was down, watching his feet move forward.

"How are you, Tom?" Taliaferro asked.

The soldier gave him a weak smile. "Oh, you know, Bill. Getting along."

"Betty looks to be doing poorly."

Smallwood looked at his mount and stroked her neck. "She's good for a few miles more, I reckon. She doesn't complain much."

Taliaferro nodded and stepped out of the line. "Well, you know best."

The lieutenant called him forward.

"Sergeant, I think we've gone about twenty miles, but I haven't seen any sight of Mr. Porter. I thought he would be just ahead."

"Yes, sir," Taliaferro said. "It probably would be alright to rest the men and horses for a few minutes."

Sweet looked over his shoulder.

"I ain't seen no sign of Indians," Taliaferro said. "I'd say we've got some distance from them."

"I wonder where Mr. Porter is?"

"He'll find us," Taliaferro said because he didn't know what else to say. "Some of the mounts, they're about played out. They've been going at it for a while now."

Sweet threw up his hand and called, "Halt!"

The line stopped. There was nothing for the men to do but hang onto their horses. It was too muddy to sit, so they just slumped against their mounts. Sweet handed his binoculars to Taliaferro. "See if you can see anything."

The sergeant took the binoculars, walked out a bit, and put them to his eyes. He scanned the prairie. Nothing but grass, a few low hills. He turned and looked ahead. He saw the outline of the Big Horn Mountains, a thin, gray band on the horizon. He returned to the column and handed the binoculars to Sweet. "What are your orders, sir?"

The question took Sweet by surprise. He slid the binoculars into his saddlebags, taking time to pad them with an old shirt he seldom wore. He closed the flap and turned to Taliaferro. "We've got to keep going. We have to get to the mountains. If we get to the mountains, we'll have a chance."

"I figure they're about fifty miles off. The Big Horns."

Fifty miles. It might as well have been a thousand miles. What are your orders, sir? Think, for God's sake, think. You're an officer, act like one. The idea came so quickly to him that he was surprised when he said it. "Pass the word to the men. Throw off anything they don't need. Ropes, picket lines, anything. Keep their greatcoats and blanket." He decided that was the right order to give. He felt better.

"It'll mark our trail for the Indians, sir."

It would. Breadcrumbs for Hansel and Gretel. "I think they already have it, Sergeant." That made sense to Sweet as soon as he said it. It sounded like something Mr. Porter would say.

"Yes, sir. Pardon me, sir." He walked along the line giving the order until he came to Mendelson. "Give it to me."

Jones stepped away from Mendelson. He knew what was coming and what Taliaferro would do if Mendelson disobeyed him.

"Give you what?"

"Listen, you son-of-a-bitch, if you make me ask again, I'll shoot you right here."

Mendelson began to speak but changed his mind. He pulled a metal flask from his saddlebag and handed it to Taliaferro. "I was keeping it in case of snake bite. That's all."

"Is that it? You'd better not be holding out on me."

"That's all."

The sergeant slid the flask into his coat. "The only snake out here is you." He moved down the line. "Listen to me," he ordered. "Throw out anything you don't need. Get rid of them cards and dime novels. Keep your greatcoats, blankets, and ponchos. Toss your lassos and pins. Everything you keep slows you down."

"Now's the time for you to get rid of that bitch," Collier said to Ashcroft.

Victoria turned her head as if she had understood.

"How far do you reckon we've come?" Ashcroft said as Collier unstrapped his blanket and pulled it off the cantle. He spread it around his shoulders so the air would dry it out. He unthreaded the lasso from the pommel ring on the near side of the saddle and threw it as far as he could. A curry brush followed. "Maybe six miles an hour at the trot," he calculated. "Eight hours at that…that's fifty miles or so. Time off for walking. Hell, I was never much good with numbers. If you figure in the time from Russell to Fetterman… So, what's that? Over a hundred miles?"

"More than that," Collier said.

"Seems like more. My ass feels like it's more."

Jones held out a small coffee grinder. "You want this, Collier?"

"Why would I want that?"

"I just thought you would, that's all." He pulled the haversack over his head and handed it to Ashcroft. "You might as well take this. There's a little food left. I won't need it."

The gesture surprised both men. "What the hell are you doing?" Ashcroft asked.

"You want it or not?"

"If I were you," Collier said. "I'd keep it."

Jones dropped the haversack and coffee grinder into the dirt and walked his horse off.

Victoria swung her rump at Ashcroft, knocking him off his feet. He tumbled to the ground and jumped back up, balling his fist and hitting the horse between the eyes. "Goddamn it, you vicious beast. Try that again and I will shoot you."

Collier watched as Jones moved up the line. "You ever seen anything like that?"

Ashcroft shook the pain out of his hand. "That boy just gave up. That's all. He gave up."

"I wonder if he knows something we don't know?"

"What?"

"I don't know," Collier said, picking up the coffee grinder. He examined it before tossing it aside. "Maybe it's something we don't want to know."

Chapter 12

Red Horse rode with a hundred warriors behind him, calling out his name and singing his song. He was no longer ignored because he was barely a man, nor did the others of the Shield Warriors Society call his father a coward. Now they only spoke of the great champion Red Horse and the bravest warrior Red Horse. The sky was filled with dark clouds, but he felt the sun on his shoulders. Red Horse! Red Horse!

The Crow pony tugged at the reins, and the hundred warriors disappeared. He jerked the Crow pony back alongside. There! Did not that pony prove he was lucky? It came to him and stayed at his side so the others could see that *Maheo* favored him. The others! They were old men who sat far from the fire and old women who haggled over every decision. They were always talking about what to do or who should go where.

I will do it, Red Horse thought. *I will go out and find Bull Bear; and finding him, I will return with him, and the others will see what a fine man I am. And the women will cast sly glances at me when they return to the village and choose me to dance with during ceremonies.*

A gust of wind spun his pony's mane and twisted the tail of the white man's shirt that he had taken from a gray-haired miner two summers before. He had cut off the sleeves and given an old woman some coins he had found in the miner's pocket, and she had sewn porcupine quills and blue ribbons across the breast. What a wonderful day. What a time filled with promise.

The Crow pony pulled again, this time so hard that his pony whinnied in protest, and he pulled to a stop. He held his coup stick high over his head as if he was about to strike, and he said to the Crow pony: "I will beat you if you do not behave. Don't you know who I am? I am Red Horse. White men are afraid of me, and warriors follow me wherever I go. I run fast, almost as fast as a pony, and I can drive a lance through a buffalo's body." The Crow pony watched him but did not shy away which, Red Horse thought, was because his previous master did not beat him enough. He kicked his pony into a trot, and the Crow pony, warned what would befall him if he did not behave, followed obediently.

"Bring me a bear, *Maheo!*" Red Horse shouted as he rode. "The biggest bear there is, and I will kill him and make a coat from his hide. Send me a herd of buffalo, and I will kill too many to count and give them all away so that others will feast and be happy. Have a dozen eagles fly down and give me their feathers because they fear and admire me. Do these things…” He stopped, catching sight of a swarm of buzzards, watching them circle. He counted them. Twelve birds. He was surprised at their presence, not because circling buzzards were uncommon, but because all the time he had been riding with the Kit Fox, he had not seen any animals. He thought once that he would say something to the Kit Fox to prove how observant he was but decided against it because he thought they might laugh at him.

He kept a white man’s pistol in a pouch slung over his shoulder, so he pulled the mouth of the pouch apart and took out the pistol. He had taken this from the miner as well, along with powder, ball, and caps. It was an old pistol, and there was rust on it so that Red Horse knew the miner did not care for his belongings, and somehow because of that, Red Horse’s kill meant less than it should have.

There were five chambers in the pistol’s cylinder, and he had four loaded with powder and ball. He got four caps from the pouch and fitted them to the nipples of the cylinder and cocked the pistol once. He knew it would not accidentally fire that way, and all he needed to do was cock it again and pull the trigger, and it would fire. He did this once after he had taken it, and there was so much smoke, he jumped because he thought the pistol had exploded. Sometimes old pistols did that. But it was just a big cloud of blue smoke. He was just a short way from a piece of charred wood he was using as a target, but he did not hit the wood or see where the bullet struck.

Now he held it muzzle up because an old man had told him to keep the barrel clear of the pony's head, so he did not accidentally shoot his own pony. He thought the old man's mind was mixed up, but he did as he suggested anyway. Later a Shield Warrior's brave said he had followed a white man across the prairie, until he thought the white man would get away; but he pulled his pistol instead and shot his own pony by mistake. When the pony fell, it killed the white man.

The buzzards continued to circle, but none of them flew to the ground to eat whatever had fallen and died. Both ponies shied away, nervous at what had drawn the buzzards. The Crow pony became difficult to manage, and Red Horse was about to strike it when it snapped the reins holding it to Red Horse's pony. Then something strange happened. The Crow pony did not run away from whatever was dead but ran in that direction.

Red Horse clicked his pony into a gallop and followed the Crow pony. He chased it down into a draw and then up over a stony ridge. The Crow pony stopped at the top of a low hill. Red Horse slowed his pony because he knew the dead thing was nearby. He could smell it, a heavy sweet scent, sickening.

He talked to his pony because he did not want it to become alarmed at the strange manner of the Crow pony or the stench. "It must be an old buffalo that has wandered off and died." He knew it was not likely killed by white men because white men killed many buffalo at one time and left their carcasses scattered in a wide area. "It could be an antelope or an elk. Maybe it was killed by a wolf." When he said that, he realized he had heard a wolf howl the day before but had not seen it. He pulled the pistol's hammer back so that it was ready to fire and urged his pony into a walk. He saw the Crow pony pacing back and forth, looking down the hill as if to say, "I have found the dead things. Come and see." Then the pony moved a short way off, still on the crest of the hill but keeping its distance.

Red Horse's pony stopped without being made to and shook the dust off its back. Red Horse let out a breath because of what he saw. Down in the draw, before it rose to meet the flat prairie, the earth was nearly black and torn up like a hundred buffalo had run over it. Scattered around were pieces of meat, parts of clothing, and some things that Red Horse did not recognize but made him afraid. He kicked his pony to go down, but the animal would not do so. Red Horse slid off his pony's back. He tightened the reins around his hand and led the pony down into the draw.

He saw part of a pony's head, the eyes and one ear, and he saw meat thrown as if a big animal had shaken it free when eating it. He looked down at his feet and saw that the dark earth was soaked in blood. He wanted to leave this place, but something would not let him. He saw a gray blanket with red stripes that had been torn up. There was a parfleche bag, which was ripped, and a rifle he had seen before, with the barrel bent and the stock broken. It was a Spencer that fired many times without reloading, and Bull Bear was proud of it. Next to it were the pieces of his rawhide saddle, and next to that, saddlebags.

Red Horse found what he knew was part of a body, but he did not know what part. There were some intestines across the ground like rope and other pieces. He saw a long bone with meat on it. Next to it, not far away, were ribs, white and curved that jutted out of a mound of flesh with a backbone sticking out of it.

There were no animals feeding on the remains. The buzzards were far overhead and would not come down. There were no coyotes standing over it to protect it from others, while they quickly ate what was left.

The stink of the place rose, and Red Horse gulped and then threw up. He threw up three times before wiping his mouth with the back of his arm. His pony pulled at the reins as if telling Red Horse, "We must leave this place! Quickly. We must leave this place now."

Red Horse jumped on his pony's back and kicked it as hard as he could. He rode it up to the hilltop and stopped, looking to make certain that whatever had killed Bull Bear was not following them. He was alone. The wind wanted him to remember this place. It brought the smell up so that it rolled over him, burning his nose and making his eyes water. He thought he would throw up again and rode farther along the hill.

He had been afraid before. On his first buffalo hunt, he clung to his pony's neck and did not fire a shot. Later a squaw ran into camp and said white soldiers were coming, but she was wrong. Now, his heart hurt, and his body ached with cold until it shook him nearly off the pony. He sent his pony into a gallop, and he rode low on its back, so the wind did not slow them down. He looked down to see both hands holding the reins and mane so tightly he could not tell one from another. He had lost his pistol. He did not have another, nor did he have a rifle. He had dropped the old weapon back where the ground was black with blood, and pieces of Bull Bear and his pony were scattered about, but he would not return for it. His eyes stung. He was crying.

He had lost his pistol and found Bull Bear. And he had lost the Crow pony as well. But then, a strange thought came to him. It was the Crow pony walking back and forth on the hill, looking down at where Bear Bull died. It did so as if it were showing Red Horse. As if the pony was proud of what he had found and wanted Red Horse to appreciate it.

Chapter 13

The Crow pony watched Red Horse ride away, and the buzzards flew overhead, waiting patiently until they could land and feast on what remained of Bull Bear and his pony. When Red Horse had disappeared over a rise, the Crow pony began to pace back and forth, shaking his head, tossing his mane about.

His body trembled, his head bouncing as if pulled by a stout rope. He became more agitated, snorting and blowing, kicking up dust. He stopped and sank to his knees, his body jerking, head swaying. A low moan came from him, not the sound a pony makes but something mournful. Finally, he screamed in pain as his head ceased bobbing. He stretched his neck tightly, eyes wide, locked on the buzzards. The skin around his head moved in waves, the bones swelling until the skin cracked around his snout. Blood poured from the pony's head as the skin split down its neck and onto his shoulder. When the skin had slipped off its head and fallen on a formless mass on the prairie, a long, white skull with yellow teeth appeared and began tearing at the skin. What had been a pony continued to scream in pain, the head of the thing with a wide, gaping mouth, its lips raw and torn, dripping blood mixed with saliva, emerged. The thing with the white skull tore itself from the pony's body and rose on long spindly legs covered in sparse, coarse hair. Then it stretched its narrow torso, drawing in a deep breath, letting it out in a growl that rolled over the prairie. The thing examined its hands in approval, flexing its long fingers with curved talons. Now twice as tall as the pony it had come from, it licked the blood from its white body, purring as a cat purrs when pleased. It prodded the pony's remains with a finger, its interest aroused, but not so much that the thing on long, white legs gave it any thought.

It stood, arms dangling, studying the terrain with dark red eyes sunken into its skull that was not of animal or man, but a corruption of the two. It took a tentative step and then another until it decided to set out across the prairie. It ran in a loping stride, arms extended, frail hands reaching out, as if it had seen prey.

It found Red Horse's trail and, grunting in satisfaction, followed it. After the warrior who had fled in fear.

Chapter 14

Walking Man led the band at a steady walk, breaking into a trot to catch up to One Eye, who was following the white soldier's trail. The others were strung out behind him, Stone Forehead, riding next to Wooden Leg, watching the sky.

"Where has the sun gone? Has something frightened it? All I see is clouds."

Wooden Leg did not bother to look up.

Stone Forehead felt the need to talk. "When we find the white soldiers, I will count five coups. Then I will kill the white chief and take his pony."

Wooden Leg nodded. He thought Stone Forehead would do exactly as he said because he was always first in a big fight.

"Do you think Walking Man was right about his vision?"

This was something new. Stone Forehead would sometimes ask Wooden Leg a question and after receiving an answer would be satisfied and ride away. But now he asked a few questions, not because he sought answers. Stone Forehead talked like a boy who was asked to watch the pony herd for the first time. He was afraid of something.

"A vision is a personal thing," Wooden Leg said. "It is meant for one man."

"This is true," Stone Forehead said. "But I think everyone is right. The old man was talking about white men."

Left Hand, who was riding behind them, shouted, "I think I see Red Horse!"

Comes-a-Pony had dismounted to tighten Wind's cinch. She threw herself onto the pony's back. "Is Bull Bear with him?"

Walking Man heard the commotion, turned his pony around, and rode back to Left Hand, pulling up sharply. "Do you see Bull Bear?"

"No. I think just Red Horse."

The others stopped and gathered around Walking Man. Stone Forehead said, "Why is he riding so fast? Is something chasing him?"

Walking Man kicked Moon into a trot and rode toward Red Horse. The others followed him. He thought something was chasing him, but the prairie here was very flat, and he could see no one, just Red

Horse. He saw the brave's pony stumble once, but Red Horse jerked its head up. They rode out to meet him near a tangle of brush when Red Horse pulled his pony to a stop so quickly that the pony dug its hooves into the ground and slid. Red Horse was slumped over the pony's neck, and when Walking Man got to him, he saw the young brave was shaking.

Before he had a chance to speak, Red Horse fell off his pony and sat heavily on the ground, pulling his head down in his arms, and began rocking back and forth. All the braves were talking excitedly, asking so many questions that the words became tumbled together.

"Wait!" Walking Man said. "Wait." He dropped off Moon and knelt beside Red Horse, putting his hand on the brave's shoulder. Red Horse jerked back in alarm and looked up at Walking Man. His eyes were red from weeping, and his face was twisted in fear. Walking Man knew something terrible had happened.

"What did you see?" he asked Red Horse, talking softly so he would not bring more fear to the brave. "Did you find Bull Bear?"

"Wait a moment," Comes-a-Pony commanded, jumping from her pony. She knelt next to Red Horse, put her arm around him and said, "Do not be afraid, brother. Here are your friends." She glanced up at Walking Man. "Give him time. Let him speak as he will." She turned back to Red Horse and said, "Tell us what you have seen, brother."

Red Horse nodded. First tears came, and then he spoke, but his words were interrupted by sobbing.

"I went back and saw buzzards in the sky."

"Buzzards?" One Eye said.

"They would not come down, and I thought it was because they saw me." He stopped speaking. The others, standing near their ponies, said nothing. "I could not tell it was Bull Bear, until I found his rifle; and then I knew it was him. Something had torn him to pieces. Even his pony was destroyed."

Left Hand asked, "Are you certain?"

Red Horse nodded. "It was him. He was cut up except for a little bit of him."

Many Horses asked, "Maybe it was wolves. Did you see any wolves?"

Red Horse shook his head. "All I saw were the buzzards, and they would not come down." He used the tail of his shirt to wipe his eyes and nose, but he would not look up. "I have never seen anything like it before."

Wooden Leg spoke, which surprised the others because he was always last to speak and used only a few words. "Where is your other pony?" It was a strange question to ask because Red Horse said that Bull Bear was dead and had been eaten up, and nobody really cared about a missing Crow pony. But the question was asked because, in times such as this, some people would speak in a way that meant they could not comprehend what had happened and looked for something to say.

"He ran off," Red Horse said. "I think he smelled blood and was frightened." He pulled up the pouch that had held his pistol and said, "I lost my pistol."

"We will find you another," Comes-a-Pony said. "When we kill the white soldiers, you can have your pick of pistols." She looked at Walking Man to speak.

"Yes," he said. "We'll rub them out, and you will have a pistol. Maybe two. That one you had was old. Now, you can get a new one."

Stone Forehead asked Red Horse, "Did you seen any sign of white soldiers?"

Red Horse spoke slowly, "I do not remember. All I remember is Bull Bear and his pony."

Many Horses said, "It was white soldiers. They did the same thing to Black Kettle and his band. They shot everyone down; and when they were dead, the white soldiers cut them up. They made tobacco bags from the breasts of women and cut off the privates of the men. They are animals. I hate them. They should all be rubbed out."

"How can one man do that to another?" Stone Forehead said. "If you cut off a man's hands or take out his eyes after he is dead, he cannot fight you in the afterlife; but the white men do not believe this. They will destroy a man or woman for sport. I do not understand this."

Standing a little back from the others was Little Raven. When he spoke, everyone turned. It was his manner of speaking that drew them. His words had no force, no will. They were simply words, spoken. "That is a bad thing to see," Little Raven said, calmly. "I am sorry that you saw such a thing." Then he pulled out his Remington pistol that he traded four ponies for. He put the pistol to his head and cocked the hammer and said, again, "I am sorry you saw such a thing." Then he blew his brains out.

The others cried out and rushed to Little Raven, but the side of his head was gone, and his body collapsed. Some of his brains was on the ground, and the earth soaked up the blood flowing out of his head as if it were thirsty for nourishment.

"No!" Walking Man shouted. He meant that he did not want Little Raven to kill himself. No one spoke as he walked to the body, which had dropped so that the arms and legs lay unnaturally. He took the pistol out of Little Raven's hand and stretched out his arms and legs, turning them so that it looked as if he had laid down for a little sleep and would arise soon. "What have you done, friend? What caused you to do this?"

Stone Forehead was next to Walking Man. "I have never seen anything like this."

Walking Man went to Moon, who kept a respectful distance along with the other ponies because they smelled blood. He took his blanket off Moon and draped it over Little Raven's body, leaving his head exposed so he could see to find his way to the Milky Way. Then he laid his arms over his chest and put the Remington pistol in his hand. He spoke to Old Turtle, "Will you help me paint him?" Walking Man wanted Little Raven's soul to find his body but that would only be so if he was painted.

Without speaking, Old Turtle went to his pony and retrieved his paint and paint pot. Stone Forehead and Fool Dog took Little Raven's belongings off his pony and laid them around him.

They painted Little Raven, and Walking Man said, "*Maheo* has given Little Raven *omotome*, which he gives all of us at birth." He was speaking of a man's spirit. White men called it a soul. Maybe it is the same thing. "For some time, Little Raven's mind had been troubling him. I have seen old people act strangely; and it is said *mahata'sooma* has left their bodies, and *omotome* will leave after that. I would like to say that in four days his spirit has gone to *Seana*." He meant the camp of the dead, which is located on the long fork of the Milky Way; but he knew that would probably not be so, and the knowledge saddened him. A man that killed himself was denied entry into *Seana*. That was understood by everyone. So, he said, "I ask *Maheo* to guide Little Raven's spirit to *Seana*. He should not go up the short fork of the Milky Way. If he does, he will return as an evil spirit; and that should not happen to Little Raven. He is my friend."

After they finished preparing Little Raven, they mounted their ponies and left that place. Red Horse's pony was worn out, so he rode with Old Turtle while Many Horses took the reins of Red Horse's pony, and it walked behind him.

Walking Man drew close to Comes-a-Pony and said, "You did a fine thing with Red Horse."

"He was frightened," she replied.

"I have not taken the time to speak to you," he said. "I should have done so."

"Maybe you had nothing to say." She thought he was not talking about what had just happened but about another time. "Anyway, that is in the past so it cannot be changed."

"This…" Walking Man began, but he could not find the words to describe it. "I was not prepared for any of it. Not Bull Bear or Little Raven, nor Red Horse."

"Do you think," Comes-a-Pony said, "that you can control the wind? If you stand before it and command it to go here or there, it will listen? I have found that is foolish thinking. Most things happen as they were meant to occur." She found herself speaking softly, with care, and was surprised. She had always thought she could never be kind to Walking Man; but for that moment, her heart was not made of stone. "You do not understand what has happened. Neither do I. I do not think that not understanding is a bad thing. It just means that the truth of a thing has not been revealed." Then she remembered the hurt he had caused her, and she wanted him to ride away. "You should go talk to the others."

"I will."

"Now," she said. "You are leading them. They have listened to you. Go and speak to them."

This time she saw Walking Man was hurt, and she felt satisfaction at seeing what she had done. But when he rode off, she felt ashamed and wished she had not sent him off.

"What do you think?" Left Hand asked her. She did not reply because she thought he was speaking of Walking Man. He said, "What has happened is terrible. Little Raven was a good man."

"You think every warrior is a good man. You said Walking Man was a good man. Not every man is good." She wished he would go away. Sometimes they would sit for a long time and talk about many things; but now, she wished he would go away.

"Not every man is bad," Left Hand said. "Maybe some will tell you I am a bad man."

"You are my brother." She stroked Wind's neck. "I wish I could be like you."

Left Hand laughed. "Little Sister, I still remember the puppy."

His words angered her. "You are mocking me," and spurred her pony forward so she would not have to speak to her brother anymore.

Walking Man made his way among the warriors. They rode, silently, thinking about what had happened. It was too much to consider all at once, he understood. They would need to settle into it before they were willing to speak about anything.

After they had ridden for some distance, Walking Man said, "It will be dark soon so we must find a place to camp. When we do, I will go out and search for the old man so I can ask him about what Red Horse saw and why Little Raven put the pistol to his head."

Again, no one spoke. They were thinking of what Red Horse told them and what could have happened to Bull Bear and his pony. They were thinking about Little Raven who seemed to have lost his way for a while, so he put the Remington pistol to his head.

They were afraid.

Chapter 15

When they stopped, they let their ponies search for grass to eat because they had traveled a fair distance. They found wheatgrass and some sandreed. They had gone past the edge of the shrublands so there would be more for the animals to eat. The warriors expected to chase the white soldiers to the Big Horn Mountains, and the land would get better. That is, until Red Horse returned.

Walking Man found a dry creek bed where the foliage was thicker than on the prairie. He thought the braves might be able to dig to find water because they did not have much left. Before Red Horse came back, the warriors talked about water and agreed that they could do with less water than the white soldiers because it is common for all white men to be careless with things.

They made camp and soon, the night came. They had built a fire, bigger than the ones they had built before, but Walking Man did not caution against it. The braves gathered around the flames and ate food without talking. Walking Man was standing guard with his Henry rifle on the edge of the ravine, and sometimes a brave would look up at him but say nothing. They knew that he would go out looking for the old man and maybe learn what was happening to them. Finally, after the darkness had covered the land, Walking Man glanced at Old Turtle, who nodded that he understood that he would search for the old man and walked away.

His hand went to his knife in its leather sheaf at his side, and he was relieved that he had the weapon in case his Henry rifle stopped working. He spoke in a whisper, calling on the old man to make himself known, so that he, Walking Man, could come and learn things.

"Today we found out that our friend, Bull Bear, had been rubbed out and cut up. Then Little Raven killed himself, which is a terrible thing to see. I know it is bad luck to hold council at night, but you came to me at night before, so I thought maybe you would come again." He looked down and saw a sagebrush, so he stepped around it.

When he looked up again, he was in a tipi.

The wind was blowing outside, making the buffalo hide cover shake, and a little snow sneaked in under the edge of the tipi. He saw a boy sitting close to a fire, watching the smoke curl up and disappear out the opening in the tipi where the lodge poles came together. The boy was plump, with a round face and thick arms. He looked up at Walking Man and motioned that he was to sit near the fire. Walking Man did so, putting his rifle next to him, which said he was not fearful. Had he been, he would have kept it in his hands. He was confused. This was another vision, a different vision.

"You were expecting to see an old man?" the boy, who was maybe ten or twelve summers old, said. He wore a fine doe-skin shirt with long sleeves and red trousers made from a blanket. His moccasins were decorated with beads. Some woman had worked a long time to make them.

"I was," Walking Man said. "Will he come?"

The boy picked up a hoop and stick. Children often played with such things. He spun the hoop on the stick as he talked. "I am he," the boy said. "And his father before him, and his father before that."

Walking Man waited, letting the boy talk.

"I was sorry to hear about Little Raven," the boy said. "Such things are horrible to see."

"Yes," Walking Man said. "And Bull Bear was rubbed out. Red Horse found him."

The boy nodded. "Chewed up." He brushed his long hair back over his ear. "Do you think," the boy asked, "that some beings are evil?"

"Yes," Walking Man said. "White men are evil. They do bad things to The People and others. I know there are evil spirits, but I have never encountered any."

"White men? No. No, I was speaking about something worse even than white men. Although, there is not much worse than white men." The boy set down the hoop and stick and put his hands close to the fire to warm them and said, "Are you warm enough? Is the fire to your liking?"

Walking Man did not understand. "What is worse than white men? They hunt us and give us blankets full of sickness. How can you say there is something worse than them?"

"Some men listen," the boy said, "but hear only what they think is said. That is a human thing. Especially, when they have never seen something different."

Walking Man grew irritated. "You are talking in circles. Before you told me about the White Devil. I know the White Devil. I have fought them and killed them, and still they come on. Crook and his army are coming. They have come to wipe us out, like The People who fled the forest."

"Did I say that to you? Is that how I spoke?"

"I have come for help," Walking Man said. "My brothers and I are in danger from something that I do not understand."

"You have an old wound, shaped like lightning," the boy touched his right arm above the wrist. "Just there."

Walking Man put his hand over his arm, remembering when a boy named White Tail shot him with an arrow by mistake. White Tail was showing off and not paying attention. He was killed later by whites, who took his pony.

"I have come to find out how to fight this thing that killed Bull Bear," Walking Man said. "When I spoke to you before, I thought you were warning me about white men. Now, it is something different, but I cannot think what it is."

"I told you," the boy said. "Before. When I came to you as an old man."

"I do not…"

"I told you a story. This thing is very powerful and cannot be easily killed. It is an ancient enemy of The People. There are not enough of you to fight it."

Walking Man thought of Black Antelope. If he could find the others, maybe they could help fight off the thing. But where was he? He said he was going north to cut off the white soldiers. Where was he?

"No," the boy said, reading Walking Man's mind. "Not Black Antelope." Before Walking Man could say anything else, the boy said, "The thing that killed Bull Bear and caused Little Raven to shoot himself is the White Devil. Sometimes people called it a demon. Sometimes others call it by another name. It changes shape. First, it is one animal and then another. It is weak until it feeds, but once it feeds, it grows larger. It is very fast, as fast as a good pony. You decided that I was speaking to you of white men. But you were wrong. "

The cold wind wrapped its fingers around Walking Man's chest, and for a moment, he could not draw a breath. "It is a thing? This White Devil? A spirit? Can it be killed? Can you tell me what I must do to kill it?"

The boy stared at the fire as if the answer were hidden in the flames. "You cannot kill it alone."

Walking Man tried to find his words without anger. "I have come looking for you because I need your help. You came to me as an old man, but I did not understand you. I was wrong; and because of that, Bull Bear has been killed, and Little Raven shot himself. You say the thing can be killed, but I cannot kill it. My brothers will die. I ask you and all who came before you to guide me."

"But we have," the boy said, as if speaking to a child. "We have given you weapons and a plan. You must look beyond what you think you heard. You are Walking Man. You go out and consider how things ought to be. Reason walks with you. That is a powerful weapon."

"When you were an old man, you said this thing was ancient. Why has it come back now?"

"Oh, it is hungry," the boy suggested. "Or The People have taken the wrong path and offended *Maheo*. Who is to know?"

Suddenly, Walking Man heard shooting floating out of the darkness.

He was alone. There was shouting behind him and more gunfire coming from the camp. Walking Man heard a scream, and he started running, his heart pumping to give him speed. The wind fought him, trying to keep him away. He cocked the Henry rifle. It must be the soldiers. They have turned around and come back.

No.

It had found them. The thing the boy spoke of had found them. There was no time for reason or planning. No time to consider what the old man and the boy had spoken.

He got to the top of the gulley and saw it in the firelight. The White Devil, tall and gaunt, stalking back and forth, holding the body of Old Turtle in one hand, as Stone Forehead threw a lance. The light from the fire danced over the creature, carving black shadows out of the white skull, bathing the hollow chest in a glow. The creature batted the lance away as if it were nothing. The others were firing their pistols and rifles; but the creature ignored them, growling as it taunted them by shaking the body of Old Turtle at them, blood dripping down his arms and legs.

Comes-a-Pony was on the other rim of the ravine. She fired her Sharps, dropped the breechblock, loaded, and fired again. She kept extra cartridges trapped between her fingers, loading, and firing without slowing.

Wooden Leg, seeing Walking Man, shouted, "Shoot it! Shoot it!"

Walking Man took aim and shot the White Devil in the head. It turned quickly, and he saw it's terrible bloody mouth and its red eyes. Then the creature held out the body of Old Turtle for Walking Man to see, and then raising it above its head, it ripped the head off Walking Man's friend and threw it at him.

Walking Man dropped to the ground as the head sailed past him. He saw a body burning in the fire. It was Many Horses, his clothes ablaze, his body motionless. The White Devil skirted the fire, howling as if in pain.

The fire. The fire.

The old man told him. He said the brave who had spoken of the thing and the other two men stayed with the fire at their back.

The boy had said, "Is the fire to your liking?"

Chapter 16

Sweet was on his feet as Taliaferro shouted, "What the hell is that?"

The other soldiers grabbed their carbines, staring into the night. They heard gunfire coming from behind them. Coming from the direction of the war party that had been chasing them.

Sweet said, "Sergeant?"

Taliaferro handed Sweet the officer's carbine. "I hope that's some of our boys, but I don't see them attacking at night. They'd be afraid they'd shoot one another."

"Yes," the lieutenant said. "Smallwood? You and Collier mount up, come with me." Jones handed Sweet the reins to his horse and held the officer's carbine as he swung into the saddle. "Sergeant Taliaferro? You stay here. If it's safe, I'll fire three rounds. If you don't hear the signal in two hours, then move out."

"Lieutenant, maybe you ought to wait until daylight before you go back there?"

"Two hours," Sweet said, forgetting his fear. "See if you can locate Mr. Porter, but by all means, keep going toward the big peak. When you strike the foothills, they'll lead you northwest. You should find Gibbons' command."

A voice came out of the darkness. "Don't worry about Porter."

It was the scout, leading his horse into camp.

"Mr. Porter, I thought you were dead," Sweet said.

Porter listened as the distant gunfire increased. "That's a big fight for certain."

"I wonder if some of Gibbons' men ran into them?" Sweet asked. "Don't you think we ought to go back there?"

Porter didn't answer. He stared into the darkness; his eyes narrowed in thought. His horse tried to pull away, and he grabbed the bridle. "Settle down, Randy."

The lieutenant noticed the dark stain across the scout's jacket. "Mr. Porter? Are you hurt? Is that blood?"

Porter slid his carbine from the boot strapped to his saddle.

"What is it?" Mendelson asked Taliaferro when Porter snapped, "Shut up!"

"Mr. Porter?" Sweet began when Porter held up his hand to silence him.

"Don't you hear it?" Porter asked Sweet.

"Hear what?"

Porter slid a cartridge into the breach of his carbine. "I don't know," he said in a voice so low Sweet almost didn't hear him. "I thought I heard something. How long's that been going on?'" The gunfire continued, scattered, dull.

The question confused Sweet. "How long? Ten or fifteen minutes, I suppose. Maybe…"

"You ought to throw out a skirmish line," Porter suggested to Sweet.

"Yes. Of course. Sergeant Taliaferro," Lieutenant Sweet ordered. "Advance carbines."

Taliaferro didn't have to give the order. The men swung their carbines forward on the slings, pulling back the hammer. They slipped a cartridge out of their cartridge belt and loaded their weapons. "Ashcroft," the sergeant said. "You and Jones take the horses to the rear."

"Skirmish line, Sergeant," Sweet said.

"Skirmishers, forward," Taliaferro said. The remaining men took position, kneeling at five-yard intervals, waiting. There was enough moonlight filtering through the clouds for the men to see each other but little else. Sweet, Taliaferro, and Porter stood next to their mounts, frozen in place.

Porter listened intently. "What is that?" he said, perplexed.

Sweet glanced at the scout. "I don't hear anything but gunfire."

"It's dying down now," Taliaferro said.

"Yeah," Porter said. "Yeah, it is."

"Lieutenant," Taliaferro said. "My ears ain't as good as Porter's, but I'll tell you what I don't hear. I don't hear no Springfields. Whoever is fighting back, there ain't soldiers."

Porter swung into the saddle. Taking the reins, he said, "I'm going to ride back there a bit."

"I thought we could capture them. You know, sneak up on them," Sweet protested. "We can hold them for hostage in case the other band showed up."

"I wouldn't worry about that," Porter said.

"You can't go back there alone. Mr. Porter, I can take some men and capture them." He felt like a boy trying to convince his father that he had grown up. He had almost forgotten that he was just a mapmaker and not a soldier.

"Lieutenant," Porter said, looking down at Sweet. "Do you know what Spartan women told their men going off to war?"

"Spartan women? Mr. Porter, I don't…"

"They said, come back with your shield, or on it. May not be the same, but I'll be back with those Cheyenne, or I ain't coming back."

"Mr. Porter, you're just one man. How do you expect to capture them? Let me send some men with you."

"No thanks. You fellas just wait here." Porter swatted Randy on the rump with the barrel of his carbine. The horse bolted forward and settled into a gallop.

"A nigger and a boy," Mendelson, kneeling in the line, said to Jones. "None of us are going to see our station again."

"His coat was covered in blood," Wagner said. "Did you see it?"

"I saw it," Jones said.

"Something bad has happened," Wagner said.

Chapter 17

"Get to the fire!" Walking Man shouted. "Put the fire to your back!" He saw Fool Dog grab Red Horse by the shirt front and drag him to the fire. The Shield Warrior's brave was screaming in horror as the White Devil sliced open a horse's belly with its claws, throwing gore over them. Stone Forehead stood next to them, firing his pistol at the creature. It paced back and forth, growling at the braves. It could have killed them all. It could have swept them off the ground and gutted them like a woman guts a buffalo. It was a game for the beast.

Walking Man cocked his rifle and fired again. The bullet hit the creature's shoulder, and a cloud of dust arose. But the beast was not harmed. It should have fallen. It should have been killed. He heard the men shouting; one of them was screaming. Blue smoke from gunfire danced in the light of the flames.

Fool Dog fired his Remington pistol, cocked it, and fired it again.

Wooden Leg ran forward, swinging a sword he had taken from a dead soldier. He ducked as the creature swung at him and sliced its leg with the sword. The brave dropped to the ground and rolled, jumping up to stab the White Devil in the back; but the beast was too quick for him and swung around, driving its fist like a hammer into Wooden Leg's skull, crushing the warrior's head. The brave's body staggered a few steps and fell.

Walking Man joined the others, kicking bits of wood into the fire. Sparks rose into the air, and in the light of the flames, he saw the beast lower itself, getting ready to spring. But it did not. It watched them. Many Horses lay near the edge of the fire, head cocked strangely to one side, twisted at the neck. He drove the butt of his Henry into the fire, using it to stir up the flames, which blazed to life. The creature roared in defiance but kept clear of the fire. Left Hand and Eagle Head were beside him, Eagle Head's left arm hanging limply at his side. Left Hand drew back his bow string and loosed an arrow at the creature. It struck him below the eye, high on its cheekbone. He swept his arm up, knocking the shaft free.

The demon paced back and forth, until it picked up Old Turtle's body.

Stone Forehead retrieved the lance he had thrown and ran at the creature.

Walking Man shouted, "No!" but it was too late. The White Devil dodged the lance and thrust its claws into Stone Forehead's chest, ripping the brave in half. The two halves of the body fell to the ground at the creature's feet.

Then it was gone.

The fire burned behind Walking Man. A horse screamed in the darkness; and Red Horse, on his knees with his hands covering his face, wept. There was no other sound to share this scene of madness. The braves began to move.

Eagle Head held his left arm so that Left Hand could tie it to his chest.

Comes-a-Pony went to Many Horses and then to Stone Forehead. She joined Left Hand, who was tending to Eagle Head. "They are both dead," she said, and then took the leather strap from Left Hand that he was trying to use to tie up Eagle Head's broken arm. "Let me do that." She had her Sharps slung over her shoulder.

Walking Man, trembling as often happened to him after a big fight, asked, "Where is One Eye?"

Left Hand nodded to his right. "He was there before."

Fool Dog said, "I do not think he is killed, but I have not seen him."

Walking Man handed Fool Dog his Henry and pulled Many Horses' body away from the fire. He found two blankets on the ground and carefully fed them into the flames. "We must keep a good fire. That is all we can do."

One Eye joined them. "I have never seen such a thing before. I will tell you now, I was afraid of it and could barely move. I hope it will not come back. But I think it will."

Fool Dog spoke to Walking Man, "Something has unleashed a great evil on the world. I think this is your vision."

"Everyone is dead," Red Horse cried. "Everyone is dead."

"Calm yourself, brother," One Eye said. "We are still alive."

The vision. "I was wrong," Walking Man said. "When I spoke to the old man in my vision. I did not see things clearly, and because of that, my friends died. I was a fool. I thought it must be white men. I should have known. I should have seen what it was."

Comes-a-Pony helped Eagle Head to the ground. "That thing killed them. You did not. I shot it four times but did not kill it." She unslung the rifle and peered into the darkness. "Did you find the old man? What did he say?"

"There was a boy tonight."

"Boy?" Left Hand said. "What boy?"

Chapter 18

"Before that thing attacked," Walking Man answered Left Hand as he walked over to Stone Forehead's body. He dragged the torso into position near its waist. He did this without thinking. The warrior's body would be reunited. It seemed the right thing to do. "I cannot do more," he said to the body. "I am sorry that this thing has happened to you."

"You sought out the old man and come back to us with stories of a boy!" Left Hand said angrily. "And then this thing attacked us."

"No man could have seen such a thing coming," One Eye said, trying to calm his friend. "You could have told me everything, and I would have not believed you. This," he gestured to the destruction surrounding them. "This is beyond any man's sight."

"We could have stayed with the others," Left Hand said to Walking Man. "We would have been safe from this thing."

"Brother," Comes-a-Pony said, still guarding the night. "It is time to speak of other things."

Before Walking Man could reply, One Eye said to Left Hand, "You cannot blame anyone for this."

"No?" Left Hand shot back. To Walking Man he said, "Red Horse is right. We are dead men. Look about you. There is Stone Forehead torn in half. There! Many Horses is dead. All this because of you."

Eagle Head touched Left Hand's chest with his good hand. "Come now, brother. No more should be said tonight."

"How is your arm?" Walking Man asked Eagle Head. The warrior nodded, but he was in great pain.

"We have a short time until the sun comes up," Walking Man said. "Let us keep the fire burning as much as we can and then decide what to do."

"I think our ponies have all run off," One Eye said. "Those who have not been killed."

"I will go see," Comes-a-Pony said, cocking her rifle.

"Sister!" Left Hand said. "Do not leave the fire. You cannot see anything out there."

"No, but I can smell," she said to her brother. "It stank like a thousand deaths." She smiled at her brother. "If it comes for me, I will shoot it four more times." She stopped and laid a hand on Red Horse's shoulder to comfort the warrior before stepping into the darkness.

"Let us gather what we can," Walking Man said.

One Eye said to Walking Man, "Tell me what the boy in your vision said."

"Does it matter?" Left Hand said.

"It does to me," One Eye said. "I do not understand all that I have seen tonight."

Fool Dog, who had listened to what had been said, asked, "I wonder if it will come back?"

Only One Eye answered. "I do not think so. I cannot tell you why I feel this way, but I do not think so."

"Why not? It can come back and kill us all," Left Hand said. "I am going to die with old women. You," he pointed at Fool Dog. "Your name says it all. All you do is listen to that one," he nodded toward Walking Man.

"Friend," One Eye said to Walking Man. "Tell me about the vision."

Comes-a-Pony walked into the darkness, cautiously, listening. The sound of the men talking disappeared as she walked toward where the ponies had been grazing. They might have run off when the thing attacked. If they did, they would come back at daylight, searching for their masters. She wondered if she would find Wind. She heard a noise and dropped to her knee. It was a gasping sound. Something was struggling to breathe.

The moon fought its way through the heavy clouds, casting a blue light over the prairie, guiding her steps. There was only stillness and faint sounds, the ground bathed in a weak glow. *It could be waiting for you. It could be anywhere in the night.* She wished she had traded her rifle for a carbine before coming out to search for the ponies. The rifle was five feet long and weighed ten pounds. A carbine was much shorter and weighed less. If the thing attacked her out of the darkness, she might not have time to aim the rifle.

The clouds toyed with her, hiding the moon, then bringing it out again.

She listened carefully. Maybe her bullets had wounded the thing. It could be lying in the darkness, dying. She stood, then advanced, stepping carefully. She drew close to the sound. Her toe hit something, and she stopped. She reached down with one hand, finger on the trigger of her Sharps.

She felt the outline of a long neck, and heard the painful, wet sucking of a creature trying to breathe. The moon reappeared. Then her hand traced the outline of a pony's ear. She felt its softness, saw it twitch under her touch.

The pony's eyes were wide with fear. It was dying.

It was Red Horse's pony. Its eyes searched her face and stopped; its chest heaved one last time, and the pony was still.

She saw other shapes scattered across the ground. "Wind?" she said softly. She heard a whinny off to her right. She stepped back from the pony and walked to the sound. A cloud covered the moon, taunting her.

"Wind?" she whispered. There was another whinny. Her ankle brushed a form. She stopped and knelt. "Wind?" The pony moaned softly. Moonlight bathed Wind's head. She stroked her pony's muzzle. "Wind? What has happened to you?" She ran her fingers down the neck and across the shoulder until she came to the stomach. She saw intestines, piled on the ground. She jerked her hand back. The pony raised its head, seeking her touch.

"Oh, Wind!" Tears welled in Comes-a-Pony's eyes as she spoke. She leaned her rifle against the pony's shoulder and drew a knife from its scabbard. "I will find you later," she told the animal. "We will ride together and hunt buffalo, and elk, and antelope. You will have sweet grass to eat, and you can roll in the dust under the warm sun."

She found the thick vein running down the pony's neck. This time the moon held back the clouds. She touched the pony's cheek, caressed its ear, and hummed a song her mother had taught her. Wind's eyes closed, and her breathing slowed. Comes-a-Pony drove the blade into the pony, severing the vein. Warm blood bathed her hand. She felt the animal shudder and then become still. She wiped her hand on the grass.

She could not abandon Wind until she forced herself to rise and move on. She found five dead ponies, legs stiff in death, bellies torn open, stinking of death and blood. She said a prayer at the body of each and then moved on.

The moon, tired of fighting for its place in the sky, finally went to sleep, sending the prairie into darkness.

Walking Man sat down with his back to the fire. The others joined him. He told them what the boy in his vision had told him. As he spoke, he peered into the darkness, straining to catch sight of the White Devil; but he saw nothing. The wind that had come with the creature had departed as well. Now, there was no noise, except the fire crackling behind them, and Red Horse's faint sobs.

He remembered as much as he could of what the old man had spoken and what the boy had told him.

"We have given you weapons and a plan," the boy had said. "Fire that will keep it away." This Walking Man understood. "You cannot kill it alone," the vision had said. The words would not leave his mind. It cannot be killed with guns, lances, or arrows. He saw that much from the fight.

He spoke to himself in a whisper. "What have I done? I was wrong about everything, and now this devil has killed my friends." His heart was heavy with sorrow and guilt. There was no certainty in anything. He was a boy, lost. "What have I done?"

Left Hand heard a noise in the darkness, and the men turned.

"Brother?" Comes-a-Pony called from the darkness. "I am coming in. Do not shoot." The light played on her as she walked to the fire and sat down. She looked up at the men and said, "I did not find any ponies alive. Maybe some got away and will come to us later. The rest are dead."

Left Hand offered her a water pouch, and she took a drink. He told her what Walking Man had said about his visions, but she did not care. She found her buffalo robe, wrapped herself in it, and lay down, crying for Wind.

The night passed and the sun parted the horizon, trying to push its way through the clouds. It could do no more than hint at its existence. Walking Man and the others watched as the unnatural gloom denied the sun's companionship. If it would only come, bringing light and warmth, then there would be hope. A terrible thing had happened. Something that could not be explained. He stared into the fire. The others joined him, except Comes-a-Pony.

The men gathered their weapons and sat with the flames at their backs. They had two bows and five arrows. This did not comfort them because they had seen the beast brush away the arrow that had struck him near the eye. They all carried knives, but these were useless because the thing's arm could reach so far. They had several Colt pistols, and Fool Dog's Remington but not very many cartridges. One Eye found Many Horses' Spencer rifle and near it a bag of cartridges. Comes-a-Pony had her Sharps rifle and some cartridges.

Would they be enough to kill the thing? Would they be enough to save them?

Chapter 19

The fire was dying. There was no comfort because the wind was strong and cold, and the clouds that should have been blown away by the wind were too heavy to move. *Everything is turned around,* Walking Man thought. *The cold will not leave, and the sun refuses to show itself. Still, the night has gone, and that is a victory, perhaps. The wind has lost its way. Some terrible thing has attacked my friends and they have been killed. I do not know what to do.*

None of them had slept. Walking Man heard some of them shift about during the night. He knew they were tired because he was tired. But no one slept. Too much had happened.

Once, when he was younger, he had gone on a war party led by Wooden Leg. They thought they would go steal some Crow horses. It was during the Deer Rutting Moon. Before they found sign of any Crow, they found sign of six white men. Wooden Leg said it was four white soldiers and two white men who were probably going from one white man's fort to another. They sometimes did that, Wooden Leg had said. The warriors caught up with the white men but could never get close. The two white men who rode with the soldiers were buffalo hunters with long guns. Walking Man remembered how excited he was, how he wanted to fight the white soldiers and buffalo hunters, and how after three days of chasing the white men, Wooden Leg said it would be better to go and steal Crow horses. The other thing that Walking Man remembered was how he came to be so tired he could barely sit on his pony, like all the life had gone out of him.

He felt the same way after the fight with the demon. He could barely move, and his arms were so heavy he could not hold his Henry rifle.

Fool Dog sat close to him. Walking Man said to him, "What do you think we should do?"

Fool Dog was silent before answering, which said to Walking Man that his friend wanted to give some thought to the matter.

"You mean about going on after the white soldiers?" Fool Dog said.

Walking Man thought how finding the white soldiers meant nothing to him, now.

Fool Dog continued. "I think we should forget about them and go home. Maybe if we went home a different way, that terrible thing will not find us. I do not want to fight it again."

Walking Man knew what Fool Dog really meant. He meant if they fought the thing again, then it would probably kill them all. "Something has troubled me." He heard Red Horse cry out, and then he became silent. The others ignored him. Walking Man thought that the Shield Warrior's brave would not regain his mind because of what had happened.

Fool Dog waited for his friend to speak.

"Suppose," Walking Man said. "Suppose this thing is a good tracker." He was afraid to say what troubled him and had troubled him all night. He thought if he said it aloud, it would become alive, somehow. His mind did not want to work, but he knew he would have to make it work. His thoughts had to be strong, like heavy rocks laid across a river, so he could step from one to the other. "What I am saying," he spoke to his friend, "is that this thing would travel back along our path and find our village."

Fool Dog sucked in a breath at Walking Man's words. "Do not say such things. *Maheo* would never let that happen. Do not say those words."

"I have tried to think of how I have offended the spirits," Walking Man said. He wiped away a tear quickly, so his friend did not see it. Too much had happened. Too many had died.

"Maybe, brother," Fool Dog said. "Maybe you should go talk to that boy again?" "No!" Walking Man shouted, jumping to his feet. "What have the spirits brought us?"

Fool Dog rose, putting his hand on Walking Man's shoulder as the others stirred.

"We are surrounded by our dead. We cannot make them ready for journey to the Milky Way. They are torn apart. Our ponies are gone," Walking Man said. He pointed to where the white soldiers were. "Our enemies live, and a terrible thing has come to kill our families. What can we do? How can we stop it?" He looked at the others. "Do you know? Tell me. Do any of you know what to do?" He jerked Fool Dog's hand away from his shoulder. "You want me to go talk to a child and an old man. What good will that do us? Tell me! Will they give us guns to replace those we have lost? Will they send ponies to us? Will cartridges fall from the sky like rain?"

Left Hand said, "Walking Man speaks as a man who has lost his way." It was a hurtful denunciation, and the words surprised the others. "Go and talk to the old man and the boy," he said, bitterly. "I will stay here and tend to the dead. At least they will be cared for."

Comes-a-Pony sat up, her eyes were red from crying and no sleep. "I will stay with my brother."

More of the sun came through the clouds. It was not much, but it spread over the ground, over the fire that was beginning to die out, and over the bloody bundles which had once been men.

One Eye spoke, his words soft, but clear. His soul was worn down by the fight, and the death of his friends, and by the knowledge that they would all die soon. Not like warriors in a fair fight, but like buffalo slaughtered by whites. "Listen to me, friends. I am tired in my heart. My brothers are rubbed out around me, and the sky is always gray; the wind never stops taunting us, and even the fire does not warm me. Walking Man has done his best, and we have followed him because of that. I do not know how to fight this terrible creature. It is not from this world and maybe not the next. I think we must do this. I think we should go as far as we can from our village. Maybe the thing will follow us. Maybe we will give it a good fight and convince it not to seek our village."

"Maybe!" Left Hand said. "Maybe this and maybe that. Every word anybody has to say is maybe."

Walking Man exploded in anger. "Fight me! All I hear is words from you. Are you afraid? Are you afraid to fight me?"

One Eye stepped between them. "We cannot do this, friends. There are just a few of us left. Look how the creature has made us turn on each other! It makes fear; and because of that, we doubt ourselves. Now, friend," he said to Walking Man. "Calm yourself. And you, brother," he said to Left Hand. "Everyone knows you fear nothing. We need your courage." He smiled at Walking Man, "And we need your reason."

Walking Man nodded.

Suddenly, a voice called to them in Cheyenne from the other side of a hill. "I have come to speak with you."

The warriors grabbed the weapons left to them, searching for the source of the voice.

One Eye pointed with a lance to the direction he thought the words had come from. They could see no one.

"It is a white man," Walking Man said. He shouted, "Who are you? Show yourself! Or are you a coward?"

"There are no cowards here," the voice came back. "Let me come and speak to you. I have news."

The words shocked the men. Left Hand looked at One Eye. "What magic is this?"

Fool Dog said, "I will go and kill him."

"No," Walking Man said. "Let us speak with him."

One Eye called, "Are you a devil? If not, come out and we will speak. If you are a devil, go away. We are tired of devils and visions."

Porter rose, holding his carbine above his head. "I am a friend of Medicine Calf Beckwourth."

"He is a black, white man," One Eye said, astonished. "Like Medicine Calf."

"Are the white soldiers with you?" Walking Man said. "Do they mean to kill us?"

Porter lowered his carbine, and leading Randy, walked slowly toward the warriors. He stopped when he saw the carnage surrounding them. "I know what did this. I know what happened here."

"Do you?" Left Hand said, watching Porter advance. "Maybe we will kill you as we killed the devil."

Porter stopped a short distance from them, the black, white man and the warriors watching each other. "If you had killed the devil, its body would be here. It is not, so it still lives. If it lives, it will try to kill you again."

"How do you know this?" One Eye said. He saw the blood covering the front of Porter's jacket. "Did it try to kill you? Is that your blood or the devil's?"

"Not mine," Porter said. "Let us talk a little. I will tell you all I know."

"Well?" One Eye said. "What news do you have?"

"He cannot be trusted!" Left Hand said. "You think this black, white man knows anything?"

Comes-a-Pony kept her rifle pointed at Porter. "Tell him to go away so we can kill him when we kill the white soldiers."

Porter slipped his carbine into its boot on the saddle. "I have a little tobacco. Let us smoke awhile and talk."

"Talk! We have no reason to talk," Left Hand said. "The white soldiers are just over the hill, and they will kill us."

"I know you," Porter said to Walking Man. "Medicine Calf told me about you. He said you are a reasoning man. If you believed him, you can believe me."

"Reasoning man," Left Hand said. "Look," his hand swept over the dead men. "See how well your reasoning has done for us?" He turned on Porter. "You are a black, white man, but you are still a white man. Why should we believe anything you tell us?"

Walking Man studied the black, white man. He was not short, but neither was he tall. He was thick in the shoulders, and his hair was pulled back, tied with a leather thong, and hung from the back of his head. Walking Man lowered his Henry rifle. "Medicine Calf was a good man. He was very old when he died."

"How are you called?" One Eye said. "If we are to talk, I must know who you are."

Porter slipped his hand into his pocket and pulled out a plug of tobacco. He held it out to One Eye. "Take this. I am Porter. When I was young, a white man kept me as his slave. He gave me his name because I did not have one of my own. He was Porter, so that is my name."

"Did you kill him?" One Eye asked.

"No. I ran away."

"I would have killed him," Left Hand said. "I will kill any white man I see. Even a black, white man."

One Eye took the tobacco, tore off a piece, and put it into the bowl of his pipe.

Porter squatted next to Randy, stroking the horse's left front leg. "The white soldiers will not come until I call them. You have chased them pretty well, and their horses are played out." He noticed Comes-a-Pony and saw her soldier's trousers and Sharps rifle.

One Eye handed the tobacco to Left Hand, who ignored the gesture at first. One Eye prodded him with the words, "The tobacco is real. Take it." Then Left Hand snatched it away from the older brave.

"Why do you come to talk with us?" Walking Man asked. "We could have killed you. We can still kill you; and, yet you come wanting to talk. Why?"

"Because of what Black Antelope told me," Porter said.

Chapter 20

Bent Horn's pony collapsed in a cloud of dust, throwing him onto the ground. He jumped up and called to the braves swirling around him, "Give me a gun!" Buffalo Skins, who carried a pistol tied to a lanyard around his neck, pulled it off and threw it to his friend.

Bent Horn caught it, cocked the pistol, and raced toward the White Devil.

The beast roared as Running Dog rode by him, unleashing an arrow that struck the creature in the neck. The other braves rode at a distance, firing and yelling taunts. Star Keeper, standing near his dead pony, had only a walk-a-heaps long gun that fired one bullet before reloading. He opened the block, slipped a cartridge in, and aimed it at White Devil's head.

Black Antelope rode close to the beast, trying to get his attention so Wolf Chief could strike with his lance. Standing Bull's torn body lay close to his dead pony. He had been the first one killed. He had ridden too close to the beast, and it had pierced his breast with its long claws, nearly tearing him in half.

"Stay away from it," Black Antelope cried. "Keep back."

Buffalo Skins had a Winchester rifle that fired many bullets without reloading. He sat still on his pony, aiming for the creature's head, but his pony was frightened at the noise and scent of blood. He shied away, and Buffalo Skins had to fight him to keep him still. He fired three shots before his pony turned and began to run away. He almost dropped his weapon as he fought to control his mount.

The devil jumped at Moccasin Lance, but the warrior's pony was too fast and escaped the claws. The brave cocked and fired his Henry twice before it jammed. The beast roared in frustration, searching for an enemy to kill.

Running Dog, on his bay pony, loaded his white soldier's gun and waited for a good shot. His pony, Stone, was like his name. He did not fear anything and would not move unless his rider wanted him to. "Aim for the head," Running Dog shouted. He raised his carbine, found his target, and fired. The bullet struck the creature in the side of his long skull but did not stop him.

"Kill it," Star Keeper urged his friends. "Kill it!"

The thing had come upon them, running at them before they saw it. It reached Standing Bull first, who did not have time to shout a warning. The beast drove its claws into the warrior, knocking him off his pony, and then the thing killed the pony before it had time to run away.

Big Wolf was the first to strike back. He threw his lance at the beast, striking him in the chest; but the beast tore the lance from its body and howled in rage at Big Wolf. The warrior rode out of the beast's reach and, taking his bow, loosed an arrow at him. But Big Wolf had been startled at the beast's answer to his lance, and the arrow went wide.

Elk Foot sat on his pony and calmly loaded and fired his white soldier's gun, while his pony did not move. It was as if nothing troubled either one of them, or there was nothing to be concerned about.

Bent Horn was a short distance from the demon when he knelt and aimed Star Keepers' pistol. He cocked it and fired. Then he cocked it again and fired once more. The beast turned on him. Running Dog kicked his pony and raced toward Bent Horn, reaching for the warrior so that he could throw Bent Horn on his pony behind him. But he was too late.

The demon sprang, landing on Bent Horn. As the warrior screamed in pain, the beast ripped off his head and threw it at Running Dog. The beast roared in a terrible manner that filled the air and made the earth shake. But they were Cheyenne braves, and they did not let fear cause them to run away. When the beast killed Standing Bear, the others became so angry that nothing mattered but avenging their friend's death.

Black Antelope called to Wolf Chief. "I will ride toward him so that he sees me and gives chase. You come up behind him as close as you can and shoot him in the head." Wolf Chief nodded. He carried a Starr pistol that did not have to be cocked. Pulling the trigger was all that had to be done.

"I have to reload first," Wolf Chief said. He took a handful of cartridges from a pouch at his side and loaded them into the pistol's cylinder. He nodded at Black Antelope when he was ready and rode behind the beast.

Black Antelope, carrying a Spencer carbine that loaded through the stock, kicked his pony in the ribs and rode straight at the creature. "I am Black Antelope," he cried. "I will kill you and all your kind. You cannot harm me." The creature ignored him. It turned on Running Dog. Black Antelope saw that Running Dog was too close to the demon, but before he could do anything, the creature's long arm flashed through the air, knocking Running Dog from his pony. The brave, stunned by the blow, rose slowly, and reacted as if he could just walk away from the danger.

Black Antelope saw blood running down the brave's legs; and after two or three steps, Running Dog fell, dead.

The anger that took hold of Black Antelope was so great that he did not hear and saw only the terrible creature that had ambushed them. He was alone on the prairie with the demon, and now his heart told him that he must kill the thing. He had forgotten White Chief, Standing Bull, and the others. He was like a man who goes wild and sees strange things that no others can see.

He pointed his Spencer toward the creature who now saw him. This was a single battle for the Cheyenne brave and the thing. Black Antelope fired as quickly as he could cock the gun, looking to strike the creature in his narrow chest.

White Chief rode behind the creature and stopped his pony so that his shots would not miss. He raised his pistol and fired three quick shots. But then the pistol jammed, and as he tried to clear it, flame-red eyes, a torn mouth covered in blood, and claws as big as a man's hand filled his vision.

Black Antelope saw the beast pierce White Chief's skull with his claws and lift the warrior high in the air. White Chief's legs kicked, and his arms fell to his side; and the creature held him up as if to admire his kill. Then he turned and saw Black Antelope, and smiling in triumph, threw White Chief's body at him. Black Antelope tried to turn his pony, but his friend's body struck him, and he fell from his pony, feeling his chest explode.

He lay there, not seeing anything except the battle and, to one side, his pony, which ran away in fear.

The sound was far away, and everything in front of him happened slowly, like when a man walks in deep snow. The creature had Elk Foot and bit his head off, spitting it out like a man spits out a seed. Elk Foot's pony was down and struggling to rise, but its legs were broken, and maybe its back too. After a while, it just stopped trying and died.

Then everyone moved out of Black Antelope's vision so that he only heard things such as guns firing and men shouting, and the scream of the beast as it killed his friends. He thought of Willow Creek, his wife, and how she was with child and how she talked about giving him a good, strong son so that he could train him how to ride and shoot, and the things a Cheyenne brave should know. His mother's face was in his mind, and she spoke softly to him; but he could not hear her because she had died of a fever many winters before. All these thoughts came to him, and he knew he must travel to the long fork of the Milky Way and reach *Seana*. Soon darkness came over him, and the world disappeared.

When he awoke, the sun was close to dying. He heard nothing. He moved to see what he could see, but his chest burned with so much pain that he cried out. He did not know where he was, but then he remembered the beast and the big fight. He realized that he was still alive.

He raised himself on his hands but with great difficulty because his whole body hurt, but mostly his chest. He thought his ribs must be broken. He coughed and tasted blood, and he looked down to see the bright red liquid paint the ground.

He looked around. Everything was still. He saw the body of Running Dog to his right. On his left were the bodies of Star Keeper and Buffalo Skins. Beyond that, he saw the pony of Elk Foot and remembered how proud of the animal Elk Foot was. "I will call him Stone," Elf Foot had told him long ago. "He stands still as if he is made of stone. His heart is big, and he fears nothing. I will call him Stone."

Black Antelope's mouth was dry, and he could make no spit. He craved water and thought that if he could reach one of the ponies that they might have water bags on them, and he could drink. Suddenly, nothing else mattered to him except finding water. He tried to get to his feet, but the pain in his chest was too great, and he fell again. He saw the sun nearly gone, and he thought he had fallen asleep again. He knew he must find water quickly because if the sun went down, it would be too dark to see. The terrible thirst prodded him.

He pulled himself along the ground using his elbows and hands. The hurt never left him, but the thirst was greater even than that, so he kept moving. He reasoned that he could pull himself to Stone and find water on the pony's corpse. He moved a short distance, stopping sometimes because he felt he could not go on. Then when his strength returned, he began again.

"You must go over to the pony and get water, little boy," his mother spoke to him as she did when he was a child. "I will help you, and everything will be as it should." He felt her hands lifting him. "When the fever took me away from you, I was sad; but I knew we would see each other again. Your father will join us but not for some time."

He heard a noise and looked up. A spirit rode towards him. His head was pointed, and he was covered in buffalo hide. He felt for his gun but could not find it and realized that even if he shot the spirit, it would do no good. He wondered why a spirit rode a pony when it could just fly across the ground. Then the spirit stopped its pony. It carried a carbine which further puzzled Black Antelope. His mind couldn't function, clouded by the pain in his chest and the thoughts of what had just happened.

Then the spirit disappeared; and he saw a man on a pony, and the man carried his carbine across his chest. He was wearing a white man's hat, but he was black. Black Antelope thought he would pass out again. He had seen three or four black, white men before, so he knew they existed. The man stopped his pony and looked around. And then he stepped slowly from his pony, holding on the reins with one hand and the rifle in the other. Black Antelope watched as the man came at him slowly, always looking about. He knew he would die because white men, even black, white men, hated The People and would kill them whenever they could. The man stopped and knelt. Then he rose and came again, and when he reached Black Antelope's side, he stopped once more. Black Antelope closed his eyes and thought, "Mother, I will come to see you."

He felt himself being turned over so that his head was supported. A canteen was placed on his lips, and a little water went into his mouth. It was wonderful. He tried to raise his hands to tip the canteen up for more water, but the black, white man took the canteen away.

Then he spoke in Cheyenne. "Not so much, brother," he said. Black Antelope wondered why he was calling him brother because they were enemies and would kill one another if they had the chance. "Your ribs is stowed in." He tipped the canteen again and gave Black Antelope a little more water. After a moment, the black, white man asked him, "What has happened here?"

Black Antelope spoke, but no words came out. His lips and mouth were still dry despite the water the black, white man gave him, and he could not make a sound above a whisper. More water came, and Black Antelope coughed, tasting blood; and his chest was on fire. He coughed some more; and every time he did, he felt the creature squeezing his chest and driving its claws into him.

"You're bad hurt," the black, white man said. "Just take your time." More water came, and Black Antelope felt better.

He said, "Are my friends all dead?"

"It looks like it," the black, white man said. "What happened? I know it was not white soldiers because your friends have all been torn up. The horses, too."

Black Antelope said. "Water?" The man gave him more water, and he coughed again, blood filling his mouth. "We came upon a creature," he said. "It was very tall with long arms and legs. We fought it, but it was too strong. I have never seen anything like it."

It was a moment before the black, white man said, "What kind of animal could do this?"

"Not an animal," Black Antelope said. "*Hea'vohe.* We could not kill it. I think it must have killed all my friends and then went off."

A bad spirit, Porter knew. More than that. He looked around at the carnage.

Black Antelope's mother was speaking again. "Come now, my son. You have done all you could. You have told your story so now you must come to me."

A little water fell on his forehead and more on his lips. There was darkness, comforting. His chest did not hurt, and the thirst had gone away. He said it again, because he wanted the black, white man to know all Cheyenne warriors were brave and fierce fighters that should not be taken for granted, "It was *Hea'vohe.*"

The black, white man whispered a word in American that Black Antelope did not know. Then the man said in Cheyenne, "A demon? A devil? Is that what you mean?"

The darkness overwhelmed him, and his mother took his hand. "Time to rest, little boy. I will carry you in my arms, and we will play games as we once did."

Chapter 21

Walking Man's legs grew weak, and he decided to sit down. One Eye and Fool Dog said nothing. Left Hand, who always had something to say, said only, "Black Antelope."

Eagle Head walked to Red Horse and sat next to the brave. Comes-a-Pony slung the rifle over her shoulder.

The black, white man called Porter did not speak for a while. Then he said, "It was a good fight. They died well."

"Good fight?" Left Hand said. "How could it be a good fight? They were all rubbed out. My brothers could not win against the beast." He pointed at Walking Man. "Look here. Look at the man who brought us to this. Bull Bear is dead. Wooden Leg and Stone Forehead. All torn to pieces. Does this look like a good fight to you?" He grabbed a rifle and pointed it at Porter. "I will kill you. At least that is something. At least that is a little honor."

Eagle Head stepped next to him and pushed the barrel of the rifle down. "Let him be, brother. Nothing can be gained by killing this man who told us about Black Antelope and the others."

Porter saw Comes-a-Pony with her soldier's trousers and gun. He had heard of women braves but had never seen one. She met his gaze with a look of disdain.

She walked next to her brother and whispered, "Maybe he is telling the truth. We should hear more."

Walking Man picked up a water bottle, stood, and handed it to Eagle Head. "Drink a little," he said. "It might help your arm."

Eagle Head took the bottle and drank, then handed it to Left Hand. "Here, brother."

Red Horse, who until this time had lost his mind, stood, wiping his face with his hands. "You said you came from the white soldiers," he said to Porter. "What will you do now? Will you go back to them and then attack us? We are but a few. We have no ponies and not many cartridges. We cannot harm you." He found his heart. "But we will not let you kill us. We will fight you until we cannot fight anymore. I am Red Horse of the Shield Warriors Society. My brothers are Kit Fox Warriors. If you come for us, we will fight you."

Porter nodded. "No need to fight just yet. I have some food on my horse. You are welcome to it. I will give you some of my water as well. I have been over this land and could find none. All the animals have gone away, so you cannot hunt them. If you want to return to your village, I will tell the white chief that I could not find you. You have my word as a friend of Medicine Calf Beckwourth."

"Did you see it?" Walking Man asked. "This thing that rubbed out our friends."

Porter shook his head. "They were dead when I got there. Except for Black Antelope. Then he died right after. They were cut up. The ponies killed as well. I looked for sign but saw only where this thing had run. I figure," he said. "A stride of seven feet or thereabout. Not a bear or any other animal I have ever seen. He called it a *Hea'vohe*. That's a demon, ain't it? Some kind of demon."

"*Hea'vohe,*" Walking Man said. "Yes."

"You see," One Eye said. "Even this black, white man says we can go home. Let us do as he says."

When Walking Man spoke, it was as if all he had seen and done had gotten into his soul and wrapped it so tightly his heart could barely beat. "We cannot return to our village. If we do, the thing will follow us and kill everyone."

"Weakling!" Left Hand spat. "We are Cheyenne. There are many braves in our village. Maybe the Lakota will come and help us make a fight. I say let us go back and make ready for battle. By the time the creature arrives, we will be ready."

Fool Dog agreed with Left Hand. "We can make a stand with the Lakota. We will be many more with guns and cartridges."

"This is sound thinking," One Eye said, but his eyes said something different. His shoulders gave way, like a man who was tired. "I would like to hear what Comes-a-Pony says."

She examined Porter before speaking. "I have never met a black, white man. Something tells me there is no difference between him and the others. Is this true?"

The scout smiled grimly. "Night and day, lady."

"You ride with them and hunt The People. If you find us, you kill us. I think you found Black Antelope, and the rest is true; but there is something I do not understand. Why did you come here? You know we could kill you. You came anyway."

Porter nodded. "Yeah, I did. I guess I'm just the curious type."

"I think we should kill him," Left Hand said. "Then we can go home and make ready for the thing."

One Eye spoke gently to Left Hand. "I know you to be a warrior, afraid of nothing. I would rather have you at my side in a fight than anyone. But what Walking Man said is true. We cannot protect our women and children. Our old people. The Lakota could come and help us because we would do the same for them. But you have seen this thing's power, as I have. We cannot go home again."

"Maybe," Red Horse said, "this thing is done with us. Maybe it will go and kill the white soldiers and then we could go home."

"You saw what I saw," Walking Man said. "This man Porter tells us about Black Antelope and the others. Red Horse tells us about Bull Bear. This thing is always hungry. It is like those braves who get a taste of the white man's whiskey and cannot let it be. No. I think it will never be satisfied. It will kill and eat until there is nothing left to fill its belly."

"There is another way," Porter said. "Come with me to the white soldier's camp. Let me tell them what I have seen. What I know to be true. We can join up together to kill the thing."

The braves looked at each other in surprise. They thought this black, white man had lost his senses. Such a thing could never happen. Only Crow and Shoshoni rode with the white soldiers. Maybe a few Lakota.

Cheyenne would never do such a thing. They would never betray their own kind.

"So that is why you came to us?" Comes-a-Pony said. "You want to make a treaty. White men always want to make treaties. First, they talk, and hand out presents, and then they make a treaty and talk some more. Then they kill the buffalo and steal our land."

Eagle Head spoke before the others had a chance to say anything. His manner was calm, unhurried. "What you suggest cannot be. White men cannot be trusted. Maybe black, white men are honest. I knew Medicine Calk Beckwourth to be honest, but white men always lie."

"Do you think we are Crow?" Left Hand said. "Do you think we will follow the white soldiers and eat what they throw to us like dogs? Go back and tell them anything you like. I would rather die than fight alongside white soldiers."

He remembered the boy's words; you cannot kill it alone. Walking Man picked up his Henry rifle and examined it. The tube that fed the cartridges had been bent so that it was impossible to load it. He threw it away. "Even the sun hides from this demon." He looked at the sky. There was light and things could be seen, but the sun was behind black clouds and refused to come out. "We have a chance to kill this thing, but only if we join the white soldiers. They have guns and cartridges. We have just a few."

"You go," Left Hand said. "You and the others go. I will stay here and wait for the thing to return, and then I will kill it, or it will kill me. Either way, I will be a Kit Fox Warrior."

"I am of the Shield Warriors Society," Fool Dog said. "All that I have seen does not make any sense to me. If a man told me this thing, I would say he had gone crazy, but I saw everything you did."

"I am as well," One Eye said, "We know the thing is afraid of fire. Maybe the white soldiers have plenty of matches. If we join them and when it comes for us, we can set fire to the prairie. Maybe that will kill it."

"Let me take you to them," Porter said. "The white chief is young, but he has a good heart. I will tell him all that has happened and how we must fight together."

Waking Man looked at the others. "Will you come with me? It is not much of a chance, but it is a chance."

"Go, then," Left Hand said. "All of you, go. I will stay and fight."

Comes-a-Pony caught Walking Man's glance. "Well? Will you go with us?"

She shook her head. "My place is at my brother's side. I will stay with him, and we will see what happens."

Walking Man saw Moon, standing at the edge of the ravine. He whistled, and the pony came to him. He stroked its neck and led it to Eagle Head. He helped the brave mount the pony. "I did not see any other ponies about. Maybe they will come back if they have not been killed." Red Horse, One Eye, and Fool Dog joined Walking Man.

"I want you to understand me," Fool Dog said to Porter. "If it comes about that you have lied, I will kill you myself. My brothers say they trust you. I am not as certain, but I will go because I cannot see any other way."

"Fair enough," Porter said. He led the others up the slope of the ravine.

Red Horse turned to see Left Hand and Comes-a-Pony standing next to the fire. The flames were going out, and only a faint trail of smoke marked its presence.

Now, Porter thought, *all I must do is convince the lieutenant that devils exist.*

Chapter 22

The wind grew angry, teasing them, pulling at their clothes, punishing them for not killing the beast. That is what Walking Man thought as he and the others trailed behind Porter. They had found another pony. She was Two Faces and had been Wooden Leg's. She was cautious as they approached, but she came over and accepted Fool Dog's hand.

"Come," he had said to Red Horse. "You ride for a while and then I will."

Red Horse nodded and mounted her without protest. He glanced down at Fool Dog and said, as if he were making an apology, "I think my legs will come back to me soon."

Fool Dog replied, "I understand. After a big fight, my arms and legs become soft; and I feel as if I cannot walk."

"Porter?" Walking Man called.

Porter turned back and hopped off Randy, walking next to the brave.

"What will you tell the white soldier chief?" Walking Man asked.

"That's a good question," the scout said. "I've been giving it a lot of thought."

"He will not believe you. White men have no confidence in spirits except the one they call Jesus."

"I've found there's a lot of talk about Jesus and not much action, so I wouldn't credit the white man with that much."

"Why didn't you kill him? The man who kept you a slave?"

"I just didn't get the chance. I ran away and joined the army; and when I got out of the army, I came west."

"Were many of your people slaves?"

"Nearly all of them," Porter said. "Those that weren't were still treated like dirt. If it makes any difference, my kind still has to fight for what's right. Hell, just to live with dignity."

"Why are they not your enemy? The whites?"

Porter laughed. "You're full of good questions, aren't you?"

They walked in silence until Porter said, "I'll ride up to them. You folks hang back until I signal you."

"No," Walking Man said. "I will not let another man speak for me."

"Listen, those boys are jittery already. It won't take much for them to start shooting."

"Did you hear Red Horse and Fool Dog? We are but a few; but if it comes to a fight, we are ready. I will go with you to talk to the soldier chief."

"I still think you oughta let me go on ahead. This fella may be a boy, but he's got some sense. Just let me talk to him alone, then you can come in and say your peace." Porter dug in his pocket and produced two pieces of stick candy. He put one in his mouth and offered the other to Walking Man.

"Still, I will go with you," Walking Man said, taking the candy. He examined it, broke off a piece and put it in his mouth.

"I don't know if that's such a great idea."

"Would you let a white man speak for you, Porter?"

"Suit yourself."

The Cheyenne's face brightened. "What is this?"

"Candy," Porter replied. "Tastes pretty good, don't it?"

Walking Man's eyes crinkled in surprise. "I have never eaten this before."

"It's peppermint. When I get low on tobacco, I just suck on one of those."

Walking Man savored the flavor.

Porter smiled at the brave's reaction. "Yep, that's the sort of thing a fella could get used to."

They walked for a little while when Walking Man said to Porter, "What if the soldier chief does not believe you? What if he calls you crazy and wants to make a fight with us?" He turned back and looked at the warriors. They walked slowly, as if they were lost in their minds.

"I just don't know. I ain't never run into any demons out here, so your guess is as good as mine. I'll tell you one thing; from what I've seen, that beast ain't nothing to trifle with."

"This man whose name you have," Walking Man asked, "If you had a chance to kill this white man, would you do so?"

Porter spat his candy out. "I'd beat him to death with my bare hands. Even if he is my pa."

"This man is your father?"

"He raped my mother when she was just a girl. She weren't the only one. Yeah, I'd go back there if I ever got the chance. I'd hunt him up and break every bone in his body, just for starters. If he's still alive. I don't know what happened to him, or her. Or any of my kin."

"Sometimes," Walking Man said, "it is better for us not to hold vengeance for too long. It is like a long, dark shadow over a man's eyes. He cannot see clearly."

"Not me. It helps me get through the day," Porter said. "Now, listen. If the soldiers try anything, I'll tell them they can find their own way home. I won't help them get back to their station. Ain't a one of them ain't got any idea how to navigate."

Walking Man turned to One Eye, "I'm going with Porter to speak with the soldier chief."

"Can you trust this black, white man?"

"I can," Walking Man said. "But not white men. You may have to make a fight here."

One Eye nodded, looking over the terrain. "This place is just as good as any other to die."

Chapter 23

"Lieutenant?" Sergeant Taliaferro said. "Can I borrow your spyglass?"

Sweet handed the sergeant his binoculars. "What do you see?"

"Porter, I think," Taliaferro said. He pointed across the prairie. "Right there." He focused the lens of the binoculars. "That's Porter. It looks like there's a bunch behind him."

Sweet took the binoculars. "What? Soldiers?" He focused the binoculars. "I don't see anything." He handed the binoculars back to the sergeant.

"I swear to God it looks like Indians. Maybe half-a-dozen."

"Are they chasing him?" Sweet said.

Taliaferro peered through the binoculars. "No. Looks like they're mostly afoot. They stopped moving; Porter's coming on. How the hell is that man not been killed?"

"I don't know," Sweet said, amazed at the scout's return.

"Yeah, that's Porter," Taliaferro confirmed to Sweet. "One of them is coming in with Porter. Don't that just take the cake?"

"Yes, it does," Sweet said. "Tell the men, nobody shoots. You stay here."

"You ain't going out there, Lieutenant?"

"Sergeant, I don't see that I have any choice. You tell the men. Make sure they understand." Sweet opened his holster flap and pulled out his Army Colt. He cocked the hammer but let it hang at his side and started walking.

The three men closed the distance. Walking Man watched the soldiers. They held their carbines ready. They would be nervous. Men like that made mistakes. If they did, nothing could help them, or his braves. Maybe better to die by a white soldier's hand than to be killed by the beast. He thought of his father and mother and of his sister Little Feather. He thought of The People who would not know how he died.

Walking Man caught sight of the officer and said, "He is a boy."

"Yeah," Porter agreed. "The army sends them young out here. He's smart though. But he's still wet behind the ears. Here's hoping nobody'll shoot with him between us and them."

The men stopped a few feet from one another. "Morning, Lieutenant," Porter said.

Walking Man watched the pistol at the officer's side. It did not move.

"Mr. Porter," Sweet said. "I didn't expect to see you again."

"Yeah, I had some thoughts along the same lines," Porter said. "This is Lieutenant Sweet," he told the brave. "This fella is Walking Man. He came for a council."

"Council?"

"Yeah," Porter said. "Why don't we just sit down here? If everybody sees us sitting, they might not be so likely to shoot."

Sweet looked beyond Porter to the waiting Cheyenne. "Can we trust them?"

"They're asking the same question about you," Porter said. "Let's sit awhile."

Sweet lowered himself to the ground, resting the Colt in his lap. The other two sat as well. "Where are the others? The ones that rode off?"

"They ain't hiding nearby if that's what you mean. They're dead. All of them."

"Dead?"

"Yeah," Porter said, pulling out his plug of tobacco. "We ain't got a pipe, so it would help the ceremony some if you take a bite. Don't swallow it, for God's Sake." The scout handed Sweet the tobacco.

Sweet took a modest bite, retched, and then handed it to Walking Man. The Cheyenne tore off a piece with his teeth and handed it to Porter, who did the same. The officer nodded at Walking Man. "Does he speak English?"

"I don't know," Porter said. "I didn't ask him."

"Where are the soldiers? That's who we heard last night, isn't it? All the gunfire? It was Gibbons' men? Or Crow?"

"No, no Crow. Or soldiers. Lieutenant," Porter said, "I'm going to tell you the damnest story you ever did hear."

Chapter 24

"What the hell's going on out there?" Mendelson said. "What's the nigger doing with a Cheyenne?"

"Talking to him, I guess," Collier said.

The men stood by their mounts, holding onto the reins, carbines suspended on slings. Taliaferro walked back and forth in front of the men without saying a word. He wondered the same thing. He held the lieutenant's binoculars, scanning the surrounding ground. He wondered where the other group of Cheyenne had gotten to. He didn't like it, not one bit. He watched the Cheyenne beyond the three men. He saw two, three guns. One man slid off a horse and stood with the others. He saw them talking. He swung the binoculars back to the men sitting on the prairie. Sweet's back was to him. He could see the Cheyenne's face, and Porter's. He saw Porter translating for Sweet and the Cheyenne.

Jones asked, "See anything?"

"Just talking," Taliaferro said. "That bunch looks like they've been in a fight. One fella has his arm bandaged up."

"A fight with whom?" Jones asked.

"With whom?" Mendelson snorted. "Ain't that just like a foreigner?"

"I'm a foreigner," Wagner reminded Mendelson. "I speak pretty good English."

"Yeah," Mendelson said. "But you're Dutch."

"Deutsch," Wagner reminded him. "German, not Dutch."

"Everybody shut up," Taliaferro said.

Ashcroft's horse jerked its head back, trying to pull the reins out of his hand. He balled up his fist and slugged the horse on its snout. "The first thing I'm going to do when we get back," he whispered to Stewart, "is get rid of this animal."

"Maybe she's thinking the same thing about you?" Stewart said.

Smallwood took a quick drink from his canteen. He slipped the cork back into the neck and hung it over his shoulder, under his arm. "I don't see why we just don't light into them. Run them off, then be on our way. We ain't getting anywhere like this."

"Maybe we don't have to have a battle?" Wagner posed.

"Have a battle," Mendelson said. "Yeah, you speak real good English, don't you?"

"The pow-wow's breaking up," Stewart said.

Taliaferro watched as the three men stood but continued talking. "Stand by," he ordered. They shook hands, Porter returning with the warrior to the other Cheyenne. Sweet walked slowly back, his head down in thought. He stopped once, looked back at Porter and the others, and then continued. Sweet slipped his pistol back into its holster. He moved like a man with something on his mind, Taliaferro thought. A man with a problem.

Collier moved to the sergeant's side. "He don't look happy."

"No," Taliaferro said. "No, he don't."

Chapter 25

Sweet watched the ground as he walked, lost, confused, going over everything that Porter had said, what he had translated from the Cheyenne brave. He couldn't think straight; everything tumbled through his mind. Words, just words.

"It's a creature, Lieutenant," Porter told him. "It ain't human. I didn't see it, but I've seen what it done. This fella," he meant the Cheyenne sitting across from him. "He fought it. There weren't no soldiers. It's not an animal. Not a man."

The Cheyenne brave said something to Porter. The scout nodded. The Cheyenne's words came faster. He gestured. Porter tried to translate, but the Cheyenne was talking too quickly, interrupting him. All the words collided with one another until the scout stopped talking and just listened. The Cheyenne became angry, slapping his fist into his palm. He stopped and began again.

"I don't understand," Sweet said to Porter.

Porter said something in Cheyenne, and the brave nodded and waited for the scout to tell Sweet. "Ten, maybe twelve feet tall. Real fast. Claws. Teeth that bites clean through a man." Now Porter talked, looking from the brave to Sweet. The lieutenant watched both struggle to find the words.

Taliaferro stood in front of him. "What happened, Lieutenant? What did they say?"

"What?"

"The Indian? Porter? What did they tell you?"

"Where are the men?"

It was Taliaferro's time to be confused. "Right here," he said. "They're right here, Lieutenant."

The men stood around him. *Tell them. Tell them what?* It started raining, a cold rain. Big drops beating on his straw hat. "Perfect for campaigning," the sutler had said. "Gets real hot out there. This will do you just fine." The men pulled their ponchos out. A flurry of black as they threw them on. Birds with beating wings.

"You don't look so good, Lieutenant," Taliaferro said.

Oh? How should I look? He saw Porter through the rain, walking with the Cheyenne, coming his way. They were like ghosts. Formless. Spirits, Sweet? Maybe they were demons?

"What are your orders, Lieutenant?" Taliaferro again. Competent, trustworthy. Just like a straw hat. This time with more urgency, "They're coming in, Lieutenant."

"Yes," Sweet said. The soldiers looked at him and then at each other. "Let them come."

Taliaferro spoke haltingly, a man uncertain of circumstances. "Lieutenant, I don't think that's a good idea."

"Let them come, Sergeant," Sweet said. "They're going to join us." One of the soldiers cursed. Another said something.

"As you were," Taliaferro snapped.

Why was it so cold? Someone handed him a poncho. He took off the straw hat and slipped it on. The hat felt as if it were melting in his hand. He put it back on. He thought it a good idea to placate the men. He should say something to put them at ease. He decided. "They're coming in to join us. There's no danger."

Wait a minute. That's not what Porter said.

"Lieutenant, that other band of Cheyenne. They was wiped out. I got to one before he died and he told me," the scout had said. "These fellas here were lucky to survive. None of this makes much sense, I know that. If I ain't seen it with my own eyes, I'd say these people were crazy. But I seen what it could do. These folks here fought it off but just barely."

"Lieutenant," Taliaferro pushed him, "we gotta do something. We just can't let that band get up on us."

"Sergeant," Sweet said. "They are coming in to join us. We're going on together." He took strength from his own words. Make some maps along the way, Sweet, a major suggested. Nothing to it. Calculate your distance, note mountain ranges and sources of water. "They weren't attacked by soldiers or other Indians. It was some kind of animal."

No, no, it wasn't. Porter told you it wasn't. "We'll be better off if we join forces." *It wasn't an animal or man. Porter told you that. A creature, he had said.*

The men were confused; they talked to one another in whispers. A few raised their carbines. The others didn't know what to do.

"Boys," Porter called out through the rain. "Keep your fingers off your triggers. I don't want to get shot. These people ain't no danger to you. They've been whipped pretty good." He and the Cheyenne stood a few feet away. Both groups watched each other. The rain slackened.

"Prepare to mount," Sweet said.

Taliaferro didn't move.

"Prepare to mount, Sergeant," Sweet said calmly.

Taliaferro broke free. "Prepare to mount," he shouted.

The men stood by their horses. Somebody handed Sweet his reins. He put a foot in the stirrup and ordered, "Mount."

Stewart said to Jones, "What the hell is happening?"

"I don't want those bastards behind us," Mendelson said.

Ashcroft's horse twisted as he tried to keep his foot in the stirrup. He was able to mount and said, "This is the craziest damned thing I've ever seen."

"Forward, at a walk," Sweet ordered. He turned in the saddle and called, "Mr. Porter?" The scout joined him. "Mr. Porter, I hope you know what you're doing?"

"Lieutenant, the only way to know for sure is if we run into that critter. And I sure as hell don't want to."

"What do I say to the men? What do I tell them?"

"The truth, I guess."

"They won't believe me."

"That boy's gonna get us killed," Mendelson said. He turned in his saddle. The Cheyenne were about a hundred yards behind them. "They're gonna wait until we're asleep and murder us."

Smallwood rode next to him. "I don't know that you're not right. He's talking to Porter about something."

"Why don't we just kill them and be done with it?" Mendelson said. "We won't have to keep looking over our shoulders all the time."

Eagle Hand rode Moon: the others walked.

"I do not trust them," One Eye said. "See how they look at us? As if we were animals."

Walking Man led Moon. One Eye was right. The white soldiers glanced back at them and talked among themselves, as if they were planning something. That is how white men behaved. They said one thing and did another. He thought, maybe they should have gone off on their own. Fought the demon by themselves. The white soldiers could turn their guns on them, kill them as they slept.

Red Horse slipped off Two Faces and handed the reins to Fool Dog. "You ride for a while, friend."

Fool Dog threw himself on the pony and took the reins. "You are feeling better, Red Horse. This is good. I was worried that you would not."

Red Horse walked a bit before saying, "That which I saw will never leave me. My heart broke when I saw what had become of Bull Bear. I could not think." He looked at the ground as they walked. "I was afraid."

"Do not be ashamed of fear," Fool Dog said. "It is a natural thing. How a man acts is what is important. I have learned this."

"What do you think will happen to us?"

"Oh," Fool Dog said. "The soldiers will try to kill us, or that beast will try to kill us."

"I can fight the soldiers," Red Horse said. "I know how to fight soldiers. This other thing…it is like nothing I have seen before."

Walking Man dropped back along the line of braves, until they had moved some distance beyond him. He could see the ground they had passed over and beyond that, the wide prairie. He thought he saw a figure in the distance, and for an instant, he became afraid. He pulled his knife from its sheaf and felt the weight of it in his hand. There was something moving far away, but he could not tell what it was. *Is it two people? The creature is following us,* he told himself. *You do not know that. You are letting your fear tell you how to behave.*

Fool Dog called. "Walking Man? What is it?"

"Keep going," Walking Man said. "Do not wait for me." He found a stone on the ground and began honing his knife blade. He would make it sharp, to kill the creature. He watched the movement until it became a man, and then two, and he thought the thing had taken a man's form and would trick them. *No,* he decided. *If it was the shape of a man, it would be easier to kill.* As it drew near, he saw that he knew the walk. She moved like the waters of a shallow stream and carried a long gun.

Comes-a-Pony and Left Hand were coming to join them. *Or maybe it was the creature. It came as two instead of one. Maybe it had killed Comes-a-Pony and Left Hand and taken their shape. Could it do that?*

When the two were close enough, he said, "I am pleased to see you." Then he thought, *maybe one of them is the creature? Or both? No, no, that cannot be.*

"It changes shape," the old man in his vision had said. Walking Man raised his knife and said, "Who are you?"

Left Hand and Comes-a-Pony stopped. "You know who we are," she said. "Why do you ask these things?"

"Maybe you are the creature that came to kill us. How do I know it is you?"

They started walking again, and Comes-a-Pony said "Because you are Walking Man. Because you always speak with reason. Even though I do not always agree with you, I know you are to be trusted. Your pony is Moon, and she is the laziest pony in the tribe. Sometimes she will throw herself on the ground like a dog and sleep. When she is not sleeping, she is eating."

"The creature could know that as well."

"Look at this," Comes-a-Pony said to her brother. "Walking Man is afraid."

Left Hand said, "If you think I am the creature, borrow someone's gun and shoot me. My feet hurt, and there are holes in my moccasins; and I am hungry and thirsty. Besides," he gestured toward Comes-a-Pony, "Little Sister has persuaded me to join you. I do not think she is right, but what do I know of such things?"

Walking Man smiled, the words lifting his heart. "Come and join us."

"If you do not kill us, we will," Comes-a-Pony said. "I would rather you did not kill us."

Walking Man showed her his knife. "This is all I have. Why did you change your mind?"

Comes-a-Pony had her rifle slung over her shoulder. "I thought, 'how would Walking Man reason with my brother?' Then I did the opposite."

"I'm glad you are here."

"That thing that attacked us killed my friends. I could not kill it. No matter what I did. I want another chance. I see the soldiers have not killed you yet."

"No," Walking Man said. He led the two to the others. "But I am not so sure that they will not try. Who knows what goes on in a white man's head? They are like *Veeho*, always spinning webs and making mischief. Maybe we will fight two enemies."

"Did you talk with the soldier chief?" Left Hand asked.

"I did. The man Porter told him what I said. The soldier chief is a boy who barely has hair on his face. I wonder what he will do."

Lightning flashed in the distance under black clouds, and a soft wind blew across them.

"I think the sun has hidden itself," Comes-a-Pony said. "I would like to feel the warm sun on my face."

Walking Man heard it first, a moaning sound coming out of the clouds. He wished he had a gun, even an old muzzleloader.

The three listened until Left Hand said, "That is the thing that tried to kill us."

"Yes," Walking Man said. "I do not know where or how far away. But it will come for us."

"Let it," Comes-a-Pony said. She held up the Sharps. "I have this and plenty of cartridges to kill it."

"Did you hear that?" Ashcroft said to Wagner.

"Hear what? I heard nothing."

"It sounded like a wolf. Way off there someplace."

"Wolves don't trouble me. But those fellows behind us, that's a different story."

The air cooled, drifting across the prairie without direction. It picked up bits of grass and clouds of dust, sending them flying. The soldiers' horses were spooked, heads bobbing, slipping sideways, pawing at the ground.

Porter noticed Sweet eyeing the Cheyenne. "They ain't the worry, Lieutenant."

"It's unnatural, having them this close. After everything I've heard about them, it just doesn't seem right."

"They ain't armed too well," Porter said. "A couple of bows, rifles, a lance and pistols. Assorted hatchets and knives."

"What are you suggesting?" Sweet asked. "That we give them weapons?"

"Nope. I just wanted you to know what they have to fight with. Let's go back and talk with Walking Man. We ought to come up with a plan."

They turned their horses and galloped to the rear.

Stewart watched them pass and then said to Collier. "I don't care what anyone says. I'm going to shoot the first red son-of-a-bitch that gets close to me."

"You know, Bill, I think that's a good idea."

Taliaferro threw up his hand. "Halt. Prepare to dismount. Dismount." The soldiers did as they were ordered and began walking, leading their horses.

"I joined the cavalry to ride," Mendelson complained to anyone listening. "If I'd wanted to walk, I'd have joined the infantry."

"You joined the cavalry just like the rest of us," Smallwood said. "Cause there weren't no jobs to be had."

"Jeff?" Jones said to Smallwood. "You still have my letter, haven't you?"

Smallwood gave him a disgusted glance. "Did you think I mailed it or something?"

"I was just asking if…"

"You ought to get that thought out of your head," Smallwood said. "We're all getting out of this and going home. Then you can mail your pa and tell him what a fine time you're having."

As they rode toward Walking Man, Porter noted the sky beyond. "There's some kind of storm brewing."

They pulled up next to Walking Man and dismounted. Sweet saw the Cheyenne warriors hesitate and spread out, suspicious of his arrival. They didn't trust him any more than the soldiers trusted the Cheyenne. Or maybe, the officer thought, they didn't trust him specifically.

"How'd they get here?" Porter gestured to Left Hand. "They weren't here before."

"They came from the place where we had the fight," Walking Man said. "He is called Left Hand. The other…"

"Yeah, I know. Comes-a-Pony. Why didn't you come with us when we set out?"

"Because, Porter," Walking Man said, reminding the scout, "they were afraid that the soldiers would try to kill us."

"Who is that girl?" Sweet asked. "She's wearing soldier's trousers. That's a soldier's gun."

"I wouldn't make too much of it, Lieutenant," Porter said. "It's a war, you know."

"She killed a soldier to get them, Mr. Porter," Sweet said.

"Probably."

"The men won't take this well. I don't know how they're going to act."

"Well," Porter said. "Lean into 'em if they get out of hand. We got bigger fish to fry."

Sweet understood. He nodded at Walking Man. "Ask him if he has any ideas how we can fight this thing."

Porter translated the question and Walking Man replied. "Tell the soldier chief that this creature does not like fire. Tell him we must build a big fire."

"That'll give away our position," the scout said.

"This thing knows where we are. It has been following us, so it always knows where we are."

Porter told Sweet, who nodded. "From what you said, I think it's best if we stay out of ravines. Except to get firewood. If we camp out in the open, we'll have a better chance of seeing this thing come upon us. We'll build a fire and stay behind it. Maybe that'll help. We'll camp well before nightfall. It'll give us a chance to find good land. I'm going back up to the detail. You should stay back here with the Cheyenne. It might ease my men's concerns."

"Yeah, they looked like they were getting nervous. When we make camp," Porter added, "maybe you ought to tell them."

Sweet said nothing but turned away and rode back to his men.

"Porter?" Walking Man said. "He does not believe you, does he?"

"Oh, he believes me all right," Porter said. "I ain't certain about his feelings toward you. I guess the real problem is how to get his boys to believe it."

Sweet stopped near Taliaferro and dismounted. "When we make camp tonight, send some of the men out to gather as much firewood as they can. This is what I want to do." He knelt, found a stick, and drew in the earth. "We'll make four big fires, about twenty yards apart. We'll make another big fire in the center. The men will take up position behind the four fires, keeping an eye outwards."

"You want fires?" Taliaferro said, confused. "I'm not certain…"

"That's what I want, Sergeant," Sweet said with more confidence than he felt. "Exactly the way I want it."

"Lieutenant? I don't understand what you have in mind."

"At Alesia, Caesar created two lines of defense. One facing out and one facing in. With these tactics, he was able to defeat the Gaul." Sweet stood as the sergeant studied the design.

"Begging your pardon, sir, but I don't know anything about Caesar or them he fought. What you've got drawed out there is going to light up the whole prairie, us included. We'll be sitting ducks for any Indians that happen along. Besides which, I don't know if we can find enough wood."

"Well," Sweet repeated, "This is what I want. We're not fighting Indians, Sergeant."

Taliaferro rose, perplexed. "If we ain't fighting Indians, sir, who are we fighting?"

"Just do as I ask, Sergeant," Sweet said. He led his mount off. *You must tell them. You must make them understand. How? What do you say to them? How do you explain?* He knew three of the men to be veterans, the others, recruits. None of them were going to believe him. All he could say, was there is a Cheyenne demon out there. They won't believe him. He wasn't certain he believed the story either, but Porter did. *Was that enough, Lieutenant? One man's belief?* Something supernatural was tracking them. Ghosts and hobgoblins. The men wouldn't believe him. They would think he was crazy. They were soldiers. They understood Cheyenne and Sioux, something they could see. Something they could touch and fight. These half a dozen Cheyenne with a handful of weapons were the enemy. But a demon? He would have to convince them, somehow. Convince them of something that he still was uncertain of. Except for what Porter told him and what Walking Man told Porter existed. But Porter hadn't seen it. Maybe he was wrong? Maybe it was some kind of Cheyenne trick? How would he explain it to the major when they returned to the column? *Are you hunting ghosts, Sweet? Did you draw on Caesar's Commentaries to defend your command from spirits, when the enemy was right behind you, the enemy you gave safe conduct to?*

Tell me, Sweet? Are you a warrior or a poet? Do you fight the Indians or uphold mystical stories of spirits and creatures of the night?

Make a map of your travels. Note sources of water. Report any unusual circumstances. Find Gibbons and give him the dispatches.

But. This…thing? You've sunk too far into your books, Lieutenant Sweet. Time to return to reality.

He thought of countermanding his order to Taliaferro. He could tell the sergeant to disregard all that he had said. They will make a camp in a gulley with a small fire and post guards to keep the Cheyenne away. In the morning, they would start out again, cut north along the foothills of the Big Horns, and find Gibbons.

But he didn't find Taliaferro and change his orders. He continued to walk, looking for good ground. Looking for a place to fight a demon.

Chapter 26

Walking Man helped Eagle Head slide off Moon. The brave was in pain, although he said nothing. The others gathered around him, watching the soldiers stop and make camp on the edge of a ravine topped with silver sagebrush.

"This is no place for a fight," Left Hand said. "We can't make a fight here."

"I will go and speak to the white chief," Walking Man said. He moved toward the soldiers, cautiously, so they were not surprised. Some of them saw him come on and put their hands on their carbines. Porter walked with him, speaking in Cheyenne.

"The white chief has us a place to fight, I reckon," the scout said. He found Sweet, and the two spoke for a few minutes.

Walking Man noticed soldiers going down into the ravine and returning with firewood. Their eyes were filled with hate. He saw them talk to one another. "We are out in the open," he said to Porter. "I do not know if this is such a good plan. That thing can come at us from any direction. We should go down into the gulley and make a fight there." He almost added, if we need to, but he knew there was no question. The creature would come.

"He has a plan," Porter said. "He will make fires, and we can see the thing before it gets up on us," he pointed. "There, there, and there. He will have a fire made in the center. You said the thing does not like fire."

"Yes," Walking Man said. "I told you that, but I am still not convinced." He nodded to the soldiers. "I think they want to fight us."

"I don't think so," Porter said. "They are not certain about you. You've been fighting each other for a long time."

Sweet came up, speaking to Porter. Walking Man studied the soldier chief. He was afraid. He spoke quickly and looked from the Cheyenne to his men. Porter said something to him in American. He was trying to calm the soldier chief. Walking Man wondered how the young white man would be in a fight. He might run away. He might freeze. The Cheyenne had seen white soldiers in a fight throw their carbines away and run or stand as still as stone when the Cheyenne approached them and killed them. Once he saw a soldier hold out his carbine as if he was tired of fighting and wanted no more of it. The brave he handed it to struck him with a hatchet in the head and killed him. Left Hand had said, "They are like deer that cannot run anymore and stop, waiting to die." Maybe this would happen when they fought the creature.

Porter turned to Walking Man and told him what the soldier chief said. "He wants you to come close up. You will be back-to-back with the soldiers."

Walking Man did not like the soldier chief's plan. "What if we turn our backs to the soldiers and they kill us? This makes no sense to me."

"It's a good plan," Porter said, and repeated, "you can watch in every direction."

"Not behind us," Walking Man said. "Not to the soldiers at our back."

Mendelson kicked a branch off the limb of a dead cottonwood tree, lying at the bottom of the ravine. "Those bastards will kill us if we don't keep an eye on them. What the hell is that boy doing?"

"I don't like it either," Smallwood said, gathering bits of wood. "I don't even know who we're fighting."

"I don't trust them," Wagner said. "I have never heard of making camp with Indians, except maybe the Crow or Shoshone. Then you still have to watch everything that isn't nailed down. They are thieves.

They steal everything; and when you catch them at it, they get angry, likes it's your fault."

"Come on," Taliaferro shouted from the top of the ravine. "Let's get this done before midnight. Mendelson? You and Ashcroft lead the horses up the ravine about twenty yards and hobble them."

"What? Just us two? Suppose them savages attack us?"

"They can have you but not the horses," Taliaferro said. "Get back up here when you get done."

Mendelson watched as Taliaferro turned away. "He don't like it either. I heard him talking to Stewart. This is the damnedest thing I ever did hear of."

"Come on, let's get to it," Ashcroft said. "I don't want to be out here when it gets dark."

The two soldiers gathered the reins of the horses and led them down into the ravine.

"Why are we taking them up the ravine?" Mendelson asked Ashcroft.

"Why don't you just go up there and ask the sergeant? I believe he'd be more than happy to explain things to you. Go ahead. I ain't seen a good fight in a while. Ain't gonna be but two hits. When Taliaferro hits you and you hit the ground."

"Keep your eyes peeled, boys," Smallwood said. "They can come up behind you and cut your gizzard out before you know what's happening."

Jones and Collier half-slid down the ravine and joined them.

"What's the general doing up there?" Mendelson asked.

"He's talking to the big chief," Collier said. "Neither one of them look happy."

"I wonder what the hell is going on?" Smallwood said. "Them Cheyenne look like they've had a hard time of it."

"Who ain't?" Mendelson said. "Did you see that squaw with 'em?"

"Squaw?" Jones said.

"Don't you like women none?" Mendelson said. "Hell, yeah, it was a squaw. She's a big one, but she's still a woman. Got soldier's britches on, too."

"Yeah," Smallwood said. "I don't like that one bit."

"I bet you that nigger got us into this," Mendelson said. "He's half Indian hisself. He used to live with them."

Collier tore a limb off the trunk of the cottonwood. "Pawnee, I heard."

"What the hell difference does it make what kind of Indian?" Mendelson said. "Ain't none of them human. I bet you that black bastard's got it all worked out with them. You watch. They'll kill us in our sleep for sure."

Ashcroft, reins threaded through his fingers, said "Come on, Mendelson." Victoria tried to pull away. Ashcroft shook his fist in her face. "Try it! Just try something, and I'll beat you to death."

Collier picked up a branch and stopped, grinning at Ashcroft. "You know the old saying, Ashcroft. Ask a stallion, tell a gelding, and reason with a mare."

The soldier wasn't impressed. "There ain't no Goddamn reasoning with this bitch. Not unless it's from the service end of a Colt."

Jones walked down the ravine, searching for more wood. He heard a low murmur, like the wind through the slats of a barracks. Moaning, mournful, a noise filled with aching and sadness. He brushed back the flap of his holster, took out his army Colt, and cocked it. He heard a noise behind him and spun around.

Smallwood threw his hands up. "Jesus Christ, Jones. What are you doing?"

"Did you hear it?"

"Hear what? I ain't heared nothing but Mendelson. What's the matter with you? You ain't got a spot of blood in your face."

Jones eased the hammer onto the cylinder and slipped the pistol into the holster. "It was the most melancholy sound I believe I've ever heard. Coming from out there." He pointed down the ravine. "Almost as if something were in pain."

"I think everyone's gone crazy," he said, picking up more branches. "The lieutenant wants fires, Porter's thrown in with the Cheyenne, and Mendelson's got us killed in our sleep."

Jones joined him, gathering wood. He stopped; his attention drawn to something else. "Banshees."

"What?"

"Banshees," he said again. "I just remembered."

"What the hell is a... whatever you said?"

"My father's estate in Ireland. He would take me with him when he had business there. Before..." Jones hesitated, and then said, "before I left. Banshees are spirits. Demons. Female spirits. The old people on the estate swore they could hear a banshee's wail before the death of a loved one. That's what I heard. A horrible wailing call."

"There ain't nothing female out here except at the Hog Farm, and even then, I ain't sure," he tore off a limb and threw it in a pile. "Anyway, quit talkin' like that. You're giving me the willies." He picked up the wood, balancing it in his arms.

Jones was about to speak when he heard shouting. It was Ashcroft, back at the camp. Then there was more shouting, Cheyenne. They dropped the wood and scrambled up the side of the ravine.

Chapter 27

Ashcroft spat at Comes-a-Pony. "Where'd you get those trousers? How many poor soldiers did you kill?"

Comes-a-Pony didn't understand the words, but she did the tone. She brought her rifle up.

Ashcroft reached for his pistol. "I don't care if you are a woman, I should kill you right here."

Porter grabbed his arm. Fool Dog picked up his lance. The other soldiers grabbed their carbines.

One Eye, confused by the commotion at first, drew his pistol from his beaded belt and tried to cock the hammer back. It was an old pistol; and the cylinder sometimes did not revolve, so One Eye had to twist it into position.

Walking Man saw soldiers appear over the edge of the ravine. Two of them had their pistols out, and two more reached for their carbines. "Stop!" Walking Man shouted in Cheyenne, as if the soldiers understood him and would follow his order. The white chief was shouting as well, and Porter, speaking American, was trying to be heard. Walking Man knew the scout was pleading with the soldiers but did not understand what he was saying.

The braves drew close to one another. Left Hand slid an arrow into his bow, and Eagle Head had managed to get his pistol out with his good arm. Fool Dog had his lance raised.

"That bitch is wearing soldier britches," Ashcroft shouted at Porter. "She killed some poor lad and stripped his body."

Porter tried to calm him. "Just settle down, Ashcroft. We'll get this sorted out."

"You taking her side? She killed a soldier. Ask her. Ask her how she got those britches."

Comes-a-Pony stood her ground, eyes on Ashcroft. She cocked her rifle.

"Everyone, lower your weapons!" Sweet ordered.

Ashcroft pushed Porter away and got his pistol out of the holster. Taliaferro yanked the pistol out of the soldier's grip and held it away from his body, barrel pointed toward the ground. The soldiers were in a line, facing the Cheyenne across a pile of firewood, everyone shouting.

"Put your guns down," Porter told Walking Man. "Tell your people to put their guns down."

"Let us kill them," One Eye said. "Look at them. Let us kill them and be done with this."

"Tell the soldiers to put their guns away," Walking Man said. "Tell them."

Porter said, "Lieutenant, you'd better do something, or we'll have a blood bath."

"Lower your weapons," Sweet ordered the men. He moved between them and the Cheyenne. He spoke calmly, and for a moment, Walking Man thought he had underestimated the young officer. "Everybody stay calm. Lower your weapons."

Taliaferro joined him, barking, "You heard the officer. I'll shoot the first soldier that disobeys."

Porter was in front of Walking Man. "Brother? Let us talk. Don't let it end like this."

"He is not your brother," Left Hand said. "You have black skin, but you are still a white man."

"Tell them to stay away from me," Comes-a-Pony said. "I will kill the first one that comes near me."

"Wait," Walking Man said to the braves. "Wait. Let us settle this. It will be dark soon. Let us settle this and prepare the camp."

"We ought to kill them now," Left Hand said, disgusted. "I should have stayed where I was."

Porter said something to the officer, and Walking Man saw the white chief talk to his men. He was trying to soothe them. He spoke slowly, walking back and forth. Some of the soldiers lowered their guns, and the ones who didn't looked as if they were uncertain of what to do.

"Walking Man," Porter said. "Help me with this. They are not the enemy. The enemy is out there. You know this. We have to make ready. Tell your men."

Walking Man walked between the braves and the soldiers, like the white chief did, talking calmly, trying to reason with them. "Brothers. It will be dark soon. Let us prepare. We cannot fight the white soldiers and the thing, too. Put down your weapons, and I will talk to the white chief."

"I did nothing," Comes-a-Pony said. "This soldier spat at me. He wants to fight me. I should kill him."

"No," Walking Man continued. "They are our enemies, that is true. They will always be our enemies. We will fight them someday. But not now. Now we have to make war with them, not against them. Remember our people. If this thing gets away, it will kill them. I think the white chief has a good heart. I was afraid at first, but now I think differently."

"What the hell is this?" Mendelson said. "Look at that bitch. She killed a soldier and then stripped his body. They ain't human. What are we waiting for?"

"Yeah, and we did the same thing to her people," Porter said. "So, it goes both ways."

"I gave an order," Sweet said. "Sergeant, if the men don't lower their weapons, disarm them."

"Are you crazy?" Smallwood snapped at Sweet. "Look at those bastards. They're just waiting for a chance to kill us. I ain't giving up my gun just to be butchered by those savages."

"This ain't no good," Ashcroft said. "Let's run them off and take our chances."

"I swear to God that the next one of you who says anything is gonna get my boot up your ass," Taliaferro said. "Now, lower your guns and take your finger off the trigger. And I don't mean maybe."

Ashcroft stepped back, as Smallwood lowered his carbine. The others followed, still watching the Cheyenne.

Walking Man said to Comes-a-Pony, "Please. We cannot do this. You know it."

"I will not be insulted," Comes-a-Pony said. "No man spits at me. If he does it again, I will kill him." For an instant, betrayal filled her eyes. "Why do you let them do this?"

Walking Man gently turned her rifle away from the soldier. "This is not the fight we need. Not now." He spoke to the others. "If we fight them, we lose. That thing will get away and kill our people. Brothers? Please?"

One Eye slid his pistol back into the belt. "I do not think it would fire anyway."

Fool Dog turned his lance upside down and drove it into the earth. Eagle Head lowered his pistol and slumped to the ground. Left Hand rushed to his friend.

"What has happened to you?" Comes-a-Pony asked Walking Man. "Have you lost your way? You used to be a warrior. Now," she shook her head in disappointment. "I do not know what you are."

"I am Walking Man of the Kit Fox, and you are Comes-a-Pony. What has happened in the past does not change who we are. I ask you now for patience. Will you let me talk with the white soldier chief to settle this?"

Then the demon came.

Chapter 28

It streaked out of the ravine, a white blur, and grabbed Jones. The soldier screamed as it carried him over the edge of the ravine, disappearing into the dwindling light.

The camp exploded in gunfire. A storm filled the air with the heavy boom of army carbines and the sharp crack of civilian rifles. Muzzle flares trapped the men in flashes, stopping them in motion, a tableau of frozen movement. Blue gun smoke swirled around the men.

Sweet cried, "Light the fires! Light the fires!"

The soldiers shouted at one another, and then at the darkness, and then in frustration over the attack.

"Where is it?" the sergeant cried.

Mendelson called back, pointing, "Over there. Right there."

Jones's body sailed through the air, landing next to Smallwood. The men fired wildly into the gloom.

"For God's sake men," Sweet ordered. "Wait until you see something."

Taliaferro threw a lit match into the center fire and then raced to the other piles, striking a match, and holding it under a dry sagebrush, making sure it caught the flame before running to the next. The light flooded the area, coating the men. Wood crackled as the flames consumed it. Wind batted the fires, throwing wild shadows all about the camp, bathing the soldiers and braves in a flickering light.

Walking Man positioned the Cheyenne warriors. Eagle Head tried to crawl next to the central fire but could not, and Left Hand dragged him close to the flames. Red Horse picked up the discarded pistol and stood next to the other braves.

"What do we do?" Ashcroft shouted. "What do we do?"

"Get your backs to the fire," Porter ordered. "Form a perimeter."

"What was that?" Stewart said. "What the hell was that?"

Walking Man drew close to Porter and said, "He will wait and then come. He threw the soldier's body back to frighten us. He feeds on our fear."

"Lieutenant?" Taliaferro said. "Keep the men spaced out."

Wagner, trying to slip a cartridge into his carbine said, "Gott im Himmel." He dropped the cartridge and reached for his cartridge belt, his hands shaking so much his fingers could not grasp the cartridge. He dropped it and three more.

Stewart stood next to Collier. They both peered into the darkness. "Did you see it?" he said.

Collier whispered, "For God's Sake, Stewart. What the hell was it?"

A low moan floated over them. The soldiers swung toward the direction of the sound. Nobody spoke. No one moved. The fire fully engulfed the wood.

"How is Jones?" Sweet asked Taliaferro.

"He don't have a face. He's dead."

"Porter?" Sweet said. "Porter? Tell us what to do."

"When will it attack again?" the scout said to Walking Man.

"It will stay out there and howl until it drives the white soldiers mad, and then it will come."

"I didn't see it," Mendelson said. He glanced at Jones's body, its blood inching across the ground. "I didn't see it."

The braves knelt, readying themselves. Weapons raised, alert.

"It will come from another direction," Walking Man told Porter.

The howling increased, a terrible trembling cry that filled the camp. The soldiers pulled back, bunching up for protection, terrified.

"Spread out," Taliaferro ordered. He thumbed the hammer back on his carbine. "Keep your eyes peeled. Don't shoot until you see something to shoot at." He moved to Wagner and said, "You pick up every one of them goddamned cartridges and clean them off before you put 'em in your belt. They go in your weapon, not the ground."

The creature's wail surrounded the men. Walking Man watched the soldiers. They will break, he thought. They will throw away their guns and run.

Mendelson seated his carbine on his shoulder and fired into the night. He lowered the trapdoor on his Springfield and quickly slid another cartridge into the breech.

"Cease fire," Sweet ordered. "Wait until you see something."

Walking Man said to Porter, "What will the soldiers do? They are too afraid to fight. Maybe they will run like buffalo."

"They ain't the only ones afraid," Porter said. "I can think of a hundred places I'd rather be than here."

"I would like to go home again," Walking Man said. "I would like to see my family."

"Maybe we'll get out of this mess."

"I do not think we will. I think I will die far from home."

"If we do," Porter said. "I'd like to take that bastard with me."

"Mr. Porter?" Sweet said. "Ask him how we can kill it."

"He wants to know how to kill it," Porter said to Walking Man.

"Maybe," Walking Man said, watching the flames lick at the cottonwood limbs. "Maybe we can use fire. It fears fire. There is a reason for that, I think."

Porter told Sweet what Walking Man said, and the lieutenant called out to Taliaferro. "Sergeant? Find a way to make torches. If that thing gets close enough, maybe we can set it on fire."

Taliaferro called, "Ashcroft? Stewart?" Distant screams filled the night.

"The horses!" Collier shouted. "That thing is killing the horses." Collier started toward the cries.

"No!" Sweet ordered. "It's trying to draw us out. Stay here." He walked calmly among the soldiers. "Steady. Keep your distance. Don't leave the circle."

"Get some wood," Taliaferro said to the two soldiers.

"Be quick about it, Sergeant," Sweet said. "We don't have much time."

Taliaferro ripped off his coat and began tearing strips of cloth. Ashcroft and Stewart pulled sticks from the piles of wood. Stewart stopped, stunned by the cries of the slaughtered horses.

"Stewart! Goddamn it, get to work," Taliaferro ordered. *The liquor. Mendelson's liquor.* The sergeant pulled the flask from the coat pocket, wrapped the cloth around the sticks, and hurriedly soaked the bundle in liquor. He did four and handed them to the men. "When that thing comes back, light them torches and stick 'em up its ass." He made a fifth torch for himself; but as he poured the liquor out of the flask, the stream slowed to a few drops and then stopped. He threw the flask down in disgust. "Okay, lieutenant."

The wailing began again, louder, and closer.

"It's coming," Mendelson said. "Oh, God, it's coming."

"Light the torches," Sweet said. He ordered the soldiers, "Set it on fire. The rest of you, aim carefully. Make every shot count."

Walking Man, Fool Dog, One Eye, and Left Hand stood around Eagle Head. "Brothers," Walking Man said, "at least we will die together."

"There!" Porter shouted, pointing into the darkness. The night erupted in gunfire.

The beast jumped into the center of the fire ring, driving its claws into Wagner. The soldier screamed as the others fired at the creature. It roared in rage as Taliaferro rushed it from behind. The beast turned just as he jammed the torch into its back. It burst into flames as Ashcroft set fire to the creature from the front. The other soldiers kept loading their carbines, shooting at its head. Blood and tissue flew into the air as the fire covered its body.

Walking Man and Fool Dog ran to the creature, Fool Dog jamming his lance into the thing's chest. Walking Man ran behind it and slashed at the back of its leg with his knife. The thing dropped to one knee. Red Horse and One Eye fired their pistol, advancing on the creature. It grabbed Fool Dog and crushed his head, throwing the body at Red Horse and One Eye.

Comes-a-Pony knelt, brought her Sharps up and fired, reloading, and firing again, aiming at the white skull with the bloody mouth. Its head swung toward Comes-a-Pony, the beast's eyes locking on her. She fired again, the bullet plowing into the creature's mouth.

Porter took careful aim at the dark, soulless eyes. He fired, reloading. He saw the thing's left eye explode.

Stewart ran at it with his torch. The creature sank its teeth into Steward's upraised arm, severing the soldier's arm at the shoulder. Steward screamed and dropped to the ground as the flames engulfed the creature. It dropped Wagner's body as it batted at the fire, stumbling toward the ravine. Bullets ripped into its flesh.

"Kill it now!" Smallwood screamed as the thing fell back over the edge of the ravine, landing at the bottom. The fire consuming its body set dried sagebrush aflame as the soldiers on the edge of the ravine kept shooting into the thing. It tried to crawl away, but the whole ravine was engulfed in fire. One Eye and Red Horse fired at it until they were out of cartridges. They picked up large stones, and heaved them at the thing, trying to smash its skull.

Comes-a-Pony took position on the edge of the ravine, loading and firing, watching each round striking the thing's body. She was not afraid. She saw only the creature and the impact of the heavy bullets. Nothing else existed.

Its arms reached out as it tried to drag itself away from danger; but soon it could not move, and it lay still as the flames covered it. The stench of burning flesh rose and swallowed the men at the edge of the ravine. Two of the soldiers retched, throwing up. Sweet covered his mouth and nose with his handkerchief.

"Cease firing," he ordered. "Cease firing."

The only sound was the crackle of burning sagebrush and the creature's body sizzling as the flames fed on it.

The men stood silently, watching their enemy being consumed. Mendelson fell to the ground, covering his head, sobbing.

The Cheyenne gathered. "Is it dead?" One Eye asked. "Is it truly dead?"

Left Hand sought out his sister. "Are you injured?"

"No," she replied.

"You have blood on your arm."

She looked down. Blood covered her forearm and hand. She wiped it on her trousers. "It is not mine."

"We should let it burn," Red Horse said. "Let it burn until there is nothing left but ashes."

Sweet said, "Ashcroft, you and Jones," then he remembered. "You and Collier stay here and keep an eye on that. If it moves, shoot it until it doesn't. Someone will relieve you shortly. Sergeant Taliaferro? See to the men, if you will. Mr. Porter? Mr. Porter?"

"Here, lieutenant," the scout said. Walking Man was with him, his buckskin shirt ripped across the chest.

"Are you injured?" Sweet said to Walking Man. Porter translated, and the Cheyenne glanced down at his shirt. He shook his head. "No." Sweet moved close to Porter and said in a low voice, "Is it really dead?"

Porter stared at the creature. It continued to burn. "Well, it's cooked anyway. I don't think it'll get up and run off."

Mendelson regained his feet, and the men returned to the camp.

Ashcroft didn't move and asked in a whisper, "What was that thing?"

Taliaferro dug a jammed cartridge out of his carbine with a knife. "You have your orders."

"Did you know about this?" the soldier asked. "Is that why them Indians threw in with us?"

"Hell, Ashcroft, I don't know a damned thing." Taliaferro lost his patience. "Get your ass over there and stand your post."

Collier joined him. "How come nobody told us? How come you let that thing get the jump on us?"

"I didn't tell Sergeant Taliaferro," Sweet said. "Porter told me."

"How come you didn't say nothing?" Mendelson asked. "You could have said something. Give us some kind of warning or something."

"Would you have believed me?" Sweet replied. He looked at the men. "Would any of you have believed me? I didn't myself until I saw it." To Ashcroft and

Collier, he said, "I gave you an order." The two men hesitated but then moved to the ravine edge.

Taliaferro knelt next to Stewart's body. "He's dead. Arm's torn clean off." He rose and said to Sweet, "Wagner and Jones, too. Mandelson, you, and Smallwood take them bodies off a bit."

"Gather what ammunition you can from the dead," Sweet said. "Get their canteens as well." He motioned for Porter to join him. "I think it best if the Cheyenne go on their way."

The scout looked at Walking Man, who was talking to the warriors. "Yeah, I believe you're right. They ain't in no shape to move now, but I figure at first light. If you agree."

"I suppose that can't be helped. I suggest they camp some distance from us. For the men's benefit."

"I know this ain't exactly playing according to Hoyle, but maybe giving them a couple of weapons and a handful of cartridges."

"Arm them?"

"They've got a long way to go. Besides, they've been beat up pretty bad. Anyway, they pitched into the fight."

"Sergeant Taliaferro, distribute two carbines to the Indians, and twenty-four rounds of ammunition. Mr. Porter? Tell them we're going to give them weapons so they can make their way home. I suppose it's the honorable thing to do."

Mendelson was reaching for Jones when he stopped. "Honorable? To give them guns?" he said. "Lieutenant, I don't think…"

"Shut up, Mendelson. Nobody asked you," Taliaferro said. "They earned it."

"Yeah, but we killed that thing already," Mendelson argued. "All that means is we're gonna get shot with our own guns."

"They're far from home, Mendelson. They helped us kill that thing," Sweet said. "It's only right. Mr. Porter? Tell them we will arm them for their journey home."

The scout nodded and translated the lieutenant's message, adding to the soldiers. "All these folks want to do is get out of here. I think their fighting days are over for a while."

"Jesus Christ, Lieutenant…" Smallwood began.

"Shut up. Strip the dead of anything useful," the sergeant said, "and put them out there."

The soldiers picked up the bodies of their dead and placed them outside of the ring of fire. They handled the torn bodies gingerly, not out of respect, but because of the blood and tissue leaking from the dead.

"Smallwood," Sweet said. "When it gets light, I want you to go out and recover what you can from the horses. Take another man with you." He saw the Cheyenne kneeling close to Fool Dog's body. "What are they doing?" he asked Porter.

"Burial ceremony. They didn't get a chance to tend to the others, so they're giving their man a good sendoff. As good as they can under the circumstances. They want to make certain he gets on the path to the Milky Way."

"Milky Way?"

"Yeah. It's their version of Heaven." He looked at Sweet. "You did all right, Lieutenant. That was a hell of a fight, but you did all right."

"I don't know how," Sweet said. He watched the Cheyenne. "Funny, I never thought they believed in things like Heaven and Hell."

"Oh, they've got pretty strong beliefs in the afterlife, angels and demons, and such." He smiled wryly. "I guess we got introduced to the demon part of what they believe. Anyway, they ain't so far from us in some things."

"I was scared," Sweet revealed to Porter, keeping his voice low.

"If you weren't, Lieutenant," Porter replied. "You ain't human."

"Were you, I mean did you…"

"Was I skeert?" Porter said. "I'm real pleased I didn't shit my pants."

Walking Man said to the others, "We have no way to prepare Fool Dog for his journey, but I think *Maheo* will see him along the way." Red Horse went back to Eagle Head and sat by him. The wounded brave did not move, his breathing was shallow. Red Dog placed his hand on Eagle Head's broken arm, hoping somehow to comfort the warrior.

"It is done, then," Left Hand said. "We have killed the thing, and now we can go home."

"How will we tell others of this time?" One Eye said. "They will not believe us."

"They will believe us," Comes-a-Pony said. "They will believe it because Many Horses is dead. Bull Bear is dead. Wooden Leg, Stone Forehead, Old Turtle, and the Shield Warriors and Dog Soldiers are dead. They will see it in our eyes and believe it." They finished what they could of Fool Dog's ritual, and then they lay down to sleep. Walking Man remained awake, watching the soldiers on guard as they were relieved.

Comes-a-Pony sat down next to Walking Man. "I was wrong to say to you what I did. When I asked why you had been chosen for a vision and the others had not."

"It does not matter," he replied.

"I was still angry at you. From before," she said. She was talking about the time on the Greasy Grass when she told him about her feelings for him. "You were right about the soldiers. They did not run away. They did not hold up their guns in surrender."

He watched the soldiers carry the dead. "I wonder why the other white soldiers do not gather round the dead and send their spirits off to the other land. Maybe Whites do not believe in such things."

"Someone told me once," Comes-a-Pony said, "about a white medicine man. He had a face like a fox with hair coming out of his ears. It was at a council with the whites. He talked loudly and the white soldier chiefs and men in black coats kept their heads down. It was a long time while everyone waited for him to sit down so the Cheyenne and white soldier chiefs and men in black coats could talk. The person who told me this said that the white medicine man was more interested in being seen to talk, than what he said."

Walking Man said, "I do not think it is necessary to shout at *Maheo*. He would listen even if a man just talked to him." They remained silent until he said, "I know you have been angry with me for some time. Before," he also spoke of the Greasy Grass when the sky was clear of clouds, and they were alone. The sun warmed them as the river bubbled around the shallows and raced down the valley. They heard the gleeful shouts of pony boys in the distance, running and playing, and a hawk kept them company, circling overhead, crying as it searched for prairie mice. "I did not know how to tell you what I felt."

Comes-a-Pony replied in a flash of anger. "You spoke well enough." It was a moment before she had calmed and said, "If I could call my words back, I would."

"I have always known you to speak from the heart," he said. "I do not. Something inside of me wants me to consider every word before I speak. It is my manner. That time, by the river, you went away because I hurt you. I did not mean to. I thought afterward about what I should have said. By then it was too late."

"You think too much," she agreed. "If you said what you felt, what was in your heart rather than in your mind, it would not be such a bad thing."

"When we return home," he said, "maybe we can go off by ourselves and talk."

"Only if you leave your reason behind."

He laughed, looking into the sky. "Little Raven wanted to see the stars again. I think if he had, he would not have killed himself. I think if he saw them, it would have given him hope."

"That is not such a bad thing to look for," Comes-a-Pony said.

The soldiers came back from carrying the bodies and slumped near the fire. Mendelson laid his carbine across his lap. "We should have gone on," he said to Smallwood. "We could have been far away from this, if it hadn't been for that nigger."

Porter's head snapped up. He jumped to his feet and rushed Mendelson, knocking the soldier to the ground, straddling his chest. He had his pistol out and jammed it into the soldier's forehead. Blood welled around the muzzle.

"Say it again," Porter said. "Call me a nigger again, you son-of-a-bitch."

"Mr. Porter," Sweet said softly. "Mr. Porter?"

Mendelson's face was twisted in fear, his wide eyes staring at Porter.

"Say it!" Porter ordered. "Call me that again."

Sweet laid his hand on Porter's shoulder. "Let him go. Let's get some sleep."

Porter smiled grimly, thumbed the hammer back, and the cylinder revolved with a click. "You came real close, Mendelson. Real close."

"Please?" Mendelson said. "I didn't mean nothing."

Porter rose, but his eyes never left the soldier. "I might just kill you later on." He walked away to the other side of the fire, holstered his pistol, and sat down.

"Maybe they will kill each other, and we can be done with them," Comes-a-Pony said to Walking Man.

Walking Man said, "When the light comes, we will go on our own. We should try to sleep." Comes-a-Pony nodded and went off. He lay down, using his arm to rest his head on. They had been given three blankets from the old soldier chief, so Walking Man handed them out. He knew it would be a cold night. There were enough so that he had one as well.

He realized he had fallen asleep and then woke up to hear the white officer talking to the soldiers on guard. They went to their bedrolls, and others would take their place. Red Horse slept next to Eagle Head. One Eye and Left Hand were asleep. Walking Man sat up, but his fatigue was so great, he knew he had to sleep. The faint stench of the burning creature floated over them, a reminder of what had happened, what they had faced. He lay down, folding his arm under his head and burying his nose in the blanket. His mind went back to the fight. He saw the thing as it rose out of the night, and he heard the screams of the wounded men. He told himself that to remember this time was no good, so his mind went to the time on the Greasy Grass when he sat next to Comes-a-Pony. He saw her smile and the way she tugged at tuffs of grass as she spoke. Her hair was pulled back into a ponytail, and she wore a red shirt that she had bought. The young girl that shared her tipi had woven tiny beads into the shape of an elk on the shoulder and tied white ribbons through the buttonholes. The ends of the ribbons danced in the wind as she spoke. What she had revealed to him was important to her, and he should have considered it a gift. But his words in return were clumsy, and he remembered her face as it turned to stone. She left him on the edge of the river. From that time, she had ignored him; but he felt her rage. Soon images began to bleed together in his mind; weariness wrapped its arms around him, and he closed his eyes and slept.

Comes-a-Pony lay down next to her brother. He rested his head in his hand and said, "I saw what you did."

"Go to sleep."

"I saw you talking with Walking Man. That is a good thing."

"Go to sleep so I can go to sleep."

He chuckled and said, "That puppy was worthless."

"So?"

"It had three legs and could not run."

"It ran well enough."

He rolled over on his back. "Everywhere I went, people would ask me, 'Why does your sister care so much for that dog? She should kill it and make a fine stew.' And I would tell them, 'Because her heart is so big, there is room even for a puppy with three legs.'"

"You are foolish, brother," she said, turning away from him. He spread out their blanket so that she was covered as well.

Chapter 29

He was on the Greasy Grass again, and the sun shone on Comes-a-Pony. Her shadow lay behind her as she spoke.

The creature.

He sat up, his heart thumping wildly. What was it? Something had awakened him. Thoughts flooded his mind. He had been dreaming about the creature. No. There had been no dream. There had been nothing. Still, something had ahold of him. Something was talking to him. Bits of thought, flashes that filled his eyes like lightning. He stood, forcing himself to think. Black Antelope was dead. The others were dead. He tried to separate the thoughts so he could understand. He peeled them away, searching for something. Searching for what had awakened him.

"We should all be dead," he whispered to himself.

He saw a soldier on guard watching him. The white man's carbine rose.

Walking Man raised his hands to his chest, gesturing to himself and then to Porter, who was asleep on the other side of the fire. He did it three times until the soldier motioned for him to move. He did so, carefully. The soldier's eyes followed him. Someone snored. Two soldiers talked softly. He knelt next to Porter and touched his arm.

Porter started awake, pistol in his hand, eyes wide. When he realized who it was, he lowered the weapon. "Jesus, you scared me to death. What is it?"

Walking Man forced himself to speak calmly. "When you found the others," it hurt to say their names, so he did not speak them. "When you found them. Where was it?"

Porter rubbed his face, trying to clear his mind. "Black Antelope? Where? Thirty-five, maybe forty miles to the northwest. Why?"

"What did he say about the thing that killed them?"

Porter's voice was drawn tight with fatigue. "I told you everything." Then he said, "What's on your mind?"

"You said," Walking man held out his arms as wide as he could, measuring a distance. "That it walked this far."

"Yeah. The stride? Seven feet, maybe a little more."

"It walked on two legs. Like that thing tonight?"

"Yeah. That's what the tracks told me. Two legs."

"We fought that thing and killed it," Walking Man said. "Fool Dog was killed and three white soldiers. But we killed it."

"Yeah. What's this all about?" Porter was about to say *I don't follow you*, but he could not think of how to say it in Cheyenne, so he said, "I do not understand you. It killed some of us, and we killed it. I told you everything I know about Black Antelope and the others."

"Yes," Walking Man said. "You say you saw their dead ponies as well."

The vision spoke to him. *You cannot kill it alone. They killed it with the help of the white soldiers. The Tsis Tsis' Tas were not alone.*

"Yeah, they were scattered all over hell's half-acre."

"They were riding when it attacked. They could move about quickly. Nine warriors on ponies did not kill it, but we did tonight. It killed the soldiers' horses because they were hobbled, so they could not run off." He had to be sure of his words. He had to set each idea as if it were a stone placed firmly on the earth.

Porter listened.

"A thing that walks that far? How tall would it be?"

Porter drew his knees up to his chest and calculated. "If you figure a man's stride at about three feet, that thing was maybe twelve or fifteen feet tall." He forgot himself and said in American, "You want to go measure that thing or something. Go right ahead, but I think I'll stay right here." The scout stared at the ravine where the body of the creature lay. An idea came to him. "It ain't that big," he said, almost in a whisper. He shook the idea out of his head. "Okay, so I was wrong. Maybe I didn't figure it right. Hell, that's not the sort of thing you see every day. Go get some sleep." He pushed his hat over his eyes and lay down. "You've got a long way to go. Better rest up."

"I remember what was told to me," Walking Man said. He was uncertain how to say what he thought. He fell to reasoning. *Be careful with your words.* Black Antelope appeared in his mind. It could not be as he thought, but it could not be otherwise. The two ideas battled each other. *Put them aside. Say what came to you as you slept and what woke you up. You have reason as a tool.* He thought of his visions: the old man and the boy. "We have given you weapons and a plan," the boy had said.

"In my vision, the boy said, 'You cannot kill it alone.'"

"Yeah, so soldiers fought with you. We both killed it."

"That is what I decided. But suppose you were thinking of the words, in another way?"

"Walking Man, I'm just too damned tired to play games."

Walking Man said, "You cannot kill it alone. He meant by itself. He meant the single creature. That thing, alone." This was when his words faltered as he spoke them, as if they were hesitant to come out and be recognized for what they said. "I have thought this through, Porter." He wanted Porter to understand what troubled him. What frightened him. When he spoke, he regretted the words even though he knew them to be true. "I think, there is another."

"What?" Porter rose. "No, no. That ain't possible. It's dead and good riddance."

"Why did it not kill all of us tonight? Why did we defeat it when the others could not? We should have all been killed. Like the others. I think there is another. One that is bigger. One that could kill warriors as they rode their ponies. I do not want to think this, but I do."

"Jesus. Now you got me going," Porter looked away. The words came reluctantly. "You said that thing we killed tonight was behind you. To the southeast. That it killed Bull Bear. It was behind you."

"Yes. Maybe not so far behind. Red Horse saw what had been done."

"After it rubbed out Bull Bear. It followed Red Horse."

"Yes," Walking Man said. "I am certain it did. That is why it found us."

"The others, Black Antelope, and the others, were killed well in front of us. Northwest, closer to the mountains." He stopped, refusing to believe. "Listen, that don't make no sense. You saw how quick that thing moved. It covered ground in no time. It killed Bull Bear and then went out and killed Black Antelope and his men. Then it came after us. That's what I think." He was satisfied with his explanation.

"Before we had guns," Walking Man said. "When we had only lances and bows and arrows. We chased buffalo until they were so filled with fear, they could not see. We chased them to a cliff, where they fell and smashed out their brains on the ground below. We drove them to their death."

"That ain't got nothing to do with nothing," Porter said, but Walking Man saw confusion in the scout's eyes. "Wait a minute. I have got to think this thing through."

He rubbed his arm where the arrow had pierced his flesh. "I think rain is coming. It is cold, but not cold enough for snow. Maybe later." He waited for Porter to think out what he had heard.

"The thing tonight," Porter said. "You're saying, it was supposed to chase us? Drive us straight to another one?"

"That is what I think."

"But what? It got too close? It got too close, and we killed it?"

"I am not sure." Walking Man sat down next to Porter. "I do not know." He had no strength, and his mouth was so dry he could barely speak. He managed to say, "I hope that I am wrong, but I do not think that I am."

The scout's eyes were drawn to the darkness. "There's another one out there," Porter said in a whisper. "God Almighty."

"Yes."

The camp was silent, the men unaware. A soldier on guard caught Porter's attention. One of the sleeping Cheyenne moved, mumbled something, and then was quiet. Taliaferro walked about, woke the other soldiers, and Sweet stood, stiffly, looking into the sky. His greatcoat hung on his shoulders, enveloping him. Clouds to the east were bathed in a faint glow by a sun that itself was barely awake.

"Porter?" Walking Man said. "I do not know how to kill it. This other one. It is too big."

"God help us, I don't either," the scout said. "It's got to be a head again taller than that one in the ravine." He took off his hat. "Does anyone else know? Did you tell your men?"

"No. No one knows."

Porter rubbed his forehead. "Well, there ain't no other way. We've got to tell 'em. If that other one is out there, it'll be looking for us, we won't have to find it. And building a few fires ain't gonna help." He searched out Sweet and called, "Lieutenant?"

Sweet acknowledged him with a nod and came over to the two men. "What is it, Mr. Porter?"

"You'd better sit down," the scout said. "I got something to tell you."

Chapter 30

One of the soldiers coughed. A thin whisp of smoke still trailed from the thing in the ravine, and the lieutenant had told the men they no longer needed to guard it. The white soldiers heated what coffee they had left to them and crumbled hardtack into the steaming mix. Ashcroft and Smallwood returned leading two horses: Wagner's and Ashcroft's. They had hung saddlebags carrying extra cartridges over the saddles. Moon did not return, nor did Two Faces. Wagner's mount favored its right foreleg heavily. Taliaferro examined the mount, unloaded the provisions from its back, and blew out a sigh. He led it away from the camp. A moment later, there was a single gunshot; and the sergeant returned, sat down, and took a cup of coffee from Ashcroft.

Mendelson slipped his arms into his greatcoat and sat sullenly next to a fire. Taliaferro carefully sipped hot coffee from a tin cup. "I hate doing that," he whispered to himself.

"This can't be true," Sweet said in a strained voice. He looked around to make sure no one could hear him speak. "This is madness. It can't be real." He said to Porter, "Maybe you misunderstood him?" He meant Walking Man. "That's it, isn't it? Isn't it? Maybe he's confused." His eyes flew from Walking Man to Porter. He was trying to convince himself that what he said was true. "Talk to him again. Ask him."

The warrior watched the two white men talk and read the disbelief in the lieutenant's voice. He did not need to understand the white soldier's words. The boy's expression said everything.

Left Hand helped Eagle Head sit up and gave him the last of the dried buffalo from his parfleche bag. Red Horse took a drink from his water bottle and then offered it to Eagle Head. The brave took it gratefully. The sun was higher overhead but still hidden behind the clouds. Thunder rumbled faintly in the distance, catching Red Horse's attention.

"I want to see blue sky again," the Shield Warriors brave said. "I think if I saw it again, everything would be better."

"What are they talking about?" Eagle Head said, watching the black, white man, Walking Man, and the white soldier chief.

"The white soldier chief is trying to betray us," Left Hand said. "That is all the whites know. I think they will kill us rather than let us go."

"He is afraid," Red Horse said.

"What do I tell the men?" Sweet asked the other two, but he knew it was a question without an answer. He saw them looking at him. Looking to him.

"If this other thing is out there," Porter said. "It's stalking us right now."

Walking Man sat as the white men talked. Porter was calm, but his voice was edged with alarm. The white soldier chief struggled with his words.

"I don't want this to be true anymore than you do. I want out of this mess, Walking Man here," Porter spoke to the lieutenant. "He thinks it's a bigger animal." He said animal because he could not bring himself to say spirit. It was a terrible thing, an unknown thing. If he called it an animal, he might make it easier to kill. "It rubbed out those other Cheyenne pretty quick from what I saw. I don't know if torches will do it. Not this time."

The soldier chief's head fell to his chest, and it was a moment before he spoke. The words came as if it hurt him to speak them. "I don't understand any of this."

"Lieutenant, I don't have any answers for you. I saw it, just like you. I saw what it did. This is a shit detail if there ever was one. None of this makes any sense."

"If I were to tell this to anyone," the young lieutenant said, "they'd call me crazy."

"Yes," Porter said. "Yes, they would." Then he added, glancing toward the soldiers, "You have to tell the others. The boys ought to know."

"What do I say? What do I tell them?"

Porter's hand came up, as if reaching for an answer. "The truth, I guess. They've got to know what they're fighting. As crazy as it sounds. They did it once. They'll have to do it again, I suppose. Hell, Lieutenant, I don't know."

"Tell him," Walking Man said to Porter. "Tell him we will fight alongside the white soldiers."

"What did he say?" Sweet asked Porter.

"They'll stay and fight. They can't go home no matter what, or that thing will likely follow them."

"Jesus," Sweet said.

"Yeah. It sure wouldn't hurt to have Him on our side."

"I'll go tell them," Sweet said as he rose, when Porter stopped him.

"Wait up, Lieutenant. Let's get ourselves a plan. It might make them feel better if we have a plan." He turned to Walking Man and said, "We have to find a way to kill it. And good ground to fight it."

"Yes. We cannot stay in the open."

"Some place where it can't get at us so easily." Porter looked over his shoulder toward the Big Horns. "It's too far to the mountains, but there are some sandstone ridges out that way."

Sweet listened to the two talk, head down. This was too much.

"Lieutenant?" Porter said. "This ain't no time to lose hope. We ain't dead yet."

"It doesn't matter," Sweet said. He wiped his eyes. "We barely killed that thing. How are we supposed to fight another one?"

"We don't have a choice," Porter said. "It's fight or give up. There ain't nothing else to it." He spoke to Walking Man in Cheyenne. "We get up to them ridges, we might have a chance."

"I know where you mean. We call them Wolf's Teeth," Walking Man said. "Sometimes they have caves or form a…" he used his hands to explain, one flat over the other. "A cave but not so deep." He noticed Sweet. "This soldier chief has given up. His heart is no longer in the fight. He sees his own death, doesn't he?"

"He's afraid," Porter said, "and I'm right alongside him."

"We have to do more than fight," Walking Man said. "If we do not kill it…"

"Yeah," Porter said. "Yeah, I know." He said this in American, and he realized this he spoke in Cheyenne. "It'll go after your people. My people, too." Porter explained the idea to Sweet.

"An escarpment," Sweet said.

Porter said, "I don't know what that word means, but it's a good place to make a fight. Maybe the only place out here."

"I suppose we can find a spot with only one way for it to get at us." His courage began to return. "We can build a fire at the mouth of the overhang and fight it from there. It's a natural defensive position."

"That's true," Porter agreed. "But we can't make it a trap. We can't trap ourselves behind the fire. If we do, all that thing has to do is wait us out."

"Yes," Sweet said. "Yes, of course." He tugged his greatcoat closer to his neck. "I don't think it's ever going to get warm again." He managed a smile. "Caesar never encountered anything like this."

"No," Porter said. "We sure got one up on him. There are some Ponderosa pine up there on the ridges. Some limber pine. We might be able to find some dried out." He spoke to Walking Man, telling him what had been said. Walking Man nodded, understanding.

"There are few of us left. I do not know how we can kill it." The brave thought of his sister Little Feather and the buckskin shirt she was so proud of. The leather gleamed in the sun, and she had worked a long time adding a blue-beaded yolk trimmed with red beads in zigzags, like lightning when it struck the earth. The shirt was almost pure white. Her face was round, and her black hair unbound so that it fell over her shoulders. She was a child entering womanhood, just before the time that she looked for a young man who would become her husband.

If he lived, he thought, he would go home, and sit outside his tipi and watch children play, and the young braves flirt with maidens, while others raced their ponies across the prairie. There would be no soldiers, no whites of any kind, and he thought he would grow old and be content. He would go for walks and sit in a vast field of yellow and white wildflowers, under a bright blue sky. Overhead, clouds would chase one another playfully. He would look into the sky and feel the sun on his face.

But his thoughts melted away. Now was the time to fight. "We have the white soldiers' carbines and pistols. The pistols are no good unless we are close to the thing. I wish we had repeaters. But we do not, so the carbines will have to do."

"Hatchets and knives…" Porter said. "If…" He did not finish the thought. He spoke to Sweet.

"That's your plan?" Sweet asked. "That's how we kill it?"

Porter rose. "That's how we try to keep it from killing us. You might as well get everybody together. We'll tell them the bad news."

"Wait," Sweet said. "You said this one is larger."

Porter took a deep breath. "Twelve or fifteen feet tall, I reckon. Look, Lieutenant. It don't matter. It's a fight no matter the size."

Walking Man told Red Horse, Left Hand, and Eagle Head to come to council with the soldiers. They were reluctant but then gathered, a safe distance from the soldiers, watching them warily.

"Sergeant?" Sweet said. "Have the men come in."

Mendelson, Collier, Smallwood, and Ashcroft stood around Taliaferro, waiting on orders. They carried their carbines loosely, watching the Cheyenne as if the fight the night before had never happened.

Now they were enemies again. If not enemies, then at least someone they did not trust.

"Listen carefully," Sweet began. "I want you to understand what we're up against."

Walking Man saw the whites listen. Their tanned faces turned pale. They looked at one another without saying a word. They were men who did not want to believe what they were being told. Porter turned to Walking Man when the officer was done talking to the soldiers. He translated what the white soldier chief said.

Red Horse began to talk when Eagle Head put a hand on his arm to silence him. Now was the time to listen. Then they could talk.

"I don't understand this," Smallwood said to Sweet. Then to the others, he said, "Didn't we kill that thing?"

"There's another one," Taliaferro said. His voice was flat as he looked at the ground. He caught the lieutenant's attention. "Isn't that what you're saying, sir? There's another one out there?"

"Yes, Sergeant."

"Oh, my God," Mendelson said.

Ashcroft said, "No. This ain't right. How the hell could there be two of those things? What the hell is it? Can someone tell me that?" His voice grew louder.

"What the hell did we kill last night? I don't even know what it was."

"Look at them," Left Hand said. "They are like frightened rabbits."

"They fought well enough," Comes-a-Pony said.

"Still, you do not trust them, do you, Little Sister?"

"No," she said. "But I have no choice. If we want to live, we have to fight alongside them."

"Yes," Walking Man said. "They are men, and they are afraid. This thing is like nothing they have seen." He spoke to Left Hand. "We have not seen such a thing before, so we are alike."

Left Hand said, "I say we go away from them. Let them fight this other thing. I say we go home and never speak of it again. If we do not speak of it, it cannot be."

"I understand how you feel," Walking Man said. "No man should ever fight something like this."

Red Horse spoke to Left Hand. "Did you not listen before? If we go home, it will kill us along the way or follow us home and kill our people."

Taliaferro said to Sweet, "If there's another one, maybe there's more. Maybe there's a whole herd of those bastards out there. Couldn't that be, Lieutenant? I mean, sure, we killed one of them but maybe there's five, or ten more."

Porter answered before Sweet had a chance to talk. "No. It stands to reason there's just them two. That little one we killed was trying to drive us to the bigger one. Kinda like what Indians do to buffalo. I only saw sign for one that killed them other Cheyenne. One's plenty."

"That's fine," Mendelson said. "That's just fine. We lost those men trying to kill that thing, and now you tell us we have to do it again. Why don't we just kill ourselves and be done with it?" He turned on the Cheyenne. "All because of those bastards. They led us into this. Let them fight it. Look at'em! They did this."

"Shut up, Mendelson," Taliaferro said.

"Could we," Smallwood offered slowly. "Could we just run from it? Get some place safe?"

"Yeah," Mendelson said. "If we get back to the column, that thing'll have to fight a thousand men." He brightened, filled with hope. "Look at those odds! That'll fix that thing. Let's ride back to the column."

Ashcroft said, "That won't work, will it, Lieutenant?"

Mendelson wasn't convinced. "Yeah, but, it's a thousand men."

"We're closer to Gibbons' command than we are our own," Sweet said. "And we have no idea where he is. It'll catch us in the open."

"We'll be dead before we reach either one," Taliaferro said to Mendelson. "Porter? Are you sure? Maybe it's just the one. It killed them Cheyenne and came for us."

Porter shook his head. "I don't think so. Maybe I'm wrong. Maybe Walking Man is wrong, and we're getting riled up for nothing. Maybe we just head for the sandstone and hunker down there and nothing happens. I wish to God that was the case, but…"

"There you go," Taliaferro said. "You said it yourself. You could be wrong."

"I wish to hell I was," Porter said. "I wish this was some sort of dream. I'd give up drinkin' and go to church every Sunday if it was. But it ain't."

"Sergeant Taliaferro," Sweet said. "Account for the ammunition and weapons. Make sure every man carries sixty cartridges of carbine ammunition and twenty-five for their pistols. Give the Cheyenne the same. Everyone walks. We use the horse as a pack animal. You don't have any more liquor, do you?"

"No, sir. I used it up last night." The sergeant glanced at Mendelson. "Well?"

"You got it all."

Sweet rubbed his forehead in thought. "Save your matches. No one smokes. Mr. Porter? How close is the nearest escarpment?"

"Ten," Porter said. "Twenty miles, maybe. If we set out now, we can reach them well before dark. We won't have time to stop for anything. We've got to get there and get everything ready."

"Very well. Tell the Cheyenne we'll move out in thirty minutes."

"All right," Taliaferro said. "You men have your orders. Let's get cracking."

"Mr. Porter?" Sweet called the scout to one side. "When you talk to them, see if they have any ideas how we can kill this one. It'll take more than torches. Right now? Right now, I just don't know how to proceed."

Porter nodded and was just about to walk back to the Cheyenne when Sweet stopped him. "Do you have any of that tobacco left? My mouth is as dry as dust."

"Sure," Porter smiled. He pulled the plug from his coat pocket and handed it to Sweet. The officer bit off a piece. "You'd better be careful, Lieutenant," Porter said. "You might pick up some bad habits."

Sweet examined the plug of tobacco. "My mother didn't want me to go to West Point. She was sure I'd get killed. I think she was just as afraid that I'd fall into bad company."

"Maybe you have," Porter said. "I ain't much more than house broke."

Sweet replied, remembering, "That's the way she talked. Bad company, she said." He handed the plug back to Porter. "Maybe she was right. I may die out here."

Porter scanned the prairie and said, as if seeing the country for the first time, "I've been out here a lot of years. I must have rode ten-thousand miles, and still, I ain't never seen the end of it. It'll kill you, make no mistake about it. But it's got a kind of…" he found the word. "Majesty. Funny ain't it? Like, I just realized it. A sky bigger than all creation, and mountains bigger than…well, bigger than anything I ever seen. Back east, everything is on top of itself, land, and people. A fella can't see more than two miles in a straight line. Out here, there ain't no limit to what a man can see." He decided. "Yep, majesty."

"You sound like a poet, Mr. Porter," Sweet said.

"I've been called a lot of things, Lieutenant. Poet ain't one of them. I was just ruminating on our situation."

They dispersed the weapons and ammunition, wrapped matches in kerchiefs and put them safely in their pockets, and started out. The soldiers, leading Victoria, were strung out in single file; the Cheyenne followed closely, more closely than they had done before, behind them, walking in pairs.

They had gone a mile or two when Sweet thought to ask Porter, "We could use some water. Do you know of any streams or springs around here?

"No," Porter said. "Game's all gone, and water has dried up. Sounds like the plagues of Egypt, don't it?"

"Maybe that thing is the devil," Sweet ventured. "I should have spent more time reading the Bible. Didn't Jesus cast the devil down into Hell?"

"Somebody did but I ain't sure who it was. I guess it's up to us now," Porter said.

Chapter 31

"Jones knew he was going to die," Smallwood said to Ashcroft as they walked. The men were spread out, heads down, one step in front of the other, feet barely leaving the ground. Clouds of dust drifted up around their ankles, settling on their trousers. Their carbines hung on their leather strap over their shoulder, pistols on their hips. Besides their ammunition on their ammunition belts, and stuffed in their pockets, blankets, and canteens, they carried little else.

"What?"

"Jones gave me a letter to send to his pa. He knew he was going to die."

"He won't be the only one," Ashcroft said. He was leading a reluctant Victoria. She pulled against the reins, fighting him. "One goddamned horse that ain't been killed, and this bitch has to be the one. I hope she's the first one to get carved up."

Left Hand sat down, pulling off his torn moccasins. He dug another pair out of his shirt and slipped them on, throwing the old ones away. Red Horse extended his hand and helped the brave to his feet.

"I would rather ride," Left Hand said. "Walking is for old men and women."

Collier, beside Mendelson, started humming softly.

"Why don't you save your breath?" Mendelson said.

"What's that song Old Martin used to sing?"

"How the hell do I know, I ain't no tunesmith."

"All the time. He used to sing it in the barracks, all the time."

Sweet turned around, walking backwards as he looked over the men following him. He turned around. "We're not making good time, Mr. Porter," he said. "I don't believe the men have much more left in them."

"Can't be helped. We gotta push on."

"How are the Cheyenne holding up?"

"Good as can be expected, I suppose."

"I don't believe we've gone more than four or five miles." The lieutenant pulled his pocket watch from his jacket pocket. Nearly two hours. "Maybe the men could take turns riding the horse?"

"Won't do us much use, Lieutenant," Porter said. "They can't go any faster than we can walk, or they'll run off and leave us."

Walking Man threw his hand on Eagle Head's shoulder. The brave managed a smile. He carried a soldier's pistol; Walking Man carried a soldier's carbine. "How is your arm, brother?"

He held up the pistol with his good arm. "I can still shoot."

"I am pleased to hear that," Walking Man said. "We are going to need you in this fight."

"I think," Eagle Head said. "I think we will fight this thing three or four times before we kill it."

Walking Man turned away so his friend could not see his face. They did not have enough men to fight it three or four times. If they did not kill it right away, it would kill them, and then it would go to their camp and kill everyone else.

"Annie Laurie," Collier remembered suddenly. "I swear Old Martin used to sing that about ten times a day."

"Don't you start," Mendelson said. "I ain't in the mood."

Collier began softly, finding his way through the lyrics. "Her brow is like…like the straw drift, her neck is like a swan, her face it is the fairest…her face it is the fairest, that the sun ever shone on."

"I ain't seen the sun in a week," Mendelson said. "Ain't no use to sing about it."

"Twas there that Annie Laurie, gave me her promise true," Collier sang softly. "I believe that was the prettiest song I ever heard."

"Old Martin couldn't sing worth a shit."

"Yeah, but he loved that song." He began singing again, his voice low and wistful, like a man remembering better times. "Where early falls the dew, Twas there that Annie Laurie, gave her promise true. Twas there that Annie Laurie, gave me her promise true." He kept singing, the words floating over the men.

"Lieutenant?" Porter said. "Give me your glasses, will you?"

The binoculars were strung over Sweet's head and shoulder. He lifted them off and handed them to Porter. "See something, Mr. Porter?"

The scout stopped, looking toward the east, and settled the binoculars against his eyes. "Don't know for certain. Thought I did, but my eyes must be playing tricks on me." He swept the prairie. "Never needed these things before. I guess I'm just tired or getting old," he said to Sweet, lowering the binoculars. "Considering how things worked out, I wouldn't mind getting old." He peered through the binoculars again. He took them down and rubbed his eyes. "Here," he handed them back to Sweet. "See if you can see anything."

Sweet pointed. "Out there?" Porter nodded. Sweet pulled out his handkerchief and cleaned his glasses. Then he looked into the binoculars, adjusting the magnification until the horizon came into focus. The image was still blurred. He dropped the binoculars and rubbed his eyes, blinking several times. He tried again, willing his eye to focus. He saw movement. His grip tightened on the binoculars, and he forced himself to hold it steady. "Mr. Porter?" he said, his voice quavering. "Mr. Porter, I see something."

Porter jerked the binoculars from the lieutenant's hands, but they were still hung around the officer's neck. Sweet pulled the strap over his head and let it fall, as Porter stared through the binoculars. "I don't see a goddamned thing," he said in disgust. "What did you see?" he asked Sweet.

"Just something," Sweet said, "moving. Something moving along a ridge."

"What did it look like?" Porter demanded. "Tell me exactly what you saw."

Sweet struggled to explain. "Just movement. I couldn't tell what it was. All I saw was something moving."

"All right," Porter said. He smiled to ease Sweet's alarm. "I'm glad you saw it." He handed the binoculars back to Sweet. "Sometimes a fella's eyes will play tricks on him out here. He kept his voice calm. "How far away would you say it was?"

Sweet said, "I guess two or three miles."

"Okay," Porter said. "Why don't you speed the men up a bit, just being on the safe side. I'll tell Walking Man what's going on."

Sweet's face collapsed in fear. "Was that it? Did you see it out there?"

"I didn't see nothing," Porter said. "But won't do no harm if we quickened our pace."

"Yes," Sweet said. He looked around for Taliaferro, and finding him, said, "Sergeant? Double time, please."

The men looked up in surprise.

"Oh, shit!" Ashcroft said.

"Come on, come on, come on," Taliaferro ordered. "Start running you bastards. Shake a leg." Mendelson was about to speak when the sergeant pushed him into line. "Move, Goddamn it. We ain't got time to discuss matters."

Porter jogged back along the line and found Walking Man. "It may be out there. I think Sweet saw it."

"Where?"

Porter pointed. "Out that way someplace. I didn't see a thing, but it's best we try to eat up some territory."

"It may not come in right away," Walking Man said.

"What do you mean? It ain't that far away."

"Remember, I told you. It senses a man's fear. It will make itself known to frighten us. That is how it tracks us."

"Well, that son-of-a-bitch is sure getting a snootful from me," Porter said. He noticed Eagle Head having difficulty moving. "He ain't gonna make it like he is." He saw Ashcroft leading Victoria. "Ashcroft? Bring your mount back here."

Ashcroft looked helplessly at Sweet, who said, "Do it!"

The soldier led Victoria to Porter, who took the animal's reins and guided her to Eagle Head. He helped the warrior into the saddle, who wedged himself between saddlebags and two extra carbines. The Cheyenne threaded his good hand through the mare's mane.

The men ran in a ragged, awkward line. If they slowed, Taliaferro pushed them to speed up. "I know you're wore out but keep going. Don't slow down." Collier grunted in pain each time his foot hit the ground. He and Smallwood were wearing heavy cavalry boots. Ashcroft, Mendelson, and Taliaferro wore lighter brogans, but they still had difficulty running.

"You ain't singing now, are you?" Mendelson said.

"If I get out of this mess," Collier said, each word separated by a gasp of pain. "I'm gonna carve you up in a hundred pieces."

"Save your breath," Taliaferro told him.

Smallwood slipped his carbine strap over his head and carried the weapon in his hand as he shuffled forward.

Left Hand, Red Horse, and Walking Man ran alongside the horse.

Sweet waited and fell in next to Porter. "We aren't going to make it, are we?"

Porter jerked his head at Walking Man. "Ask him. He seems to know all about this animal."

"What did he say?" Walking Man asked Porter.

"Nothing," Porter said. "His feet hurt him, that's all."

"We can't keep up this pace for long," Sweet said.

"If that thing catches us out in the open," Porter replied. "We won't have to worry about it. Lieutenant, give me your binoculars, and I'll get up there a bit and see if I can see a cave."

"Yes, of course," Sweet said, handing the binoculars to the scout. Porter ran as fast as he could until he thought he was far enough ahead of the others to stop and put the binoculars to his eyes. He searched for the sandstone formations. There they were, four miles or so ahead. "Thank God," he breathed. He turned and shouted, pointing, "They're just up there."

He saw it out of the corner of his eye, a white flash, eyes glowing red, mouth twisted in an evil grin, long arm upraised, talons reaching.

Porter had time to say, "Oh, God," before the demon drove its claws deep into the scout's head, splitting open his skull and ripping out his chest. His limp body collapsed in a bloody mess, Sweet's binoculars falling from his hand.

Smallwood screamed, skidding to a stop. Mendelson collided with him, and the two soldiers tumbled to the ground. Taliaferro dropped to one knee, raised his carbine, and got off a shot, the flat boom floating across the prairie. Ashcroft had his carbine to his shoulder but wasn't quick enough. The thing raced out several hundred yards before he had a chance to aim his weapon.

Sweet had his pistol up, hand frozen. He thought he was squeezing the trigger. He thought he heard the gun firing, and he saw the smoke. But he was too frightened to know if he had done nothing but stand like a statue.

"Put it up," Taliaferro said as he ran past the lieutenant toward Porter. Ashcroft was with him, hands gripping his carbine. Taliaferro knelt beside

Porter's body and picked up the binoculars. The blow had driven the scout's head deep into his shoulders and pushed his ribs out of his chest. The sergeant rose and made his way forward, signaling to Ashcroft to move to his right. He cocked the carbine and brought it to his shoulder.

"Do you have a shot?" he shouted to Ashcroft.

The soldier did not answer. The thing walked back and forth, silent, watching the men. Porter's blood was splattered across its chest. Then it squatted, long arms folded on the ground in front of it. It hunched over, waiting.

"Ashcroft! Do you…"

"No!" Ashcroft said. "It's too far out. How's Porter?"

"Deader than five o'clock," Taliaferro said. The others joined him, Mendelson halting well away from the dead scout. Walking Man and the other Cheyenne approached cautiously.

Left Hand, leading Eagle Head on Victoria, ran his hand softly over the horse's muzzle to calm the animal. It could smell the blood and become frightened. He talked soothingly to it and turned her head away from the scene.

Red Horse, wielding a soldier's carbine, joined Ashcroft and Taliaferro. The old soldier said something to the other one. Red Horse did not understand, but he smiled at the old soldier and nodded. He held the weapon up to show he was ready to fight.

Sweet gripped his pistol tightly as he walked up to Porter's body. He stared at the blood-soaked figure.

Taliaferro said something, but Sweet did not hear him. All he could hear was the sound of his heart, pounding in his chest.

"Lieutenant?"

Sweet's dull eyes settled on Taliaferro. He was in a tunnel, watching the sergeant speak.

"Lieutenant, we got to keep going. We can't stop now."

The idea was ludicrous. Something had to be done. They just couldn't leave the man's body out like this. He felt Taliaferro's hands on his shoulders.

"There ain't a damned thing we can do for that poor soul. If we don't get a move on, we're all dead."

"I saw it," Sweet said in a whisper. "I know I saw it. It was out there. How did it get this close?"

"Let it go," Taliaferro urged him.

"It's my fault. I killed Porter."

"You did no such thing, Lieutenant."

"It was my fault. I thought I saw it, but it was right on top of us."

Left Hand shouted, pointing to the southwest. The men looked.

The creature had risen and began howling.

"It is laughing at us," Walking Man said. "It has won a victory, and it is celebrating."

"I didn't see him," Sweet said helplessly. "I thought he was out there. I didn't see him."

"Come on," Taliaferro said. "We got to skedaddle."

Comes-a-Pony walked past Walking Man, towards the beast.

"What are you doing?" he said.

She stopped twenty feet from the Cheyenne brave, unslung the Sharps from her shoulder, and kneeled. She raised the Vernier tang sight into position, adjusting it for distance and windage. She took a deep breath and nestled the buttstock into her shoulder. She rested her left elbow on her knee, gripping the weapon, and settled her cheek along the butt, right eye locked on the sight.

"What the hell's she doing?" Mendelson asked.

"She ain't got no shot," Smallwood said. "I don't care how good she is, it ain't going to do no damn good."

"Come on, you bastards," the sergeant ordered. "Let's go." The men started off again, but slowly, their eyes drawn to Comes-a-Pony.

"That's just a waste of ammunition," Smallwood said before he trotted off after Taliaferro.

Walking Man watched as Comes-a-Pony blew out a deep breath. She and the rifle were one and the same, the barrel of the weapon unwavering. Her finger tightened slowly on the trigger.

There was a loud bang and Comes-a-Pony was engulfed by a cloud of powder smoke. The creature tensed, as if his eyes followed the bullet's trajectory. Then it jerked and fell over. The men, frozen by the spectacle, cheered.

"That's a 45-70 calling card if there ever was one!" Ashcroft said.

"Did she kill it?" Mendelson asked Taliaferro.

"I do not know," the sergeant replied.

The creature rose slowly. It stood, unmoving. It showed the men that it was unharmed. Then it dropped to all fours and ran toward the mountains.

"That son-of-a-bitch is tricking us," Taliaferro said. He nodded to Comes-a-Pony who stood, slipping another cartridge in the breech of the rifle. "Well, you might have got his attention, but you didn't kill him. Still," he admitted, "that was a hell of a shot. Let's go."

The men set out in a steady run, the soldiers leading. Walking Man and the Cheyenne followed. Left Hand guided Victoria, Eagle Head holding onto the horse's mane. Comes-a-Pony ran beside Walking Man.

"I did not kill it," she said, defeated.

"No," Walking Man agreed. "But I think you hit it, and that was no small thing."

Sweet finally came around as he and Taliaferro ran side by side. "When we get there," he said in between breaths. "When we get there, keep two men on guard and have the others gather wood."

"Yes, sir."

"I'm sorry Porter is dead. I feel responsible."

"Yes, sir. But it weren't your fault. This ain't like fighting Indians. Not by a long shot."

Sweet looked up, searching for the sun. The clouds around it glow faintly to mark its passage. It was just above the horizon. "We might not have much time when we get there. Before the thing shows up."

Walking Man dropped back and spoke to Eagle Head. "How are you, friend?"

Eagle Head smiled grimly and nodded.

"I wish I had some other moccasins," Left Hand said. "Or maybe a fast pony."

Walking Man did not reply but increased his pace so that he was even with the white soldier chief. He touched his breast and swept his arm forward. He hoped the boy understood. He would go up a bit to see if he could find the sandstone cave. The soldier did not understand at first, and then when he did, he shook his head violently. The Cheyenne motioned to the binoculars in Taliaferro's hand. "Go ahead," he said. "They ain't doing me any damn good."

The soldier chief talked to Walking Man. It was obvious he did not want him to go on.

Walking Man ignored him and started out. It was a struggle. His legs burned, and he gulped deep breaths, but he forced himself to keep a steady pace. He heard the soldiers running behind him.

He felt her presence before Comes-a-Pony joined him. "Stay with the others," he said.

"Do not give me orders. I go where I want. Besides," she added, "I want to shoot that thing again."

"Where the hell are they going?" Taliaferro demanded.

"I think he's going to look for the formation," Sweet replied. He stumbled but regained his footing. He fell into a loose jog, forcing himself to run. His clothes were damp with sweat, and a chill ran over him. "Come on men," he shouted. "Almost there. Keep going. Don't slow down."

Walking Man stopped and raised the binoculars, sweeping the distant mountains. Comes-a-Pony stood next to him. She saw the creature. He was too far away, even for the Sharps. "Why don't you come a little closer," she said. "I have plenty of cartridges. Come this way, and I will give you one."

Walking Man swung the binoculars toward the creature. "I do not think it is listening to you." He lowered the binoculars and smiled at her. "One day you must teach me how to shoot like that."

She returned the smile. "One day I will."

"He gets out any farther, and he's gonna get himself killed, just like Porter," the sergeant said.

Sweet felt as if he had been slapped. He was the reason Porter was dead. He had failed.

Walking Man and Comes-a-Pony ran on. The thing kept pace with them. "It wants us to see it," he said. "It could come and kill us, but it will not. Not yet. It wants us afraid."

"The soldiers stink of fear," Comes-a-Pony said. "I can smell it."

Walking Man stopped. About a mile away was a high ridge covered sparsely with Ponderosa pine flowing over the crest of the ridge. Splitting the ridge in two was a pitiable sandstone fortress, yellow against the green grass that lapped up the base of the ridge. A scattering of twisted limber pine jutted out of the layers. Even in the dim light, he could see the shadows in the overhanging tiers of sandstone. One of these would become their haven. One of these could become their grave.

He fired his soldier's Springfield carbine into the air to signal to the men. The old soldier fired his pistol in response, signaling that he understood. The faint sound of cheers told him the soldiers understood.

Walking Man pulled a cartridge from his parfleche bag to reload his carbine; and as he did, he saw the demon on a low ridge, motionless, watching him. He felt the cartridge in his hand as he lowered the breech block. He stretched out his hand, holding the cartridge high in the air for the creature to see.

"I have this for you," he shouted. "This one and many more. You will try to kill me, but I will not die so easily."

Comes-a-Pony said, "That is not the talk of a reasonable man."

"Come on men," Sweet ordered. "Come on. Don't give in now. Keep going."

They were slowing, a straggling band of desperate men. Collier dropped to his knees. Sweet ran back and grabbed his arm. "Get up! Get up, we're almost there."

"I can't do it. I can't run no more," Collier cried. "Leave me be. Let me die here."

"No one's dying. Get up. Look! There's the sandstone. It's just a short distance. You've come this far."

"Why don't you leave me alone? Let me die in peace, why don't you?"

"Get up, Goddamn you. I'm not losing anyone else. You want to die? Die fighting."

Collier rose slowly, stumbling, as Sweet pushed him forward. "That's it. Keep going. We need you." The soldier staggered forward and broke into a clumsy run. "That's it! Run. Keep going. We're almost there."

They caught up with the other men.

They closed on the rise that led to the sandstone escarpment. They pulled themselves up the ridge, holding onto the low branches of the limber pine, one foot in front of the other.

"Come on," Taliaferro called to the men. "I ain't going to carry you."

Walking Man climbed over some sandstone boulders and waved the men on. They straggled into the coolness of the cave. It was small, less than thirty feet deep, and no more than twenty feet wide. The sand-covered floor was level, with clumps of fallen sandstone scattered about. The entrance was eight feet high, a jagged rim of sandstone.

The men dropped to their knees, sucking in air. Collier collapsed into the sand and rolled on his back. Left Hand led Victoria to the cave mouth and helped Eagle Head dismount.

"Get your breath," Sweet said. "Five minutes and then I want everyone to gather wood." He scuffed a line in the sand near the end of the overhang with his boot. "Pile it here. Right here."

Walking Man tapped Sweet on the shoulder, pointed to his eyes, and then swept the surrounding ridge with his hand. Sweet nodded as he held up two fingers.

"What is it?" Taliaferro asked.

"He's going to have two men stand guard while we gather firewood," Sweet said. "Get the men's canteens. We'll have to ration water. I don't know how long we'll be here."

"Maybe," Taliaferro said, "we can send one of the men on Victoria there. He can ride out and find Gibbons. Gibbons will have patrols out from the column. If we send one of the men out, he can lead them back to us."

"No," Sweet said. "He won't make it past that thing out there, and we need every man here."

Taliaferro lowered his voice. "You know we ain't got a chance in hell."

Sweet ignored him. "Five minutes," he said. "I want a pile of firewood here before it gets dark. That's the only chance we have, Sergeant."

Taliaferro nodded. He walked from man to man, gathering canteens. "Fill your pockets with cartridges. Wipe them down so your weapons won't jam."

"What about them Indians?" Mendelson said. "They gonna get wood, too?"

"Don't worry about them."

Sweet walked over to Collier. "How are you, soldier?"

Collier looked up at him. "I'm sorry, sir. About before. My back just gave out."

Sweet knelt next to him. "Well, rest a bit and then get some wood." He saw Walking Man unloading Victoria, handing out extra cartridge belts, two carbines, and a pair of pistols. Walking Man stopped when he saw the officer. The Cheyenne held up his carbine. Sweet stood and pulled his pistol out of the holster. He raised it and nodded at Walking Man. They would make a fight together.

Here in a makeshift fort, fighting a thing that would likely kill them, they would make a fight.

Chapter 32

Walking Man examined Eagle Head's bow and the five arrows he had left. The fire's light flooded the sandstone cave, filled with piles of dry limber and Ponderosa pine. They had gathered what they could safely retrieve under the watchful eyes of the sentries. Two soldiers replaced the two Cheyenne after an hour and then were replaced in turn by Mendelson and Sweet, one on either side of the cave. Sweet sat on a sandstone boulder that had fallen from the ceiling.

The sun had gone down, and the wind had picked up. It lacked the strength to reach into the cave, barely batting at the flames.

Before they built the fire, Taliaferro had asked the officer what he wanted to do about Victoria. The sergeant offered his own solution. "I guess we could eat her if we had to."

Sweet thought for a moment and then said, "Let her go. Somebody ought to get out of this alive."

"I'll do it," Ashcroft had said. "It'll do my heart good to get rid of that bitch." He approached the horse to remove her saddle and bridle. But she bolted through the cave entrance and raced down the hill when she sensed his presence. "Keep the saddle, you bitch!" Ashcroft had shouted after her. "I don't need it anyway." He sat down next to Smallwood. "I hope she gets eaten by that thing."

The wood crackled as the flames consumed it. Red Horse and Left Hand acted as sentries, staring into the darkness. Comes-a-Pony sat on a piece of fallen sandstone, rifle across her knee.

Smallwood started laughing. Ashcroft, lying next to him with his hat over his eyes, sat up.

"What the hell is so funny?"

"I just remembered," Smallwood said. He pulled an envelope out of his pocket and showed it to Ashcroft. "Jones gave me this to send to his pa 'cause he thought he was gonna get killed."

"That ain't funny," Ashcroft said.

Smallwood continued laughing. "No, it ain't. I just thought it was funny. His pa ain't gonna get the letter, after all."

Sweet, sitting next to Taliaferro, flipped open the cover of his pocket watch and held it up to the light from the fire to read the time.

Taliaferro nodded toward Smallwood. "What the hell has he got to laugh about?"

"Time to switch out," Sweet said. He looked out into the darkness. "Wind's picking up."

"Collier?" the sergeant said, standing. "Let's go." As he picked up the carbine, he added, "Smells like rain." Then he realized. "We'd better keep an eye on the fire. If it comes a bad storm, we could be in real trouble."

Sweet chuckled dryly. "I don't think things could get much worse, Sergeant."

Taliaferro realized what he had said. "Yeah. I guess you're right." The sergeant took position with Collier. Sweet sat alone with his doubts. Maybe they should have kept on, found a better place for a defense. Where? Here the creature had only one avenue for attack, and that was partially blocked by the fire. But they were nearly out of water. Maybe if it rains, they can collect some.

You are besieged, Sweet. Now you are the Gaul, while Caesar surrounds you at Alesia. If only it were Caesar, and not this… this abomination. How long can you and your men last? A few days. Maybe. Not more than three. Water will be the problem. Perhaps the creature will grow impatient and move off in search of other prey?

Gibbons would have patrols out; Taliaferro was right about that. They might spot the smoke from the fire and come to investigate. What if they did? There would be no more than twelve or fifteen men. Not enough. Not nearly enough. But if the general decided on a reconnaissance in force? That was logical, wasn't it? A hundred men. A hundred men would do it. Even that thing out there couldn't fight a hundred men. The thought gained strength and blossomed into hope. It was a hair's breadth from reality. They would come over a rise, flankers out, a dozen men in the point, column of fours, guidons fluttering in the wind. Two full companies. They could sally out to meet them. There would be a captain in command, and Sweet saw himself making his report. No. No, first they would fight the thing. The captain would throw out a skirmish line of twenty men. Then divide his force and come at the creature from two sides. A double envelopment.

Sweet remembered Neufeld. At the Point. Neufeld and Tactics. "You young gentlemen," he had addressed them. "White hair, pedantic, demanding. You young gentlemen"

He remembered where he was. There are too many maybes, Lieutenant Sweet. Where are the certainties? Sweet was on his feet, ignoring the question. Collier was just climbing a pile of sandstone when he stopped.

"Hey?" the soldier whispered to Taliaferro. "I think I heard something."

The sergeant threw a pebble at Ashcroft and Smallwood to get their attention. The two men jumped to their feet. The Cheyenne warriors followed them. Everyone peered into the darkness over the flames. Sweet made his way to Collier.

"What did you hear?" he asked. He realized that the soldier was too far out. "Come in a little."

Collier turned to him and said, "I thought I heard something." He looked back into the darkness and said, "I don't know…" He saw the creature's face and screamed. It grabbed him with both hands and jerked him off the sandstone. Red Horse ran to the soldier and took hold of his leg. The creature bit into Red Horse's head, and the lifeless torso quivered once and fell back among the startled men.

Half a dozen carbines went off in the confines of the cave in a thunderous roar. But there was nothing to shoot at. Collier's screams move farther into the darkness. The men quickly reloaded. The screams didn't stop.

"Jesus Christ," Ashcroft gasped.

Left Hand ran to Red Horse's body, but Walking Man stopped him, dragging him away from the body as it jerked, pumping blood across the sand floor.

Left Hand angrily pulled his arm away. "Let me go! He was my friend."

"Brother," Comes-a-Pony said, "he was only trying to keep you out of the creature's reach."

"I do not need his help. I do not need anyone." He found a rock and sat down.

Comes-a-Pony said to Walking Man. "He is hurt and angry. He cannot fight the thing like a warrior fights his enemy."

"I know. I understand his anger." Comes-a-Pony turned away, but he stopped her. He wanted to say something, but the words would not come. She left him and went to her brother, but Walking Man saw her eyes search for him.

Mendelson fired and Smallwood had his carbine to his shoulder when Sweet ordered, "Don't fire. You might hit Collier."

"It would be a Godsend for that poor bastard if we did," Taliaferro said.

The screams stopped, replaced by the creature's roaring. Collier's mangled body flew out of the darkness and landed in the fire, rolling into the cave. The men jumped back, and Mendelson fired again.

"Stop it!" Sweet ordered. "Don't shoot unless you see something."

Taliaferro examined Collier's body. "It bit clear through him." He said to Ashcroft, "Help me drag him to the rear of the cave."

"Smallwood?" Sweet said. "Take his position."

Smallwood looked helplessly at Sweet, hesitating. "Lieutenant, I…"

"Get up there."

Smallwood took post behind a mound of sandstone. "I don't like…"

Taliaferro's hand shot up. "Listen!"

No one moved. There was a burst of thunder, and a stream of lightning pierced the darkness. Rain, heavy. The wind went wild, blowing rain into the cave. The fire sizzled, hissing at the men like snakes.

Walking Man ran to the fire. The flames closest to the entrance sputtered as the rain soaked the wood. Walking Man threw his carbine to Left Hand and pulled chunks of burning wood farther into the cave. Ashcroft and Left Hand joined him and then the others, working frantically to move the fire away from the rain. Pools of water drifted into the cave, running under the fire.

"Get it all," Sweet said. "Don't let it get wet."

The men ignored the flames, jerking wood out of the rain's reach.

From outside, the wind moaned piteously. The creature howled as if answering the wind. The noise echoed off the cave walls.

The men tore at the fire, throwing burning branches a few feet back to build another line safe from the rain. The rain, born on the wind's fury, followed them. Comes-a-Pony swept the burning wood back with the butt of her rifle.

"Hurry," Taliaferro shouted. "Get all of it! Hurry."

Sweet saw a cartridge belt under the new fire line. "Stop!" He reached into the fire, his hand grasping the belt and a pile of burning wood fell on his hand. He shrieked in pain.

Walking Man saw what happened and jerked the lieutenant's arm out of the fire. The officer still held the smoldering cartridge belt. The Cheyenne warrior knocked it to the ground and kicked sand over it to smother the fire.

Smoke filled the interior of the cave choking the men. They coughed as the air thickened. Mendelson dropped to the floor of the cave, gasping for air. The men's eyes teared from the smoke as they struggled to see. Ashcroft drew his sleeve across his face to rub the smoke out of his eyes and began to retch.

"Get down low," Taliaferro ordered. He dropped to the ground, reached up, and pushed the lieutenant to his knees. "Get down, goddamn it, so you can breathe."

Sweet cradled his hand, fighting back sobs.

The wind shifted, eased, and the smoke rolled out of the cave into the night. The rain slowed to a steady hum as it beat off the sandstone formation.

Walking Man motioned for Left Hand to guard one side of the cave entrance while he took the other. Eagle Head had collapsed against the wall. Mendelson was lying on the ground, face down, crying. Ashcroft and Smallwood, cradling their carbines, rose slowly as the smoke found its way out of the cave.

Taliaferro tried to pry the lieutenant's burned hand away from his body. "Let me see it, sir."

Sweet wept uncontrollably, fighting the sergeant. "It hurts. Oh, my God, it hurts."

Walking Man turned his parfleche bag inside out and showed it to Taliaferro. "Here. It is covered in grease. Rub it on his hand." He knew grease from buffalo and deer meat soaked the bag. It might offer some relief for the soldier chief's wound.

Taliaferro pushed the Cheyenne back, but Walking Man showed him the bag again and made a rubbing motion.

Comes-a-Pony took the parfleche bag from Walking Man. "Here. Let me do it." She showed it to Taliaferro.

The sergeant understood and nodded, holding up the lieutenant's hand. The skin was leathery. His entire hand – an angry, deep red. "Hold still, Lieutenant. This is gonna hurt like hell."

Comes-a-Pony gripped the bag. She smiled at Sweet and nodded. He hesitated and then looked away. She patted it carefully over the wound. Sweet screamed in pain and tried to draw his hand back, but Taliaferro pinned it against his chest. "I know it hurts but let her do it."

Comes-a-Pony continued as the lieutenant slumped against Taliaferro; the only sound coming from him was a low moan. She rubbed the bag with her thumb. It was dry, the grease transferred to the wound. She held up the bag to show he was finished. Taliaferro pulled a faded red handkerchief from around his neck and carefully wrapped the lieutenant's hand. "I don't know how good this will be, but it's all I got." He looked over his shoulder. "Ashcroft? Smallwood! Keep your eyes peeled."

She returned the bag to Walking Man.

He took it and tied the parfleche bag to the soldier's cartridge belt that he wore. He pulled the other one out of the sand. He brushed it off and showed Comes-a-Pony. "This is what he took out of the fire."

"Brother," Left Hand gestured toward Eagle Head. "Our old friend is dead."

Walking Man crawled over to Eagle Head. His eyes were closed, and his mouth sagged open. The Cheyenne warrior touched his face, but Eagle Head did not move. "What is this?" he said to Left Hand.

The warrior shrugged and turned back to the night. "Nothing happened to him. He sat down and decided to die."

Walking Man patted Eagle Head's shoulder tenderly and then stretched out his body so he would be comfortable in death. He sat back against the wall. Now, there were five soldiers, but one was wounded and would probably not be any good in a fight. Of his friends, only Left Hand and Comes-a-Pony remained. He sat with his back against the wall and slipped the cartridges out of the belt loops. He brushed each against his shirt to wipe off the sand so they would not foul the carbine.

Comes-a-Pony sat next to her brother. She put a pebble in her mouth to draw out saliva. It would help quench her thirst.

"I thought the fire was gonna keep it out," Mendelson said, pushing himself up on all fours. "I thought we were safe."

Left Hand spoke without looking at Walking Man. "Even the wind fights us. And the rain. We must have done something to anger *Maheo*."

Walking Man let his head fall against the wall. "No. I do not think so."

"What did your visions tell you about this?"

"We do not need Walking Man's visions to tell us what has happened," Comes-a-Pony said. "There is only so much a man can do." The words were without malice. She was saying what was true and without blame. To Walking Man she said, "Now it is time for you to reason."

Walking Man said, "I was told not to do that." He smiled at Comes-a-Pony.

She returned his smile with her own, but it quickly flew away. "Whoever said that to you must have been mistaken. It is your strength. It is something we need now."

Mendelson rolled to a sitting position, his carbine lying on the ground next to him. "I ain't gonna die like that." He jerked his head at Sweet. "All because we listened to the general, there."

"Pick up that weapon and clean the sand out of the action," Taliaferro ordered.

"Pick it up yourself," Mendelson said. "I'm done taking orders."

Left Hand glanced at Comes-a-Pony. "He will be next. He will run away, and the thing will eat him."

Mendelson heard him and said, "What did he say? What did that filthy savage say about me?"

"Ask him yourself," Taliaferro said. "After you pick up that weapon and clean it. If you don't, I'll throw you out there." He finished tying the kerchief around the lieutenant's hand. "That took a lot of balls, Lieutenant. If we get out of this mess, I'll ride with you anyplace."

Walking Man studied the cartridges as he cleaned them. They could have exploded if it weren't for the young soldier chief. He pulled the parfleche bag off his belt. He held up a brass cartridge and turned it end over end. Hawk, a young brave, had a bad cartridge blow up in his rifle, scaring his cheek. For a while, he thought he would be blind; but his eyes repaired themselves. Walking Man found a rock, laid it on the ground, and placed a cartridge on it. He pulled his knife out of its sheath and, gripping the cartridge to hold it in place with his left hand, dug the point of the knife into the brass casing with his right. The knife tip slipped off, but he tried again. He split the cartridge casing and poured the powder into his hand. He pushed it around his palm with his thumb, feeling the grains.

"Sergeant?" Sweet raised his tear-stained face. "What's he doing?"

Taliaferro watched the Cheyenne work the knife tip into the soft brass. "Hell, if I know. Maybe he's just bored."

Chapter 33

Outside the sky was still a deep gray of shattered clouds, but the wind had lost its desperation. The rain had gone on, and the sun tried its best to pierce the sky; but the clouds were too strong and fought it into submission.

The cave stank of smoke, piss, and sweat. The air was heavy and still, wrapping the inhabitants in despair.

They were running out of firewood.

Ashcroft and Smallwood guarded the cave entrance. Mendelson sat sullenly in one corner. Sweet was in a deep sleep on the floor of the cave, and Taliaferro fought to keep awake.

Walking Man had restrung Eagle Head's bow to tighten the sinew and had the five arrows laid on the ground next to him. Left Hand watched as Walking Man's knife pierced another cartridge. Two dozen split cartridges lay scattered around the rock. He looked at Left Hand and smiled. He poured the powder from the cartridges into his parfleche bag.

"Do you think my mind has gone?"

"No, but I am too tired to ask what you are doing."

"I will watch if you want to sleep. The soldiers take turns sleeping," Comes-a-Pony said to her brother.

Left Hand cocked his head at Mendelson. "That one wants to run away, but he is too afraid. I think he is also too afraid to stay here and fight."

Comes-a-Pony dug into the deerskin bag she wore over her shoulder. She opened her hand filled with cartridges. She silently counted them. "I have thirty-eight cartridges."

Left Hand watched as she dumped them back into the bag. "The soldier's cartridges should work in your gun."

"I will try them to see," she said. She glanced at her brother and motioned toward Walking Man. "He has something in mind."

Walking Man poured the powder from an opened cartridge into the bag.

"You are reasoning again," Left Hand said to Walking Man. "Every time I look up, I see your mind working. Was there ever a time it was not so?"

"Let him be," Comes-a-Pony said.

Left Hand was surprised at his sister's response. "You are not angry with him anymore, Little Sister?"

"Not so much," she said. "Now is not the time for anger."

"Were you at the council when the soldiers fired the big gun that speaks twice?" Walking Man asked, pulling another cartridge out of the belt at his side.

"At the soldiers' fort on the Platte? No, why would I? I went hunting. Why should I go and listen to lies?" Left Hand said. "But I heard about it."

Walking Man dug the knife tip into the cartridge. "It was very loud. Broken Tree's pony was scared by the noise and bucked him off. He was very angry. The gun spoke once and then again, and the earth exploded some distance away. I think the soldiers were trying to impress us before the council. They thought their magic was big enough to make a difference."

"It did to Broken Tree's pony," Comes-a-Pony said.

The Cheyenne worked the knife tip back and forth to enlarge the hole in the cartridge. "They put bags of powder and a big iron ball in the gun. There was so much smoke it was hard to see the soldiers."

Taliaferro and Mendelson replaced Ashcroft and Smallwood at the entrance to the cave. The sergeant stopped Smallwood. "Wake up the lieutenant. Do it nice and easy."

Smallwood nodded wearily.

Mendelson took position, looking back into the cave. He settled his carbine on the pile of sandstone rocks, watching as Ashcroft picked up some wood from the dwindling pile and put it on the fire.

"Your post is out there," Taliaferro reminded Mendelson.

Mendelson muttered something but turned toward the entrance.

"Well?" Left Hand said to Walking Man.

"I think," Walking Man said, pouring the powder into the parfleche bag. "Maybe we can kill it with this." He held up the bag.

"That little thing?" Left Hand pulled his hatchet from his belt. "I think this is better. I will chop off its head, and we can play ball with it. Little Sister will shoot its eyes out."

Ashcroft knelt and shook Sweet gently. "Lieutenant? Hey, Lieutenant?"

Sweet sat up, rubbing his eyes with his good hand. He moved his right hand gingerly, wincing in pain. "What is it?" His hand felt his face. "My glasses? Where are my glasses?"

"Here you go, Lieutenant," Taliaferro said. He tossed them to Ashcroft, who handed them to the officer. "I thought you might roll around in your sleep and bust them."

Sweet cleaned them with the tail of his shirt.

"Goddam it!" Taliaferro cried. Mendelson was gone. "That son-of-a-bitch skedaddled!"

Sweet and Ashcroft were on their feet when Smallwood said, "He took some canteens."

"What?" Sweet said. "How many?"

"Two, I think," Smallwood answered. "There was six there. Now there's just four."

"Ashcroft?" Sweet said. "Take his post. Sergeant? Can you see him?"

"No," Taliaferro muttered. "I should have been paying attention. He's probably gone over the ridge. I don't see nothing."

"What happened?" Walking Man said, knife tip poised over a cartridge.

"That one I told you about," Left Hand said. "He has run away."

"That may not be such a bad thing," Comes-a-Pony said. "I would not trust a coward to fight alongside me."

Shrieking filled the cave. The men ran to the entrance, standing on either side of the fire. They saw, down at the bottom of the ridge, the demon, standing erect, holding Mendelson up with one hand. The soldier's feet kicked in the air, his hands trying to pry the creature's grasp from his neck.

"Jesus Christ! He's still alive." Taliaferro raised his carbine and fired. The demon held Mendelson higher, and with the other claw, drew its talons across the soldier's chest. Mendelson struggled frantically, crying out in a high-pitched scream. Then, the creature dug its claws into the man's right leg, drawing them slowly down to his foot. Blood dripped onto the ground, and his body jerked violently.

"It is showing us what it can do," Walking Man said to Left Hand. "It is showing us its power."

Comes-a-Pony had her rifle up when Walking Man stopped her. "The man is dead already. Wait until it is closer, and you can put a bullet in its brain."

Taliaferro quickly loaded his carbine and took aim. He lowered it, rubbed his eyes, and took aim again. "It's too far," he whispered. "It's too far." He fired anyway, the boom filling the cave. He pulled another cartridge from his belt and slid it into the breech. "He's laughing at me. That bastard is laughing at me."

The creature threw its head back and roared. It walked back and forth, showing the men in the cave its prize. He sunk his claws into Mendelson's other leg, raking them down the full distance before raising his hand. Blood rolled down its thin, white arm, dripping from its elbow, and falling into the grass.

The creature took hold of Mendelson's legs and held him high over its head for the men to see. The soldier's arms dangled lifelessly, his head swayed back and forth. Then it tore the man in half, letting the blood cascade over its head and shoulders, running down its torso, and over its legs. It raised the two halves in triumph, guts streaming from Mendelson's stomach, covering the creature's arm.

The men did not speak. They watched, frozen in horror. When the creature was satisfied, he tossed the two pieces away, and dropped to all fours, prowling back and forth in contentment, eyes never leaving the cave, bloody mouth twisted in a grin. It stopped, sat down, picked up Mendelson's torso, and began eating it.

"He wants us to see," Smallwood said. "He wants us to see what he's going to do to us."

"We have to kill it," Sweet said. "We can't wait. We have to kill it now."

"How!" Ashcroft demanded. "What are we supposed to do? Shoot it? How do we kill it?"

"I think the soldiers want to fight it," Left Hand said.

"We have to let it get close to us," Walking Man said, as the soldiers spoke to one another.

Left Hand looked at him, stunned. "What are you saying?"

"As long as it remains out there, we have no chance of killing it."

"You want it to come closer?" Comes-a-Pony asked.

Smallwood said to Sweet, "What are they talking about?"

"I think the big one has an idea," Taliaferro said.

"How do we know what to do?" Sweet said. He gestured expectantly toward Walking Man with his good hand. He did it several times, trying to make his question known. "Do you have an idea?"

"What does he want?" Left Hand asked Walking Man. "Is he telling us to go? Maybe he wants us to go out there and feed the beast. While it's eating us, they can run away."

"I do not know," Walking Man said. He dropped to one knee. He smoothed the sand and began drawing. He drew an arch, and then out from it a stick figure. He pointed outside, gestured to the figure, and then pointed again.

Sweet knelt next to him and tapped the stick figure. He motioned outside and then to Walking Man. Comes-a-Pony and Left Hand stood over them.

"We ought to make a run for it," Ashcroft said. "Let's get out of this goddamned cave and fight it in the open. Maybe we'll have a chance to get away. We can split up. It can't catch all of us if we do. Can it? Some of us can get away. Some is better than none."

Walking Man nodded and smiled at Sweet. The soldier chief understood. The brave used two fingers to draw parallel lines leading from the stick figure to the arch. He did it several times.

"What the…? He wants us to charge it," Taliaferro said. "He wants us to go out and fight it. That ain't no good."

"There," Ashcroft said. "You see? He's got the right idea."

"No," Sweet said. "Look at the direction he's making with the marks. He wants the thing to attack us."

Ashcroft exploded. "What? What the hell kind of an idea is that?"

Smallwood joined in. "No, no. I ain't gonna do it. That's crazy. We're supposed to let that thing in on us?"

"This don't make no sense, Lieutenant," Ashcroft said. "Let it get in here? We're dead men if we do. Let's fight it out there."

"I'm with Ashcroft," Smallwood said. "We can rush it and then split up."

Walking Man watched as the soldiers spoke. Left Hand said, "I do not think they want to do as you wish."

Comes-a-Pony knelt down with the others. She pointed at the drawing. "You want that thing to come in here?" She looked around at the confines of the cave. "We would have no room to fight."

"What choice do we have?" Sweet responded to the soldiers. "What's it doing now?" he asked Taliaferro.

"Just walking back and forth," the sergeant said. "Like it's waiting for something."

"Yeah," Ashcroft said. "It's figuring who it wants to eat next. That's all it needs to do cause we ain't got a chance. Now," he pointed at Walking Man, "he wants us to invite it in. Just stand back and let it kill us."

"Wait a minute," Sweet said. He motioned to the drawing in the sand and looked at Walking Man. *How can I understand what he wants? How can I talk to him?* He held out his left hand. Tell us. *Tell us what you have in mind.* His eyes pled for something, anything. A way to make the Cheyenne understand him. Please, please tell me. What can we do?

Walking Man saw a question in the soldier chief's eyes. He took the lieutenant's good hand and pushed it gently into the parfleche bag. He forced the fingers closed, and then helped the lieutenant pull out grains of powder. He smiled at the boy and nodded. He flipped his fingers over his head, like fireworks on a summer's night. He looked expectantly at Sweet and did it again. This, this is what I want to do. We can use this. Maybe it will work. It might be a chance. A way. He pointed at the arrows. He saw the soldier chief's eyes glisten. He was afraid. He was crying for his own death. Would he fight? Can he overcome his fear and face that thing?

Can you do the same? Walking Man asked himself.

"I think I know what he wants to do," Sweet said.

"He better make it quick," Taliaferro advised. "I don't know how much longer that thing is going to wait."

"What difference does it make?" Ashcroft said, slumping against the cave wall. "We're dead no matter what we do."

"Will you quit saying that?" Taliaferro demanded. "I ain't so all fire ready to die. You want to get dead? Run out there like Mendelson did."

Smallwood kicked at the fire. It blazed briefly. He stared at the last of the wood. "That's it," he said. "That's all we got."

Sweet stood. "Get all the cartridges. Use your knives to split them open."

"What's that supposed to do?" Ashcroft asked.

Sweet picked up the parfleche bag. "We can make a bomb." He looked from man to man, his voice filled with desperation. "We can use the cartridge powder…" He searched the cave with his eyes. "Look for something else we can use. Anything to hold powder."

"There ain't enough powder in the world to kill that thing," Smallwood said.

Left Hand took Mendelson's position, settling into the pile of sandstone rocks. He watched as the thing walked slowly back and forth, its eyes seeming to pierce the gloom of the cave. He began to speak, not to Walking Man, but to the beast. "Our brother fought with Red Cloud during the Moon of the Popping Trees." He wanted to include Little Sister.

"Little Horse," Walking Man supplied the name. Left Hand would not speak it. The words were too painful. Comes-a-Pony stared at the ground. She remembered Little Horse. He was a fierce rider who could hang from his pony's neck and shoot arrows from under its head. His eyes burned with hatred for the whites.

"Yes. They tricked a bunch of white soldiers into coming out. Walk-a-heaps and pony soldiers. They split them up and rubbed them all out. My brother said that the white soldiers went crazy when they saw what was going to happen to them. They tried to run away. Two soldier chiefs shot each other on a hill. He said it was so cold that blood froze on the rocks. They called it 'the Battle of a Hundred-in-the-Hands.'" Now he looked at the men. "I think these white soldiers have gone crazy, too." He jerked his head in Sweet's direction. "That boy cannot control them anymore. They will run out like that other one and die. The thing will feed on their bodies."

Ashcroft's hand tightened on his carbine. "That one is sure doing a lot of talking. Maybe they plan on going out on their own."

Smallwood thumbed back the hammer of his weapon. It clicked twice, ominously. "Yeah. These jaspers are up to something."

Sweet spoke. His voice was calm. It sounded out of place in the cave. "I know you're scared. All of us are. What's happened to us… what's happened to our friends, isn't right. They didn't deserve to die like they did. We're all carrying knives. We can cut open the cartridges and pour the powder into something. Anything to hold it." He reached into his trousers, pulled out a pocketknife and opened the blade with his teeth. "I can't do much with one hand, but I'm willing to try."

"The way I figure," Taliaferro said, his eyes following the creature. "Either way, if it comes in here or we go out there, we've got our work cut out for us. We've got most of our cartridges. If we get it to come in here, it won't have room to move about. We'll be fighting it toe-to-toe. Maybe that's the trick. I don't know. Anyway," he glanced at Sweet, and added softly, "the only way this plan will work is if we shove the powder right down its throat."

"All right," Smallwood said. "Suppose we do, how do we set it off? We ain't got no fuses. By the time anyone gets close enough to set off the powder, he'll be dead."

Sweet nodded. He walked to Walking Man and picked up an arrow. He held the flint tip close to the remains of the fire and looked expectantly at the Cheyenne.

Walking Man picked up the other four arrows and held them close to the fire. He drew his fingers over the point several times, as if his idea sprouted from the tip.

"He can do it," Sweet said. "We can wrap some cloth around the arrow tips, light it, and shoot the powder bags. That should set it off." He sought out Taliaferro. "That should do it, shouldn't it, Sergeant?"

Taliaferro shook his head.

For the first time, Sweet saw defeat in the sergeant's eyes. "Sergeant Taliaferro…"

"I know what you're asking me. You want me to say we can do it. That we can kill that thing with leather bags and a bit of powder. Well, I don't know that we can, Lieutenant. That thing is twice as tall as a man and faster than greased lightning. If we get it in here, we have to keep clear of its claws. There ain't room enough in here to swing a cat as it is. We'll have to use our pistols."

"Sergeant…"

"You want to fight it that Indian's way? All right. Give me the order. I'll fight it anyway you say. I ain't disobeyed an order yet, and I ain't about to start now. But you ought to know, if that thing gets in here, nobody's leaving this cave alive. There ain't no other way to say it."

"You may be right, Sergeant," Sweet said. He considered his words. "Likely, you are right. But it's a chance." He pulled his shirt tail out of his trousers, and ripped out a piece of cloth, wincing at the pain in his right hand. He handed it to Walking Man who took it and began wrapping it around an arrowhead.

Walking Man spoke to Left Hand as he wound the cloth, tore the end, and tied it off. "I think this soldier chief is better than we know."

"Good," Left Hand said. "It will be a hard fight."

"You want the powder to explode?" Comes-a-Pony said. "You think that will kill it?"

"No," Walking Man said. "But maybe it will injure it enough so that we can."

"Sergeant Taliaferro," Sweet said. "How do you suggest we lure that thing in here?"

Taliaferro leaned his carbine against the cave wall, pulled a plug of tobacco out of his coat, bit off the end, and offered the remains to Left Hand. The Cheyenne took it and tore off a piece. He found his calumet pipe, most of the stem broken off, and pushed the tobacco into the bowl. "I ain't got the slightest idea."

"Jesus Christ," Smallwood said helplessly. "I guess we don't got no choice, do we? I wish the hell I'd never joined the army."

"Well, you did," Taliaferro said. "For sixteen dollars a month and all the beans you can eat."

"So that's it, is it?" Ashcroft asked. "We get that thing in here and try to blow it up?"

"That's it," Sweet said.

Left Hand motioned to Ashcroft, pointing to his pipe.

Ashcroft struck a match on a stone. It hissed into life, throwing shadows into the cave. He handed it to Left Hand, who lit his pipe, tossing the plug back to Taliaferro.

"My pa's got a store in Springfield, Ohio," Smallwood said.

"What's that got to do with anything?" Ashcroft said sourerly.

"When I headed west, he told me, when you get this nonsense out of your system, you come home and help me run the store. I couldn't get away from that place fast enough. Now…that store don't look too bad." He pulled a D-ring Bowie knife out of a sheaf on his belt and began sliding cartridges out of his belt. He sat down, found a rock, and began prying open the casing.

Left Hand threw Walking Man his parfleche bag. Sweet unrolled the kerchief around his hand and laid it on the sand, smoothing the fabric. He stepped on a cartridge to hold it in place and drove his knife into the brass. The blade rolled off and he tried it again. The blade finally bit into the soft metal. He twisted the blade, opening the cartridge. He looked up. "Smallwood? Bring me a canteen. Pour the water in another and bring it to me."

The soldier rose, found a canteen that was almost empty and, removing the cork stopper, poured the water into another canteen. "Here it is, Lieutenant." He handed it to the officer. "I ain't got no idea what you want with an empty canteen, but here it is."

Sweet took the canteen, shook the remaining drops of water out of it, and scooped up a handful of sand. Smallwood looked to Taliaferro for an explanation. The sergeant shrugged.

The officer filled the canteen with sand, swirled it around, and emptied it. "I was thinking," he said to no one in particular. He held the split cartridge over the canteen mouth and watched as the black grains emptied into the canteen. He looked up at the soldiers around him and said, "Give me as many cartridges and as you cut up. Hurry."

The soldiers did as they were ordered, handing the cartridges to Sweet, who poured them into the canteen. "I was thinking the most effective way to make a bomb is to compress the powder."

This time Taliaferro glanced at Smallwood, who had no answer. The sergeant said, "I don't follow you, Lieutenant."

Walking Man watched with interest as Sweet said, "Powder only works in a cartridge because the fire is concentrated in a container. The cartridge case." He continued pouring powder into the canteen. "Like a powder bag in a cannon barrel." He held up the canteen. "This will be effective. I hope."

"Ain't you forgetting something, Lieutenant," Smallwood said. "How you gonna set it off?"

"I don't know," Sweet said, upending a cartridge.

Comes-a-Pony sat down beside Walking Man and pulled out her knife. She was about to reach for her cartridges when he stopped her. "Use the soldier's cartridges. Save yours."

Ashcroft opened the blade of his pocketknife, grabbed a handful of cartridges, and spread his kerchief out.

"How many of those bombs do you want to make, Lieutenant?" Taliaferro asked.

"As many as we can," Sweet said. "We'll fill up the canteen. He's got five arrows, I guess five bags for him." He watched as the men began slitting cartridges, piling the powder into pitiful, little mounds. "We have to get at it the moment it comes in. It won't give us time to think." The men worked steadily, Taliaferro cutting cartridges and glancing out of the cave.

No one spoke until Ashcroft said, "How we going to get it in here?"

The men looked at Sweet. It was a moment before he said, "I'll go out there and let it see me. When it comes after me, I'll run back into the cave. Then, you can kill it."

The men and Comes-a-Pony worked silently, splitting cartridges, and pouring the powder into the makeshift containers. The carcasses of empty cartridges lay near them.

"What if it gets you first?" Smallwood said.

Sweet shrugged. "Then someone else has to go. I don't know what else to do." He lifted the canteen, testing the weight. "This ought to do it."

Walking Man and Comes-a-Pony finished tying rags to the arrowheads. He examined their work. "I wish I had some grease. It would burn properly if the rags were soaked in grease." Left Hand poured the powder into his parfleche bag and started on another cartridge.

"There may be enough grease left in the bags," Comes-a-Pony said. She untied Eagle Head's parfleche bag. "I am sorry to take this from you brother. You may need it when you travel over." She handed it to Walking Man. "We have this one, mine, and Left Hand's. Yours too, but it does not have grease in it. How will you light them?"

"What if we tie the bags to the arrow, and light the cloth?" Left Hand said. "The arrow only needs to reach the creature." He studied the interior of the cave. "If you are back there," he pointed to the rear of the cave, "you will be just a little way from it. The arrow will hit it right away. What do you think?"

Walking Man slipped an arrow into the bow, drawing back to test the tension on the sinew. "I will have to be quick about it. If the fire gets to the powder before I fire the arrow…"

"You will be on your journey to the Milky Way," Left Hand said.

"What if it does not explode?" Comes-a-Pony asked. "Suppose it just burns?"

"Then I will have to reason out another plan," Walking Man said. He considered what she had said and looked at Sweet and the canteen in his hand. "Maybe his plan will work. Perhaps you are right. I do not know what else to do."

Sweet walked to the back of the cave. Here, the roof was low, the passage narrow. "If we station ourselves right here," the lieutenant instructed the men. "There won't be room for it to get at us. We'll have an advantage. We can keep out of its reach. For a bit at least."

"What if it doesn't take the bait, Lieutenant?" Ashcroft asked. "I mean what if it smells a rat and don't chase you in here?"

"I hadn't thought of that," Sweet said.

"I'll go out with you," Taliaferro said.

"Sergeant, I don't think that's necessary."

"If it sees two of us, it might make it greedy."

"Are you volunteering?" Smallwood asked. "Ain't you told us never to volunteer for anything?"

Taliaferro folded his kerchief stuffed with powder and tied the ends. "I just want to get out of this stinking cave. That's all."

Sweet went to Walking Man and pointed to the back of the cave. He bent down and drew in the sand. An arch, and out from it, the stick figures of two men. He tapped his chest and pointed at Taliaferro. Then he drew two lines back to the arch. Walking Man read the drawing and saw what the soldier chief was telling him. He understood.

"That boy is going out," Left Hand said, but not as a question. He had seen the men talk and read each of their faces. It was not difficult for him to determine what they planned.

"The old soldier with him," Walking Man replied.

"It will not work," Left Hand concluded. "They will go out there and the beast will eat them up before they get away."

"Perhaps."

"I will go instead," Left Hand announced. "I am the fastest runner. I have never lost a race." He reached down and jerked off his moccasins, throwing them out the cave entrance. "These things are worn out. I do not need them."

Comes-a-Pony stared at her brother in shock. "No. Let me go."

"No," Left Hand said.

"Why not? Do you think I am weak because I am a woman?" She was angry and frightened for her brother and spoke heatedly. "I can outshoot and outride you, Brother."

"This is true," Left Hand said. "No, you are not weak. You are a warrior."

"You should both stay here in case something happens to me," Walking Man said. "These white soldiers do not know how to use a bow."

"If you are killed, brother," Left Hand said, "then we are all dead." He said to his sister, "You cannot run as fast as I. No one can." To Walking Hand, he said, "You are better with a bow than I am." He smiled slyly. "But not so much better." Comes-a-Pony was about to speak when he stopped her. "Little Sister, you must use some of Walking Man's reason. I will go. I count on you to shoot because you are a better shot. Shoot out its eyes so that it cannot see me."

She thought about what her brother had said but was still reluctant. "Do not be foolish when you go out there, Brother," she said. "Do not get too close to that thing."

"I will not."

"I mean it," she said. "Do not get too close and do not get between me and it. I want to have a good shot at it."

Walking Man turned to the soldier chief. "I will speak with you as if you and I understand each other." He placed a hand on the boy's shoulder. "Left Hand reminded me he is a very fast runner. This is true. I have seen him run and would not wager against him. You are brave as is," he nodded to Taliaferro, "the old soldier. But it is likely the beast will catch you before you have gone very far, and then it will not come into the cave so that we can kill it. Let my brother go out and tease it so that it grows angry and chases him. He has the best chance."

Left Hand spoke, slapping himself on the chest. "I will go." He walked two fingers through the air and slapped his chest again.

"What's he saying, Lieutenant?" Smallwood asked.

Sweet nodded and looked at Left Hand. "He wants to go. That fellow there. Walking Man agrees with him. That's what I get at least."

"Well, hell," Ashcroft said. "Let him. One less redskin."

"Ashcroft," Taliaferro said. "You just don't know when to shut up, do you?"

Chapter 34

Walking Man tied the last of the bags to the arrows, slid one into the bow to test it, and then said to Left Hand, "It is not balanced very well, but I think it will work." He pointed at the wood piled near the rear of the cave. Sweet understood and noticed the Cheyenne glance at the canteen. He stuck a cork stopper in the neck, and nodded at Walking Man. "It's full of powder," the lieutenant said. "At least it'll make lots of noise. Keep the fire burning Ashcroft. If it goes out…" There was no reason to finish the thought.

"I guess he's ready," Taliaferro said, glancing at Left Hand.

Left Hand had his own pistol and another one given to him by the soldiers. He handed it back, and pulled his hatchet out of his belt, holding it for everyone to see. "If that thing gets too close, I will cut off the head. Then I will skin it and use the skin to make a shield." He grinned at Walking Man, but it faded away as he said, "If that thing kills me, I want you to tell the others when you get home about my bravery. Have the women sing songs to celebrate my courage."

"I will tell everyone about my brother Left Hand," Walking Man said, "and his fight with the demon."

He turned to Comes-a-Pony. "Now, Little Sister, pay attention to what I have to say. *Maheo* may see fit that the thing kills me. If so, I will go on to *Seana* to wait for you. Do not come so quickly or I will be cross."

She hugged her brother and took a necklace from around her neck. It had a blue stone drilled out with a leather strand passed through it so she could tie it around her neck. Painted Feather had found it and using a ramrod from an old musket as an awl, had bored a hole through it. Comes-a-Pony draped the necklace over Left Hand's head and touched the stone when it fell on his chest. "This will go with you and protect you. Keep this in your heart. Stay clear of the demon so I can shoot it. Do not let it get you."

Left Hand smiled, which he rarely did. "I will do everything you say."

She stroked her brother's arm and then stood back. There was nothing left to say.

Left Hand climbed over the pile of sandstone boulders, looked back once, and then walked out of the cave into the open. The thing, seated on the ground, eating the last of Mendelson's body, watched him with interest. He dropped the corpse and rose. It stood, long arms hanging at its side, immobile.

Left Hand walked slowly toward it, calling out, "Are you ready to die? I see you standing there. Are you afraid to move? Are you afraid to face me?" He shook his hatchet at it. "Look what I have for you. I am Left Hand, Kit Fox Soldier. I have killed twelve white soldiers with this hatchet and counted a hundred coups. You think I am afraid of you?" He stopped and spread his arms wide. "Come! Come and fight me if you are not too afraid. Come and fight a Kit Fox Soldier and see what it is like to die."

Taliaferro cocked his Springfield carbine and raised it. Ashcroft and Smallwood did the same. Comes-a-Pony rested her rifle on a pile of rocks. Sweet held the powder-filled canteen close to his body and took out his pistol. Walking Man looked back at the fire and strung an arrow in the bow. He had left a small piece of fabric dangling from the cloth tied around the arrowhead, close to the parfleche bag filled with powder. He whispered a prayer to his ancestors and to his friends who had been killed by the thing. He asked them to make his aim true. He asked them to give him courage. He asked them to walk by Left Hand's side and protect him from the creature.

The thing's interest in Left Hand increased. It dropped to all fours and paced slowly back and forth.

Ashcroft took aim. "It looks like a goddamned cat."

"Don't shoot," Sweet warned him. He cocked his pistol awkwardly with his left hand. "When that thing comes at us, fall back to the rear of the cave. Nobody shoots until it's at the mouth of the cave. Aim for its head. Be careful not to hit the Indian."

Left Hand advanced a few feet. "Don't you hear me? I am all alone. There is no one else."

The creature stopped moving and stood up.

"Jesus, that thing's big," Ashcroft whispered.

"The bigger they are…" Taliaferro said.

It took several steps toward Left Hand, stopped, and seemed to sniff the air.

"It's figuring what to do," Taliaferro said. "Come on, you son-of-a-bitch!" he yelled.

"Come on," Smallwood shouted. "Come and get it, you ugly bastard."

Sweet and Ashcroft joined him, screaming at the thing. Walking Man watched the creature. It knows, he thought. It knows we are trying to trap it.

Left Hand ran a few steps and stopped. "Come and fight me! Here I am. Here is Left Hand, son of Running Bear, grandson of Red Leaf. They are here with me. They will help me kill you." He moved again, closing the distance. The creature's arms came up as if it was ready to grasp its prey. Left Hand moved again, and the creature crouched in readiness.

"Don't get too close," Taliaferro muttered. "Too close."

Left Hand screamed a war cry, holding his hatchet high over his head, shaking it at the thing.

The creature shot forward, and Left Hand turned and raced toward the cave.

"Dammit!" Taliaferro shouted and was out of the cave before Sweet could stop him. The sergeant fired his carbine on the run, flipped open the breech, and loaded it. The thing turned toward Taliaferro. Left Hand gave a quick glance toward the thing and ran toward the cave. Taliaferro dropped to his knee, aimed carefully, and fired. The bullet struck the thing in the chest, but it did not slow down.

Comes-a-Pony's Sharps fired. The bullet struck the creature's shoulder. She had another cartridge seated in the breech, aimed, and fired again. "Run, Brother. Run." She got off two more shots.

It was almost on Left Hand when Ashcroft and Smallwood fired. The crash of both carbines shattered the interior of the cave and smoke rolled out of the entrance. Ashcroft's bullet went high, missing the thing, but Smallwood's struck it on the arm.

Left Hand stopped next to Taliaferro, who slammed the breech of his carbine closed, raised the weapon, and fired again. The Cheyenne had his pistol out and fired. He cocked it and fired again as Taliaferro loaded his carbine. The creature was a few feet from the pair when Left Hand threw his hatchet. The creature knocked it aside and sprang on Left Hand, knocking Taliaferro backwards. The soldier jumped to his feet, jerked out his pistol, and jammed the muzzle in the creature's head as it drove its claws into Left Hand.

Comes-a-Pony sprang over the rocks, but Walking Man grabbed her arm, jerking her back into the cave. She swung her rifle at him, but he ducked and pushed her to the ground, kneeling on her chest. "You cannot go out there!"

"Let me up," she screamed. "Let me up, or I'll kill you."

Walking Man spoke softly. "It is too late. You cannot help him." Her face melted into sorrow. He saw that she understood. She climbed back up to the rocks, loading and firing her rifle. She kept her eyes on the creature, avoiding the crumpled body of her brother.

The thing spun on Taliaferro, mouth open, blood dripping from its claws, eyes dark red, yellow teeth covered in gore. Left Hand, chest torn open, managed to raise his pistol and fire. The creature's claws flashed through the air, ripping Taliaferro's head from its shoulders.

"Oh, Lord!" Ashcroft screamed. "Oh Lord." He ran to the back of the cave, dropping his carbine. Sweet picked it up, rested it on a pile of sandstone, took careful aim, and fired. The bullet hit the creature on the leg.

"Ashcroft get up here, Goddamn it. Load this thing." Sweet dropped the carbine and took aim with his Colt revolver. He fired, cocked, and fired again. He was too far away. The creature stood over Left Hand's body, driving its claws into the warrior's corpse. Then it turned and shrieked at the cave in triumph, crouched, and leaped forward. It covered the ground in an instant. It was at the entrance, its body blocking the cave's mouth. It screamed again, a foul stench rolling into the cave, tearing wildly at the sandstone.

"Fall back," Sweet shouted. He fired his pistol in the creature's face. He turned to Walking Man. "Now! Now!"

Walking Man dipped the fabric in the flames, the stand of cloth catching fire. He pulled the bowstring back and released it. The arrow bounced off the creature's shoulder, spinning into the air. Smallwood fired, cocked his pistol, and fired again. Ashcroft had his pistol out, sobbing. He cocked the pistol but didn't pull the trigger.

The thing pushed itself into the cave, trying to squeeze its huge body into the narrow opening. His claws tore at the sandstone as it shrieked in frustration. Dirt and debris flew into the air as Walking Man drew another arrow, flames eating at the cloth. He waited, glancing from the fire to the creature. It forced itself deeper into the cave, its long arm shooting out, grasping Smallwood's arm. It pulled the screaming soldier to him and smashed his body against the cave wall. Ashcroft dropped to the floor of the cave, placed the pistol under his chin, and this time, remembered to pull the trigger. The blast threw brains and blood onto the cave roof.

Walking Man released the arrow. It struck the thing's chest and exploded in a bright flash, knocking the creature back.

Comes-a-Pony screamed in defiance. There was no room to aim her rifle. She grabbed a carbine and cartridge belt. She loaded the weapon, pointed it at the creature's head, and fired. The bullet missed the thing's eye but blew off a portion of its cheek. It dug furiously at the walls, trying to get at the survivors. It squeezed deeper into the cave, arms shooting out, trying to reach them.

Sweet gripped the canteen tightly in his left hand. He felt the creature's hot breath, rank with decay, surround him. Now. Do something. Walking Man saw the look in his eyes. Sweet ran forward, jammed the canteen against the thing's leg, pushed the muzzle of his pistol against it, and pulled the trigger.

The powder exploded in a bright flash. The thing screamed in pain and threw Sweet's body against the cave wall. It dropped to the floor.

The creature managed to fight its way deeper into the cave. The survivors fell back as far as they could, their backs against the sandstone. Comes-a-Pony slipped another cartridge into the carbine and raised it to fire.

Walking Man saw her and shouted, "Comes-a-Pony!"

She nearly had the carbine up to her shoulder when the creature drove its talons into her chest. She squeezed the trigger and the carbine fired, the bullet ricocheting off the cave roof. Blood spurted out of her mouth, as the thing drove her body into the floor.

Walking Man dropped to her side. Blood bubbled around her lips as she tried to speak. Her eyes were wide with fear.

She was gone.

His strength drained from him. He felt himself raising the bow, saw the last parfleche bag, and the trailing fabric smoking. There was no sound. He saw blood bubbling from the thing's leg where the canteen had exploded. It was a hideous wound of torn and burned flesh. The creature's body blocked any light coming into the cave, and what little did glow around the demon's head. Its body seemed to be on fire. He felt the tension of the bowstring in his hand, running up his arm and into his shoulder. He saw the creature's eyes, dark and fathomless: a thing without a soul, a living thing without life. The right eye. The right eye.

Walking Man released the arrow. It penetrated the eye and exploded. The thing wailed in pain and stumbled backwards out of the cave. Walking Man threw the bow down, took the cartridge belt and a carbine from Comes-a-Pony's hands, and loaded the weapon. The creature was still on its feet, swaying uncertainly, its right eye replaced with a smoldering hole, blood cascading down its cheek. He aimed the carbine at the thing's head and fired. He saw the bullet impact and heard the thing shriek in pain. He loaded again, continued toward the cave opening, and fired again. He saw Eagle Head's hatchet and pulled it from the dead man's belt.

They were out of the cave and into the faint light. The thing roared, turning its good eye on Walking Man. It lurched toward him, arms grasping.

Walking Man fell back, climbing the rise around the cave. He stopped and fired down at the advancing creature.

The demon staggered backward, shaking its head in confusion, batting at the air, trying to find Walking Man.

The Cheyenne warrior aimed again and fired. The bullet blew off a chunk of the thing's neck. He loaded and fired. He didn't see where the bullet struck, but now the thing had seen him and rushed forward. Walking Man tripped and fell near the edge of the escarpment. He crawled backward up the ridge, loading and firing, striking the thing in its chest. It howled in pain and pulled itself up the ridge.

It would not die. Its hands reached out, digging onto the earth as it pulled itself upwards, blood and saliva dripping from its mouth. Its eyes were fixed in hatred on Walking Man. It came on, slowly, doggedly. It would reach him and tear him to pieces. He would die like Comes-a-Pony. Like Left Hand. Like the young soldier chief.

Walking Man fired again, crawling to keep distance between himself and the demon. He loaded, and fired, bits of the thing flying into the air.

He pulled himself behind a boulder, resting his carbine on the edge of the rock. He fumbled with a cartridge, slipped it into the breech, and locked it into place. He took aim, the creature filling his vision—just feet away.

Comes-a-Pony was a better shot, and Left Hand ran like the wind. The young warrior chief was brave, and Bull Bear was the best tracker in the tribe. Who are you? Walking Man, the reasoning brave, your mind never still, your thoughts flowing like the waters of the Greasy Grass. He saw Comes-a-Pony's face under the warm sun and felt the wind pick at his shirt. She was smiling, and the hawk overhead cried out in delight.

You will not see us anymore, he said to the creature. I will blind you, and you will not look upon my friends or offend us with your foul breath.

His finger slowly squeezed the trigger, and the gun fired. Smoke rose into the air, and he saw the creature jerk upright, crying out in pain. The bullet hit the thing in the left eye and tore a part of its face away. It rose, stumbling forward, and a high-pitched scream filled the air. It did not die. It still came on, but Walking Man could see it struggle. He held Eagle Head's hatchet in his left hand. He dropped the carbine and pulled a soldier's pistol out of his belt. The thing moaned, grabbing at its head as if trying to find the source of the pain. Walking Man stopped a short distance from the creature. Blood flowed down its face and covered its narrow chest. He aimed the pistol at the thing's head and fired. He saw his bullet hit the thing. It stumbled over the rocks. Walking Man knew it was dying.

It dropped to its hands and knees and began crawling, searching for Walking Man. The Cheyenne brave rushed forward, raised the hatchet, and brought it down with all his strength on the creature's neck. The thing roared in defiance but did not strike out at Walking Man. He buried the blade deep in its neck, again, and then once more. The thing's body shook, and its shoulder dropped as Walking Man brought the hatchet down again. The thing tried to rise as he pointed the pistol at the back of its head. He fired and a piece of skull flew into the air. He cocked and fired again. Blood spurted out, covering the warrior's face and neck. He tasted of it and spat it out, aiming again. He fired and brought the hatchet blade down. The thing had stopped crawling and fought to rise.

Walking Man pushed the pistol into his belt, took the hatchet handle with both hands, and raised it over his head. He brought it down with all the strength remaining in him. The blade sunk deeply into the creature's neck, and the handle broke off in his hands.

The thing shuddered and dropped. Walking Man pulled out the pistol, placed the muzzle against the back of the thing's skull, and fired. He cocked and fired again, but the third time, the hammer struck an empty cylinder. He returned and found his carbine, loaded it, and shot the thing once more.

It did not move. Blood came from its wounds and streamed down the hill in a dozen fingers. Walking Man stepped back and slumped to the ground. He began to cry. Gunsmoke stung his eyes. He cried until there were no more tears; and he sat still, staring at the thing.

He rose and found dried wood from Ponderosa pine and piled it around the thing's body. He jerked dried grass from the ground and stuffed it between the pieces of wood. He had no flint or matches, so he put the muzzle of the carbine into a patch of dried grass that he had gathered and fired it. A wisp of smoke appeared and then a flame, and the fire spread over the wood covering the thing's body. Brown smoke rose into the sky, where the wind batted it back and forth. He watched the fire eat at the thing, the stench of burning flesh filling the air. He raised his carbine to the sky and shouted, "My name is Walking Man. Do you hear me? I am Walking Man of the Kit Fox Warriors, and I have killed this thing. Send me another one, if you dare; and I'll chop off its head and burn its body. Send the wind and rain to carry its away, and let the sun bleach the bones. I am Walking Man." He returned to the boulder that he had used to aim the carbine and sat down with his back against it.

He felt a terrible thirst and realized he could not remember the last time he had water. He sat for hours. Walking Man sat but did not think. His mind decided it was time to rest. There were no thoughts to trouble him. Just the flames, consuming the thing on the hillside. Gray clouds disappeared as night covered the prairie. The fire burned into the darkness; and there was no rain, so it continued until the thing was burned up except for a blackened carcass, shriveled and twisted by the flames.

He fell asleep; and when he awoke, the sun was just above the horizon. The clouds, which had been so strong, chose to move away and give the sky back to the sun. He sat, letting the sun's warm rays comfort him. He rose and stumbled down the rise, carrying the carbine, passing the creature.

He went to Left Hand's body, carefully picked up the dead warrior and took him into the cave. He laid him next to Comes-a-Pony, found a soldier's greatcoat and covered them as best he could. He had no paint and could not make his mouth water to moisten the sand, so he picked up a handful and sprinkled it over Comes-a-Pony and Left Hand's foreheads. "I want you both to go on together. You will see the others. Tell them how sorry I am at their deaths. I will come later."

He touched Comes-a-Pony's shoulder and stroked her cheek.

He was tired and wanted to rest more, but his thirst was too great, so he searched the cave for canteens. He found two.

One was empty, but the other had some water remaining, so he drank a bit and washed it around in his mouth. He stripped down and scooped up sand and used it to scour the blood from his face and body. He threw his shirt away but kept his trousers. He wiped them in the sand and then put them on.

He saw Eagle Head's blanket and put it over his shoulders, thanking the warrior for the use of it and telling him that he would speak of his courage.

He found fourteen carbine cartridges and twenty-seven for the pistol. He went to the edge of the cave and said a prayer for those who had died and stopped at the body of the old soldier and said a prayer for him and the young soldier chief.

He went out of the cave into the sunlight and saw three elk on the crest of a ridge in the distance. Two does ate while a stag kept watch. It seemed to be looking at him. He thought that they were really a spirit that had come to say there was nothing left to fear. He watched them until they were satisfied to move on. One doe lingered, watching him, and he thought for a moment, it was the spirit of Comes-a-Pony reminding of their time on the Greasy Grass.

He began walking, and after a while, he saw a horse standing near a limber pine. It looked strange, misshapen, but as he got nearer, he saw that it was a soldier's horse and its saddle had slipped so that it hung from its belly. The animal watched him as he approached but was more interested in the grass at its feet. He recognized it as the soldier's horse called Victoria. He talked softly to it so that it did not get frightened and run off. When he was close enough, he held out his hand for the animal to sniff. The horse did and then resumed grazing, barely moving as he undid the saddle cinch. The soldier who rode this horse had used two saddle blankets, so he kept both, one to ride on and the other to wear. He took the bit out of the animal's mouth and threw it to one side.

Walking Man swung onto the horse's back, wrapped his hands in the animal's mane, and kicked her into a walk and then a gallop.

A flight of sage grouse followed him for a while, but then they set off for the southeast and left him alone.

About the Author

Steven Wilson is the author of *Voyage of The Gray Wolves, Armada, Between the Hunters and The Hunted, President Lincoln's Spy, President Lincoln's Secret,* and *Roosevelt's Jubilee.* He was the former curator of the Abraham Lincoln Library and Museum, and Managing Editor and contributor to The *Lincoln Herald,* as well as an Instructor of History, at Lincoln Memorial University.